The
Willing
Spirit

The  Willing Spirit

Piers Anthony
and
Alfred Tella

TOR®

A Tom Doherty Associates Book
New York

This is a work of fiction. All the characters and events portrayed in this novel are either fictitious or are used fictitiously.

THE WILLING SPIRIT

A Tor Book
Published by Tom Doherty Associates, Inc.
175 Fifth Avenue
New York, N.Y. 10010

Tor Books on the World Wide Web:
http://www.tor.com

Tor® is a registered trademark of Tom Doherty Associates, Inc.

Design by Basha Durand

Library of Congress Cataloging-in-Publication Data

Anthony, Piers.
    The willing spirit / Piers Anthony & Alfred Tella.—1st ed.
        p.   cm.
    "A Tom Doherty Associates book."
    ISBN 0-312-86266-0
    I. Tella, Alfred.   II. Title.
PS3551.N73W49   1996
813'.54—dc20   96-29211
                                                                          CIP

First Edition: December 1996

Printed in the United States of America

0 9 8 7 6 5 4 3 2 1

Acknowledgment

*Thanks to Professor Krishnamurti Chandrasekar
for sharing his knowledge of Indian mythology,
and to whom this tale owes so much*

Contents

The
Willing
Spirit

Prologue

Finally Mohini turned to face him. *Ravana!* she exclaimed in a petite fury. *Why won't you leave me alone, you repulsive horny monster?*

Ravana smiled, revealing grotesque ragged tusks. He angled his ugly head to show the horns to better effect. **Because you are an Apsara, the most beautiful creature of Indra's heaven, and I am smitten by your lovely features. You will not easily be rid of me.**

But I am not smitten by YOU, you horror from no realm I would care to know. I am a lesser goddess who prefers to associate with personable folk. What can I do to make you go away for a century or two so I can have some peace?

Ravana considered. **You might deal with me. Perhaps we should wager on a game with suitable prizes.**

Now Mohini considered, realizing that while she could never escape the evil male spirit through flight or avoidance, she might do so by means of wit. *What kind of game?*

He shrugged, causing his discolored scales to grind against each other. **Why not a game with mortals as ignorant pawns? They are often entertaining in their confusion, especially when their gore spills out just before they die.**

Mohini winced, but remained lovely regardless, for she was incapable of ugliness. *I much prefer romantic games that tweak mortal heartstrings and lead to expressions of tenderness, music, and poetry.*

Ugh! But Ravana knew that he could never make her submit to his desire without her cooperation; he had to compromise. **Perhaps a game of romance and violence.**

Mohini was intrigued. *The romance for me, the violence for you, as befits our natures.*

Rape and vengeance, he suggested.

Love and loss, she countered.

They were getting somewhere. **For what stakes?**

A century of peace from you.

A century of erotic frenzy from you.

She paused, reconsidering. The prizes did seem fair. Surely she could beat this monster, if the game was fair. *Agreed.*

Agreed.

Having settled the fruits of victory and defeat, they focused on the nature of the game itself. In due course they hammered out a situation that offered a number of intriguing ramifications. They would choose a single mortal man, whom neither of them would touch directly, though both could read mortal thoughts. The man would go where he wished and do what he wanted, except when they deflected his course by indirect means, taking turns. Mohini would act only through mortal females, and Ravana only through mortal males, touching each with a single act or emotion, then allowing the consequences to proceed in their natural fashion until the other spirit acted; then the turn would change again. Each act had to appear natural to the mortals, so as to attract no suspicion of supernatural intervention. If any such suspicion arose, the one responsible would forfeit the game.

If Mohini could seduce the mortal man in seven different guises, through different women, without Ravana killing him, she would win. Since she would enjoy the seductions, and he would enjoy the mayhem, the game should be interesting throughout.

Now we must find our innocent mortal man.

And soon thereafter I shall be slavering over your dainty quivering posterior.

Or propelling your own brute buttocks rapidly elsewhere. We shall see, Ravana.

We shall indeed.

〜 1 〜

The Palace of the Zamindar

Many village maidens wept when young Hari announced he would don the white mantle of austerity, take leave of his friends and family, and set out upon the open road in search of truth and wisdom.

Beloved for his beauty, cleverness, and gentle ways, he would not heed the pleas of his mother and sister, uncles and neighbors, to remain among them in his ancestral home. It was not because he was the only son of a widow or for need of his labor that they wished him to remain; rather, it was for the joy he brought to his family and all who knew him.

Ravana!

Who calls me?

Tall, slender, sturdy of limb, blessed with the cherished lightness of skin the color of ripe wheat, sharp of feature, unspoiled, and in the fullness of his youth was Hari. Yet, if the gods had smiled upon him, still he was not content. Restlessness gnawed at his heart and wanderlust tugged at his soul.

I, Mohini, am calling you, dullard. Here is the one! Come and see if it is not so.

Of late his thoughts and fancies drifted to imaginary far-off places, like shadows in a waking dream. He remembered the stories his father had told him as a child, of strange peoples and customs in distant lands and the talking animals that had illuminated the many subtleties and foibles of human character. And had not his venerated teacher, Bava, the village pundit, taught him to love and seek out knowledge, to value and learn from all experience? Surely, he told himself, such experience encompassed the outside world and the senses as well as the mind and spirit.

This idiot mortal? Mohini, his naiveté is grotesque. He thinks that mortal creatures exist for some purpose other than the entertainment of immortal spirits.

Hari had refused to consider offers of marriage, though it was a village custom that eligible bachelors of high caste take a wife before reaching the age of twenty-one. The time had come when he could no longer deny the longing within. He had to reach out for the promises that ever lingered on the horizon, beckoning him, filling his imagination. And so it was that one month before his twenty-first birthday he announced his decision to leave the village of his birth. He promised his mother and sister that he would return before too long and would keep his vegetarian habits.

I don't care, Ravana. I think he's cute, in body and mind. He means so well, with so little experience of evil.

His mother wept as she tied an amulet of yellow string from the family altar around his arm to protect him on his travels. His sister marked his forehead with a stripe of ash and admonished him to watch out for snakes on the road. Refusing all but a few coins and some meager provisions, he bade his family farewell and in the pale light of a summer's dawn set out upon a path through the hills to the south.

I will make short work of this one, Mohini! If he's the one you want, you are as great a fool as he is.

Glad to be on the road, Hari kept a brisk pace, in time with the beating of his heart. He heeded not the brooding hills, laden with premonitions, or the baleful eye of Surya, the sun, as it rolled upward across the cloudless sheet of sky. But he laughed at the young mynah birds that chattered and argued among the leaves of the tamarind, and he mimicked the merry chirpings of crickets in the brush.

Then we are agreed, you grotesque evil spirit. This is the mortal we shall use to decide our issue.

The earth and sky and their offspring were his ever present companions. The shade of the banyan gave him relief from the late afternoon sun, and the coconut, mango, and jackfruit trees that grew in abundance provided him ample nourishment. The many streams that snaked along the base of the hills served to slake his thirst and provide for his ablutions. What more could he ask of life than this? A simple yet satisfying tour of the countryside, with ample time for contemplation.

We are agreed, you beautiful daughter of pleasure. This is the fool we shall focus on.

The hills became taller and the land greener as he traveled southward, and though his body ached from climbing, his heart was light with expectation. At day's end he stretched out upon a soft cushion of grass beneath an overhanging acacia tree and soon drifted into a carefree dreamless slumber.

I shall go elsewhere and divert myself alone, for I can see that it will be days before this sweet mortal man encounters any seduceable women.

You are merely dawdling because you have the first move, O lovely Mohini, and I can't kill him until it is my turn.

How unfortunate for you, O hideous one. Perhaps you should divert yourself by chewing on your warts.

It was on the morning of the sixth day of his journey, from the crest of a high hill, that Hari saw spread out before him a broad lush valley extending to the distant mountains. It shone like a great emerald set into the breast of the earth, a coruscating river cutting through its center. Upon the near side of the riverbank stood a magnificent palace the likes of which he had only heard about in stories. Its golden domes and turrets glistened in the sun, and its white marble wings extended outward like some great mythical bird in flight.

Mohini! Come play the game, you winsome creature. A situation arises.

The sight overwhelmed him, and it was many minutes before Hari could quiet his heartbeat. Then, with all the resolve he could muster, he started down the hill toward the great edifice.

I see no women here, you curmudgeon. How can I work a seduction?

There are women in the palace. Give me leave to touch the master of this residence, and we shall soon have the fool mortal man inside.

I have no wish to let you touch a mortal out of turn. You will stir in him a killing fury against all isolated travelers, and win the game before it starts.

No I won't. We agreed: no baseless killing furies. I merely wish to start the game.

Then touch him. But I will be watching. If you cheat, you brute, you forfeit.

Then watch, luscious. At the key moment I will make the tiniest nudge, so delicate that no one suspects.

As Hari approached the massive wooden gate of the palace, he saw that it was intricately carved with figures of the gods in acts of worship, combat, and lovemaking. He was especially intrigued with the depictions of the goddesses and lingered a moment to study their voluptuous beauty. But his musing was interrupted by a loud creaking and cracking, and the great gate began to slowly swing open. He hastily stepped aside.

You, delicate? You strain my credulity, you creature of mayhem.

Your credulity is a tender flower, like yourself. Observe, and despair of any hope of victory.

Through the now open portal marched a cordon of soldiers, four abreast, uniformed in bright red and carrying shoulder spears. Once outside the gate, the soldiers split ranks and quickstepped to one side to make passage for a following retinue on horseback. The equestrian formation passed majestically through the gate, then halted and parted to make way for a magnificent black stallion that trotted to the fore. Astride the stallion sat the leader of the cavalcade, as his bejeweled saddle, richly embroidered uniform, and dignity of bearing testified.

The leader, espying the young stranger standing alone before the palace gate, reined in his steed.

"Whom have we here?" he said in a commanding but not unfriendly voice. "A young swami, perhaps? Hmm. I see that you are highborn by the sacred thread you wear, and that you have traveled some distance. Tell me, who are you and what brings you to the palace of the zamindar?"

This man is dangerous when affronted. Remember, if you try to take advantage—

Hari swallowed. "O Master," he replied, his tone humble but unwavering, "I am Hari by name, a student on a pilgrimage in search of truth, who six days past set out from my village to the north upon a path chosen by the Goddess of Fortune. Surely, O Master, she has permitted me to travel with her to this blessed land only that she may now visit with the zamindar."

Now! Instead of interpreting this as insolence, he takes it as cleverness and is graciously inclined.

The horseman laughed and slapped his saddle. "Well spoken!" he said. "Know that I am the zamindar and that your words please me. Goddess Lakshmi is indeed welcome, and I thank you for delivering her to me. I would speak with you further, young traveler, but I must be on my way. The Great Rajah has called his servant to his palace to celebrate the month of our Lord Krishna. The Goddess of Fortune will be welcome company on the journey, at whose end she will find rest in most comfortable and familiar surroundings. But tell me, Hari, what gift should I present in homage to our Lord Krishna?"

There is still danger.

Hari's heart raced as his brain searched for an answer.

"O Zamindar," he replied, "Lord Krishna is a playful god, and it is said that he is best worshiped when his worshipers enjoy the earthly pleasures that it pleases him to bring them."

"Hah! Well said, again, O Hari. You are clever beyond your years. Pray you, then, stay this holy month in my palace as my guest, if you will. And if you choose to remain until my return, we will converse again at length and leisure. But now I must go. Farewell, O child of the gods."

That mortal man is not as dull as I took him for. He helped himself that time.

Hari watched the zamindar and his retinue ride off through the hills until they disappeared from sight. He was then led into the palace by a guard and turned over to a portly berobed man of middle years who bowed politely and introduced himself as Balu, the zamindar's chief advisor. Without further ado, the advisor escorted Hari through the great halls of the palace to a guest suite in the west wing. After ascertaining that Hari had no further needs, he bowed and took his leave.

Hari was overwhelmed with his quarters, ornate and spacious, yet also private. Such wealth and finery he had never seen before, and he could not resist touching the bejeweled urns and golden censers and running his fingers over the inlaid tables, carven walls, and intricate tapestries.

From the veranda adjoining his apartments, he looked out upon the western hills, so stately and serene, glimmering beneath the golden eye of Surya. Although he was not especially religious, he gave silent thanks to the God of Gods for his good fortune that day.

Now I will start my first seduction, instilling in a comely young woman a passion for the visitor.

Hari's reverie was broken by a knocking at the door. At his spoken consent there entered into the room a maidservant who, upon crossing the threshold, bowed low before him and raised her joined palms to her chin, her eyes cast downward. She remained fixed in that position awaiting the command to rise.

She is so shy she will never make the attempt, despite her mys-

*terious sudden passion for the guest. You have wasted your move,
honey breast.*

Hari failed to give the expected sign, but could only
stare at the bowed figure before him. Here, he thought,
was a female to rob one's very soul, a maiden in the fullness of her youth, fair beyond compare. Blessed she was
with skin the smoothness of the lotus petal, full plum lips
embracing milk-white teeth, almond eyes gray-flecked
and slightly cowled, hinting of mysterious secrets, and
fringed with long eyelashes guarded by high brows arched
like drawn bows. Her hair was shining sable, fine as gos-
samer, falling freely about soft slim shoulders, framing a
narrow forehead and long slender neck. The loose sari
she wore failed to conceal her full round breasts, sylph-
like waist, rounded hips, and long graceful limbs.

*Give it time, obnoxious one. She may be shy, but she is show-
ing her wares, which are formidable.*

Never had Hari looked upon such feminine beauty,
wholly sensuous yet possessed of a quiet dignity worthy
of reverence.

Only when the maidservant's head inclined upward
slightly and he saw her look of demure puzzlement did
he realize his unintended discourtesy. He quickly bade
her to rise.

"O Swami," said she, "I am your servant, Meena, sent
to do your bidding. If it is your wish to sup, I have
brought fruits, sweetmeats, and cow's milk for your pleasure."

"Yes, thank you, Meena," he replied in a voice that
gave no hint of his inner disquiet. He was trying to lead
a simple life, if not an ascetic one, and desires of the flesh
were not appropriate for that. Was the maiden unaware

of her beauty? "I will take some fruit. But pray do not call me swami, I who am only a traveling student. My name is Hari."

Meena, placing the platter of food on a low table, replied, "But it is said you are very clever and have amused my lord, the zamindar." She seemed about to say more, though hesitant; she seemed to be suffering some gentle uncertainty or conflict of emotions.

"I am grateful for the zamindar's kindness and generosity," Hari politely interjected, if only to discourage any further recitation of his perceived, or misperceived, virtues. "But come, Meena, will you not sit awhile and partake with me of this fruit?"

"Oh no, Master," she exclaimed. "That I cannot do. It is forbidden for a servant—"

"Do not speak so," Hari interrupted. "Are we not near together in years? And can we not be friends during my brief visit? None need know of our friendship."

See how her passion guides her mind, she not yet understanding its nature.

Meena was silent, considering, and as she looked upon his beauty, his pleading eyes and earnest smile, she felt her reservations slipping. Then she too smiled and sat down beside him, though at a respectful distance.

Women were ever devious, even to themselves. A man would be straightforward.

That is easy for one whose attention has but a single channel.

From their conversation Hari learned that Meena was not of humble birth, which did not altogether surprise him, but was the daughter of a regional prince who three years past had been killed in war by soldiers of the zamindar. As was his right, the zamindar had taken Meena to be a servant in his household. She had been well treated and cared for, and gradually had come to accept, even to find some pleasure in, her new position in life. She had her own room in the palace, her duties were few, and she had ample time to walk in the garden, embroider, and play tunes on the veena. In truth, she had come to respect and even to like the zamindar, who was a fine man when not opposed.

Hari in his turn told Meena of his life in the village and of his desire to learn more of the world. She seemed to be so rapt with attention that he talked rather more than he had intended, being flattered despite his effort to be objective.

The time passed quickly and soon Meena announced she must depart. Not unmindful of her obligations, she offered to bring Hari fresh hens' eggs in the morning for his breakfast, if it would please him.

"O Meena," he replied, "know that I am a vegetarian. Although eggs are to my liking, I can only eat those which are infertile. Tell me, in the chicken house, are the cocks kept separate from the hens?"

"There is but one cock," she answered, "a great white cock which the zamindar keeps to announce the coming of day. And a proud and magnificent bird he is," she added enthusiastically, as if there were something about the subject of breeding that appealed to her. "Now," she continued almost breathlessly, "although the cock is kept separately in an enclosed pen next to the henyard, he on occasion somehow manages to transgress the intervening fence and move among the hens."

"Does he then tread the hens," asked Hari, "and so fertilize the eggs?"

"He does that," replied Meena, "but not with all the hens. There are among the hens those of many colors— red, white, gray, speckled, a few yellows, and a single black. The white cock has interest only in the black hen, and it is only her eggs that would be fertile. But since I know the nesting place of the black hen, when I fetch the eggs in the morning for your breakfast I will be sure to gather only from the other nests."

Hari pictured the black hen in his mind as Meena spoke, and it was as if the feathers were as sleek and dark as Meena's glossy hair. He could appreciate why the cock had desire only for that one. And, it seemed, that desire was returned.

"But Meena," said he, "although hens are among the gods' blessed creatures, they are not known to be overly intelligent, being somewhat fickle and not always certain of their place. Therefore, is it not possible that one hen might occupy and deposit her eggs in the nest of another? And so might not a fertile egg find its way into a nest other than that of the black hen?"

"Be not concerned," Meena assured him, "for I have long been gathering the hens' eggs and observing their habits. Know that the eggs of the black hen are of a slightly darker hue than the other hens' eggs. As I gather from each nest, I will observe the color of the eggs and choose only the whitest to insure against the possibility of selecting one that is fertile."

Hari, satisfied that all risk had been eliminated, thanked Meena for her solicitousness. They then bade one another good night, each looking forward to their meeting again the following morning. In fact, had Hari not known better, he might have supposed that the intensity of her parting look suggested a desire to remain longer in his chamber.

It was not yet dark and Hari decided he would take a stroll about the palace grounds before turning in. As he walked along the winding pathways he marveled at the beauty and grandeur of the terraced gardens, manicured lawns, and tall hedges, the flowering trellises, carven statuary, and elaborate dovecotes. How plain and insignificant by comparison seemed the gardens of his native village. Yet, he thought, as he gazed upon the climbing purple bougainvillea, were its blossoms really any more beautiful or fragrant than those which grew in his own yard?

Following the walkway around to the rear of the palace, he came upon the area where the livestock and poultry were kept. He walked over to the fence that separated the henyard from the demesne of the white cock whom he could see pacing about in apparent discontent with his confinement. He seemed a fine bird, but it was not evident that the cock was all that worthy of the acclaim and admiration Meena had heaped upon him.

Hari saw too in the adjoining yard some of the hens picking about on the ground, though the black hen was not among them. He guessed that she and others of the hens must have already gone indoors for the night, judging from the clucking he heard coming from the henhouse.

An idea suddenly came to him which brought a smile to his lips and a sparkle to his eyes.

Slowly he made his way along the line of the fence that separated the hens and the white cock, carefully examining the fence and ground as he went. As he neared the far end of the fence, his brow wrinkled in puzzlement. But then at the very bottom of the fence where it was partly hidden by an overhanging bush, he saw what he was looking for.

Darkness was descending: time to return to his quarters. As he walked along he silently named the constellations scattered across the star-filled sky, the smile on his face now mimicked by the rising moon.

He arose early the next morning, and no sooner had he finished bathing and dressing than there came a familiar knocking at the door. Meena entered carrying a tray upon which was a silver platter of fresh fruit and a bowl containing three ivory-white eggs. Hari saw that today she wore a garland in her hair and was adorned in a shining white sari embroidered with tiny red flowers. Her fragrance was of sweet lotus. If his pulsebeat quickened, he did not show it. He was relieved that his memory of her had not deceived him, and indeed the face that now assailed him was beauty and perfection itself.

"Good morning, Meena," he said, giving the traditional hand greeting. "I thank you for the breakfast, and not least for the unseeded eggs which are so white and perfect it seems a pity to eat them."

"Good morning," she replied. "But you must eat to keep your strength." Her tone was gently admonishing, yet also motherly and slightly coquettish. She seemed more familiar and less shy than before, as if her natural reticence was being vanquished by some more intense emotion.

"Very well, Meena, but you must join me," said he.

"My thanks, but I have already eaten. However, I will keep you company." So saying, she sat down beside Hari who proceeded with his meal.

"These eggs are most tasty," he said. "I should have thought to thank the benefactors when I passed the henhouse during my evening stroll."

"Oh?" exclaimed Meena with interest. "Did you see the hens while on your walk?"

"Yes, but only a few, some reds and yellows. I did not see the black hen, who must have been in the henhouse."

"And did you see anything more?" inquired Meena.

"Oh yes, I also saw the white cock in his yard, though he seemed restless and not at all happy at his confinement. I watched him awhile to see if he might attempt to cross the fence and visit with the hens and so reveal the secret of his means of transgression."

"Oh! And did he do so?" asked Meena somewhat anxiously.

"No, he did not," answered Hari calmly. "But curiosity overcame me and I decided to inspect the fenceline that separated the white cock from the hens to see if I could discover anything that might help to solve the mystery."

"And—and did you find anything?" Meena's voice was now nervous and agitated, though she tried to disguise her unease.

Hari stopped eating, turned toward Meena, and looked her full in the eyes as he placed his hand on hers. He could feel her hand trembling and knew it was not because of his touch. He answered gently, almost in a whisper.

"Yes, Meena. I found the white cock's place of entry at the corner of the fence, covered by an overhanging bush. The fence had been pulled up by someone to allow the cock's passage."

There was a long silence as Meena stared into Hari's eyes and he into hers. His thumb caressed her still trembling hand, as much to reassure her and allay her trepidation as to express his feeling for her.

Meena knew she had been found out, that he knew her secret. All that he had said, his manner of speaking, and now his understanding smile and caresses, and, above all, the message in his eyes, told her that he knew.

Hari saw the utter helplessness in her eyes, the naked exposure of her innermost longings, and he knew that he had found the key to open a window into her heart.

Look into her mind, Ravana. She is shy, but her passion caused her to linger overlong in his presence, so that he noticed her charms, and now he will take her.

Bah!

There was no longer any reason to pretend, Meena thought. Her hidden passions, so long suppressed, she now saw mirrored in Hari's eyes. Yes, she now admitted to herself, openly, even boldly—yes, she had made the opening for the white cock to enter. Yes, and many were the times, her heart racing triumphantly beneath swollen breasts, she had watched the white cock gloriously tread the black hen.

A softness came into her eyes, a softness which spoke of resignation, surrender, and desire. Hari said nothing, but gently pulled her to him, and she knew from his touch that he cared and understood. She felt no guilt or shame as her body bent to his, as the flame of passion rose within her breast.

She desired adventure with a man, but only with one of quality, and of course the zamindar is married. It required only the slightest nudge to orient her on Hari.

Hari took her to his bed, and the goddess Lakshmi smiled upon the union, bringing to them bliss and delight, happiness and fulfillment, joy and ecstasy. For was he not the white cock and she the black hen, he the buck and she the doe, he the bull and she the heifer, he the boar and she the sow, he the ram and she the ewe, he the stallion and she the mare?

Even so will I do with you, Mohini, after I kill him. But I will take you without the mortal man's foolish gentleness. Now it is my move, and I will make it at my convenience.

It was not until the sun was near its zenith that Meena finally arose, explaining that it was time for her to go to the kitchen and inform the cook of Hari's dietary requests for the remainder of the day. Were there any special dishes he would like?

"O Meena," he replied in as serious a tone as he could muster, "since this is the holy month of our Lord Krishna, who in his wisdom has seen fit to deliver the zamindar to the distant palace of the rajah that our Lord may be worshipped in splendor, it is only appropriate that I too should give Krishna thanks and do him homage through the traditional means of self-sacrifice. Therefore, commencing this very day I will fast by foregoing the middle meal of every day of this holy month. And at the first and third meal I will restrict my consumption of food which, for the pleasure of Krishna, will also serve to honor the sacrifices that our Lord's creatures of the earth have made by their provision of my daily nourishment. And surely the zamindar's hens are to be counted among our Lord's most worthy creatures. And so, O Meena, beginning this evening, and also in the morning, and on the morrow's eve, and on each and every day of this holy month, let each of Hari's meals consist of but some milk and fruit, and three fresh white hen's eggs gathered by your own hand."

At that, Meena rushed into Hari's arms, hugged him tightly, and they both laughed long and heartily. He realized that he was not yet destined to live a life of privation, and decided to accept what seemed to be destined.

✻ 2 ✻

The Zamindarini

Now I have seduced him once. It is your turn to try to kill him, Ravana. But remember, it must seem to stem from natural mortal events, or it doesn't count.

Have no concern. I have no need to influence events. They will take care of it themselves. Consider the host's woman.

You must not influence a woman!

Nor must you, damsel spirit, until it is your turn. But we both can look into any mortal mind, as we have been doing, without acting. Study her mind, and despair.

I see no point, but I will look.

And peek at the advisor's mind, too; he is integral to this seething mortal brew. There is excellent potential for bloodshed here.

Now the zamindar had a beautiful young wife, Leela by name, who had decided to forego the discomfort of the long journey to the palace of the rajah and remain home instead. Upon learning of Hari's presence in the palace, she became curious and asked Balu the advisor to deliver a message to Hari saying that she would be pleased to receive him in her rooms the following day at the hour after midday. Balu, knowing the zamindarini's ways, was not at all pleased at this request, and feared the possible outcome of such a meeting. So he attempted to dissuade her from issuing the invitation by hinting that the zamindar might be displeased. When that failed, he suggested alternative activities for the morrow that she might prefer, such as riding in the hills or visiting the house of her father.

But Leela was adamant, so Balu had no choice but to agree to do her bidding; at least that is what he told her. But in fact he did not deliver the message, hoping that by the following day something would occur to divert her attention to other matters, or that she might simply forget about the meeting. She was after all prone to whims and had a short attention span.

Balu sighed as he recalled when three years past, his master, upon returning from a tax collection trip, arrived at the palace with a new young bride, much to the surprise and consternation of all. She was the youngest daughter of a local landowner who was financially in debt to the zamindar, and whose debt was erased from the ledgers upon the arrangement of the marriage. But, after all, Balu had told himself, the zamindar was a lonely widower approaching his middle years, and Leela was a voluptuous beauty less than half his age and no doubt well schooled in the art of pleasing men. Little wonder that the master had succumbed. Balu, however, had been offended that he was not consulted about the marriage, for he well knew that in the life of a zamindar there can be no separation of personal and political matters; one invariably carried implications for the other. It would have been better had the zamindar married a woman of known qualities, such as Meena, who was of royal lineage herself. But Meena, though of rare beauty, was the very last to presume—which was one reason she would have been a better wife.

And, indeed, the zamindar came to regret his hasty decision. It soon became evident that the zamindarini did not possess the maturity or character equal to her station. Worse, she proved to be of an exceptionally passionate, if not lustful, nature, requiring frequent conjugal attention lest she become restless and moody and a constant irritant to the palace staff and servants. At first the zamindar (who lived in separate quarters, as was the custom) paid her frequent nocturnal visits and so pacified her carnal needs. But his visits, of necessity, became less and less frequent. He was no longer young and could not keep pace with his energetic wife, whose demands were draining his strength.

Also, the duties of office required more of his time, and more tax collection trips became necessary because of financial crises brought about by droughts and poor harvests. And, in truth, he visited her less to avoid her continual complaining.

As a consequence of Leela's frustration, Balu suffered most of all. She required his presence with increasing frequency, calling upon him for the most trivial and contrived reasons, whereupon she would regale him mercilessly for hours on end. And to make matters worse, as if to take revenge on all males for her husband's neglect, she teased and tormented him with her abundant physical charms so as to drive him near to distraction.

She knew that Balu was a bachelor and suspected—correctly so—that he was virginal: all in all an ideal victim for her coquetry. So she would summon him and prattle on about such weighty matters as the reallocation of household chores among the servants, all the while squirming about on the floor in a sea of cushions, assuming the most provocative positions and generously revealing the curvaceous perimeters of her thighs and breasts.

After repeated exposure to such torments, Balu found he had trouble sleeping, and when he did sleep he dreamed of making passionate love to Leela. He knew her nature, and had contempt for it, but her blandishments were strong and his resistance weak. The desire grew potent within him, and during one of his visits he was tempted to hint of his willingness to collaborate with her that their mutual needs might be satisfied. But he dared not, not so much because of his position in the palace, but because he feared she would laugh at him and reject him in the cruelest way possible. He did not think that she would tell her husband, since his denial would doubtless be believed because of his trusted relationship to the zamindar. It was the ridicule and rejection he could not bear. So he suffered silently, never failing to maintain his outward composure even though the flame of desire burned ever hotter within him.

When Hari did not appear before Leela at the appointed time, she became furious and summoned Balu for an explanation. Balu begged her forgiveness, saying that he had been unable to deliver her message because of an urgent political matter that had unexpectedly arisen. But she cut him short, berated him severely, and demanded that he personally deliver Hari into her presence forthwith.

Obviously she has seduction in mind. But that will merely give me another score for my count.

You underestimate the perversity of mortals.

Balu found Hari reading in the garden, whereupon he dutifully, albeit morosely, delivered the zamindarini's message. Hari was surprised but honored at the invita-

tion and immediately accompanied Balu to the zamindarini's chambers. Balu coolly, but with dignity,
presented Hari to the zamindarini, who was now all
sweetness and calm, and at her sign the advisor withdrew, leaving the two alone.

Hari greeted the zamindarini with upraised palms and
waited for her to speak. But she was silent and only gazed
intently at her visitor.

Hari was surprised at the zamindarini's youth and was
admiring of her loveliness; nor could he help but admire
her earthly attributes, which her silver-flecked gown was
cleverly designed not to hide. She, in her turn, fairly
consumed her guest's youthful beauty with her stare.
When finally she spoke, she asked Hari to please be
seated beside her and proceeded to inquire of his back-
ground and how he had happened upon the palace of the
zamindar. He gracefully answered her queries, whereupon there ensued another long silence. That caused
him some uneasiness, for he was beginning to suspect
that there was something on her mind.

Indeed there is! He is a fortunate mortal.

**But also an idiot. It requires two to dance in this manner, and
it is a dangerous dance.**

"I see, Hari," she said, "that you carry a book. Pray
tell, what are you reading?"

"O Zamindarini," he replied, "this is the ancient book
of fables, which I borrowed from the zamindar's library,
wherein I have been reading stories about the making of
friends and enemies."

"Well then, sit closer to me, here, and read me a tale
of friendship. And since we are alone, you may call me
Leela."

"Gladly," he replied, moving a little closer, but not as

close as she had indicated. She reached out and placed her hand on his. He pretended not to notice, but calmly turned the pages of the book looking for a story to tell her.

Thereupon he related the tale of the hound and the wolf queen. Of how, despite their differences in kind and station, the hound and she-wolf became fast friends, like brother and sister, and how they prayed and played together, demonstrating to all their virtues of trust and friendship.

Leela withdrew her hand from Hari's and listened with growing impatience and annoyance. The message was clear enough: Hari would be her friend and nothing more. Her intentions had been detected and as quickly rejected. Even though the manner of negation was gentle and clever, it was a rejection nonetheless—something she could not accept.

You idiot, Hari! Take what offers!

You see what a dolt he is.

"An interesting and amusing story," she said coolly, suppressing her anger. "Now let me tell you a tale, also of the hound and the she-wolf.

"It happened that one day the hound decided to leave the village of his birth in search of knowledge and adventure, and he traveled long and far until, weary and hungry, he came upon a den of wolves. There he stopped and asked the leader of the wolves for food and shelter. The wolf, being favorably inclined toward the well-mannered hound, gave him nourishment and the use of an empty cave near his own. Not long after, the wolf king and his pack went into the forest to hunt. But the wolf king's wife remained behind. Now, she was greatly admiring of the hound, of his long slender body, lithe limbs, and sleek coat, and she greatly desired him. So she invited the hound into her den and offered herself to him. But, even though the wolf queen was comely, the hound, ungrateful cur that he was, spurned her, much to her dismay.

"Later, when the wolf king returned from the hunt, he found that the hound had departed and his wife was in great distress. The she-wolf proceeded to tell her mate how the hound had attempted to force his will upon her, though she had successfully fought him off, and the cur had fled.

"Thereupon the wolf king, in his fury, sent his pack out in search of the traitorous hound. The hound was soon tracked down and held at bay by the pack until the wolf king arrived to deliver his justice. And swift it was: the wolf king grasped the hound by the neck with his sharp teeth and tore out his throat. The pack devoured the remains.

"That ends the tale, O Hari. I pray the moral has not been obscured in the telling."

Now perhaps you see the relevance. Your mortal man is doomed—and you can not touch the she-wolf out of turn.

Hari swallowed as the dread meaning of Leela's words sunk into his consciousness.

"O Mistress, the moral is clear enough," he replied. His mind whirred, searching for some way out of the dilemma. He had little doubt that the zamindarini was capable of lying to the zamindar about the transgressions of a stranger in their midst, and she would surely be believed over him, assuming he would even be given the chance to explain. But how could he yield to her? The zamindar had been kind to him. He could not be an ingrate and a traitor. And even if he did capitulate, what new risks would he then face? No. He must hold firm and try to find a solution.

Yet my mortal man is clever. He will find a way.

Then, of a sudden, as if from the brow of Krishna, an idea came to him.

"O Leela," he said, "do not misunderstand, for surely my eyes have never beheld such beauty as yours—and who am I that I should be so greatly honored by your attentions? Surely I am blessed by the gods this day. If I seem reluctant it is only because there are circumstances which prevent me from giving rein to my heart's desire. Though you have kindled a flame within me, alas, I must strive to extinguish it lest we both commit sacrilege and blaspheme the God of Gods."

Leela was aghast as this declaration and for a moment was speechless.

"I will explain," continued Hari. "Know that when, these many years past, I reached the age of manhood, the time came for me to undergo the sacred religious ceremony wherein I would receive the holy Brahminical thread, this very one that winds about my body. At that time, as is the tradition, I made a sacred vow to Lord Brahma. As all know, a vow so given can not be broken lest Moksha be forever foresaken and future rebirths be as the lowliest creatures that crawl upon the earth.

"My vow to Brahma was this: that nevermore in this life would I look upon the nakedness of woman, nor lie upon the breast of woman.

"And so, O Leela, such is the reason I can not avail myself of the sweetness which is yourself, though my heart be sorely inclined."

A curse on his lying cunning!
What is he doing?

Leela listened in utter amazement. Hari's words rang true, for vows of celibacy on such holy occasions were not uncommon. And knowing the sanctity of such vows, she could not take offense at Hari's unwillingness to succor her. She could not expect him to break his vow.

Though no longer angry, and her pride now repaired, she was still deeply disappointed and pondered the situation mightily. She asked Hari to repeat the exact words of his vow once more. Fortunately, having an excellent memory, he was able to do so. Suddenly Leela's face brightened as though lit by a thousand candles.

"Hari, I have found a way!" she cried, grasping both his hands in hers. "There is a way we can make love without you breaking your vow. Recall in my story of the hound and the she-wolf: had the hound complied with the wolf-queen's wishes, he would have mounted her from behind in the manner of the beasts. Well, then, so can you do the same with me. And you will not—by the very words of your vow—have lain upon the breast of woman. And if all the lights are extinguished with only the blackness of night to keep us company, so then will you have kept your vow not to look upon the nakedness of woman."

Oh, the deviousness of women!

I could not have said it better myself. She will put him into criminal conduct yet, and the zamindar will have his trusted guest's head when he learns of this—as he surely will. Even if some disreputable male servant has to be mysteriously moved to inform him.

Leela clapped her hands in glee, immensely pleased

with her own cleverness. Hari stared at her wide-eyed, benumbed with astonishment. He had been outwitted.

Thereupon Leela bade Hari to leave and return to her that very evening at three hours after sunset. All would be in readiness. She would dismiss her servants, darken the room, leave the door ajar, and be waiting upon the floor cushions in anticipation of his coming. She waved him off with a smile.

No sooner did he return to his room than came a knock on the door, and Balu entered. The advisor hoped to learn what had occurred between Hari and Leela, and from Hari's gloomy look he suspected the worst. Balu knew that Hari would not be forthcoming unless he, Balu, could convince him that he knew of Leela's ways and could be trusted for advice. So with artful indirection the advisor revealed something of his knowledge of Leela and promised that he would keep any secret Hari might care to confide. And if Hari was in difficulty, he would try to help.

Hari would have preferred to keep his own counsel, but he was sorely pressed and time was growing short. So he decided to confide in Balu, who seemed sincere, and thereupon told him the whole story of his visit with Leela.

Balu pursed his lips and shook his head. "A serious problem," he muttered, "very serious. And I fear an insoluble one. Hari, you must flee. Take yourself as far from the palace as you can before the zamindar returns." The advisor then sighed wistfully. "Ah, if it were only I whom she desired!"

"O Balu," said Hari, "I have reason not to flee. Nor am I inclined to do so since I am innocent of wrongdoing. If I run, it would appear an act of guilt. Doubtless the zamindar would track me down anyway."

Together they pondered the problem in silence. The advisor sighed again. Hari looked at Balu and a glimmer of light came into his eyes.

But what is this? The deviousness of a man?

"Tell me, Balu," he asked, "were you in earnest when you said you harbored desire for the zamindarini? Please be candid, I beg you, for much is at stake. If you were, then there may yet be a way out of this dilemma, and perhaps a way to satisfy your desire."

Balu perked up. "I will confess such a desire, fool that I am, for she has long tormented me with her feminine wiles."

Hari then proceeded to tell Balu of his idea, and as Balu listened his heart beat faster, for he saw it was clever indeed. Together they worked out a precise plan in which the advisor readily agreed to collaborate.

They are plotting their way out of it! Disgusting.

At three hours after sunset Hari made his way to Leela's quarters. There were no guards about and Leela's door was ajar as she had promised. He took a deep breath and eased the door open. It was pitch black inside, as also had been agreed upon. He quietly entered, but was careful not to fully close the door behind him.

"Leela?" he whispered.

"I am here, Hari," came the soft reply, "in the center of the room among the cushions where you last saw me. Come to me. I am ready."

"Yes," he answered. "But first I would ask one thing of you. So that our joy may be complete, and so that we may be transported to the lofty realm of the gods and our minds and bodies be merged in perfect union, pray let no words pass between us this night from this moment hence. Let only the sweet silence of darkness mingle with your fragrance and bathe us in the stillness of bliss."

"Oh gladly, gladly," Leela replied, her passion redoubled by Hari's words. "Now come to me, for my flesh is burning."

Quickly, Hari slipped soundlessly through the door and into the corridor as Balu, just as nimbly, entered the room and eased the door shut. The advisor hastily disrobed, dropping his garments by the door, then proceeded to grope his way on all fours through the darkness in search of the waiting object of his desires. Guided by the sound of Leela's belabored breathing and the fragrance of her body perfume, he had no difficulty locating her among the floor cushions. His outstretched hand came first in contact with her smooth pulsating buttocks. He soon ascertained that she was bent over in the stipulated position. Thereupon, without delay or hesitation, he assailed the waiting bastion of delight with leonine eagerness, and henceforth the stillness was interrupted only by moans of labored ecstasy: a serenade of the night newly sung, yet as ageless as man and the gods before.

Hari returned to his rooms and prayed that the charade would be successful and that Balu would be able to satiate Leela's appetite so that a repeat performance would not soon be necessary.

A scullery servant, meanwhile, was searching the kitchen for a lost earring, a favorite bit of jewelry his father had given him as a child. Unable to find it, he concluded that it must have fallen sometime during the afternoon while in the performance of his duties. With the aid of an oil lamp, he immediately began retracing his steps through the dimly lit halls of the palace. As fortune would have it, and much to his relief, he found the earring in a corridor not far from the rooms of the zamindarini.

As he passed the door to the zamindarini's suite on the way back to his room, he heard a strange noise coming from within—a low moaning sound. Puzzled, he stopped to listen for a moment. He again heard the moaning, which was now louder, and could only think that the zamindarini must be ill and in pain. Concerned about his mistress, he knocked lightly on the door. There was no reply. He realized that he should report this to his superior, the majordomo, who would send a discreet woman to investigate, but the hour was late and the majordomo would not appreciate being disturbed over what was probably nothing. Yet suppose it wasn't nothing?

No, mortal moron. You must investigate yourself, this instant. This makes sense in the circumstance.

So the man, believing this to be his own thought, quietly opened the door and entered the room, holding up the oil lamp to illuminate the darkened interior.

Oh! You are exposing the liaison! But to what purpose? Hari is not here, so will not be blamed.

His breath caught. There, squatting naked on the floor amidst a multitude of cushions, was the zamindarini, and attached to her from behind was the advisor, Balu. The servant saw that the moans were indeed those of his mistress, but moans of pain, he now realized, they were not.

As the lamplight flooded the room, all activity within ceased. Leela shot a look of surprise mingled with threat at the intruder, but her expression transformed into one of utter amazement as her eyes fell upon Balu behind her. Balu, stupified and benumbed with shock, a look of abject terror on his face, silently prayed for death to strike him swiftly.

But the zamindarini will blame Hari for tricking her like this, and have him promptly executed along with Balu and the servant, thus covering her shame and protecting herself from exposure.

The servant was the first to gain his wits, and he slipped out of the room without uttering a word. Balu started to pull away in fear, but Leela cried out: "Hold, Balu! I command it!" Balu froze, not daring to move a muscle.

"So, I have been tricked!" Leela's words slithered like a cobra.

A cunning ploy, Ravana. But I shall counter it by putting a thought into her head—a thought to which she is not averse.

Then Leela smiled slyly. "But Krishna works in wonderful ways, does he not? You, Balu, have long lusted after me, not entirely due to discouragement on my part. But I would never have considered you because I thought you unmanly. I know now that I was wrong. Had it not been for the little game you and Hari have played, I would never have discovered your virtues. For, know you Balu, never before have I experienced such pleasure as I have this night. Your endowment is indeed generous and would put a bull to shame, and your skill at its employ is that of a master.

"So! I command you now—nay, I entreat you." Her voice softened to a purr. "Will you not continue to employ your talents on your zamindarini's behalf? Will you not resurrect your virtue and complete what you have so well begun? Fear not, our secret will be safe. I will even forgive Hari, for without him this night's pleasure would not have come to pass.

"And besides," she added, laughing, "now we need not be restricted to the position of the beasts, but may indulge ourselves in the full range of exotic delights that the great Vatsyayana has bequeathed us."

Balu could hardly believe his ears, but neither did he question his fate or hesitate before it. Rather, he offered up a silent prayer to Brahma, and proceeded forthwith to engage with Leela, bringing to her and himself the manifold pleasures and delights that the great God of Gods, by so fashioning his children, intended for them to enjoy.

Then he remembered the scullery servant. "Suppose the servant tells the zamindar?"

Leela shrugged. "Must I turn advisor to you, as well as lover? Surely you can advise him that his choice is between a promotion to more comfortable employment, such as night guardian of the palace to ensure that no other person learns of our liaisons, or the untimely loss of his tongue? Is there any doubt of the nature of his choice?"

"No doubt at all, my mistress."

So you have countered me, Mohini, this time. You have accomplished your first seduction, and balked my first kill. But six more such challenges remain, O luscious one.

Six more remain, you ugly spook.

When late in the night Balu departed the rooms of the zamindarini, promising he would meet with her again soon, he stopped by to briefly visit with Hari. Thereupon he related all that had occurred with Leela, and they both laughed until tears came to their eyes.

The next morning when Meena delivered Hari his

breakfast of fresh eggs, he told her the happenings of the previous day. Though she was not at all amused by the tale, she could not help but admire the boldness of Hari's plan and his courage in carrying it out. Most of all she was relieved that the zamindarini no longer had any romantic interest in Hari. She had no wish to share him with anyone.

❖ *3* ❖

The Cave of the Guru

This episode is done. We must move on to the next challenge.

I find this interlude pleasant enough. The mortal man is a fine lover, and I enjoy occupying the mortal woman as she indulges his passion.

Then I shall call time on you, you succulent spirit, for you are not indulging my passion. If you will not agree to urge your mortal man onward to the next challenge, you must indulge me during the delay with a portion of the lustful activity I shall command when I win this contest between us. This is the nature of our deal.

I shall give you no early sating of your lust, you monstrosity. I shall arrange to nudge the cute mortal man to develop a desire to travel again. It will be easy enough to cause the mortal woman Meena to press upon him too closely.

And I shall nudge the regional rajah to issue an invitation that the dull mortal man will be obliged to accept. I think there will be interesting opportunities in the rajah's palace. We are agreed that such nudges do not constitute moves in our game, beautiful?

We are agreed, tuskface.

The days that followed were pleasantly uneventful. Hari spent many idle hours strolling in the palace gardens with Meena, talking and laughing about nothing in particular, reveling in nature's wonders. They picked flowers, fed the parrots and peacocks, and chased butterflies and one another. Too, Hari met often with Balu, who was a veritable fount of knowledge and who patiently answered his endless questions about palace life and neighboring lands and peoples. Other questions he sought answers to in the zamindar's great library, where he immersed himself in books on history, geography, and literature.

Yet, despite the many pleasures that palace life offered, a growing restlessness crept upon him and once again he felt the pull of the open road. Also, Meena was becoming overly attentive and possessive. She would lovingly fuss about his deplorable lack of neatness, insisting on smoothing out every wrinkle in his tunic and was forever straightening out the sacred thread around his shoulder. When he retreated to some remote corner of the palace to read, she would seek him out and find some real or imagined imperfection in his appearance about which she would gently chastise him and insist on putting right. Always he politely submitted to her attentions, never being so ungracious as to show discomfort or annoyance.

Though he desired Meena and felt a genuine fondness for her, he did not think he loved her, for he still slept well, retained his interest in the world about him, and suffered no feelings of lightness in his stomach or head. She would make some man an excellent wife, but marriage was not what he sought.

No sooner had he decided to leave the palace than news came of the zamindar's return. He knew now he would have to postpone his departure, for courtesy and custom required he pay his respects to his host and not absent himself so abruptly.

Balu confessed to Hari his mixed emotions about his master's homecoming. He would enjoy returning to his advisory duties, but would sorely miss his secret meetings with Leela. He took solace in the knowledge that the zamindar would be making a tax collection trip before too long.

It occurs to me that tracking the mortal man constantly as he trudges about will grow tedious. Let me brand him, so we can readily locate him when we wish to.

Don't brand him! I want him to remain as handsome as he is. Give him a marker instead, and we shall orient on that marker.

As you wish. There is the zamindar's enchanted medallion. That should do. It will be easy to spy, because of its magical aura.

That amulet is dangerous!

Only when invoked. This will add spice to the contest, lest it grow wearisome.

Very well. We shall give him the amulet. But if you cause the amulet to be invoked, it shall then be my move, regardless of its effect.

Agreed.

The zamindar invited Hari to a private dinner in his chambers on the evening of his homecoming, at which Balu was also present. He spoke about his recent visit with the rajah and how he had amused His Majesty by repeating the witty remarks that Hari had made at their first meeting at the palace gate. The rajah had been so delighted that he asked the zamindar to invite this clever lad to visit him and perhaps verbally joust with the court advisors, whom, the rajah felt, could well use the competition.

"And so, Hari," said the zamindar, "it seems you have

an invitation to visit the rajah. It is an honor indeed, one that I hope you will appreciate and accept. But there is no hurry. Tarry awhile and give us the pleasure of your company a few days longer."

Hari was overwhelmed and flattered by the news. "O Zamindar, I am indeed honored, though I am unworthy. But I humbly accept, as it pleases both you and his highness."

"Well spoken," said the zamindar. "And do not be frightened at the prospect of gibing with the rajah's advisors, for you are equal to the best of them.

"Now, in appreciation of the pleasure you have brought me and my household, and in consideration of the long journey you are about to take, I grant you a boon. Name what you will, and if it be within my power I will grant it. Well, what say you, Hari?"

Taken by surprise, Hari did not immediately respond as he searched for an answer. He had no strong desire for jewels or fine clothes, and felt that an extravagant request would be unseemly. A good horse would serve him well on the journey ahead, but he really preferred to walk that he might better observe the world about him. What he did wish was that the goddess of good fortune would continue to journey by his side, but the zamindar had no power to command that. Yet he knew he must ask for something lest he offend the zamindar.

Now touch him, in the manner we agreed.

Done. This does not count as a move.

"There is one small thing I would humbly request, O Master," Hari replied, having a sudden notion. "The goddess Lakshmi traveled with me on my way here, as she accompanied you on your recent journey. Let me borrow that good luck charm which hangs about your neck that I may wear it on my journey to the rajah, and perhaps the goddess will again follow and protect me."

At these words Balu sucked in his breath and all but jumped out of his chair. He hurriedly pulled the zamindar aside and whispered anxiously in his ear. Hari heard only snatches of the conversation, but he surmised that Balu was urging the zamindar not to give up the charm and to offer something else instead. But the zamindar apparently refused to heed Balu's counsel, judging from the shaking of his head, and finally he said in an angry tone, loud enough for Hari to hear, that a man's word was his bond, and sobeit. The zamindar and Balu returned to their seats.

"I will grant your request, Hari." The zamindar's voice was now somber. "But in entrusting you with the medallion, I ask that you guard it well, for it is dear to me. Know that it is very ancient and has been in my family for many generations. I must have your solemn promise that you will return it to me after your visit with the rajah. Whether the goddess of fortune will be lured by the amulet, I can not say, but I wish you well. I will give it to you on the day of your departure. Now, let us do justice to this fine dinner lest the chief cook take his vengeance on us in dinners to come."

Meena withheld her tears when Hari told her he would be leaving soon. She did not ask when he would return, knowing that he himself did not know. On their last night together she stayed with him longer than usual, giving wholly of herself as though to imprint her love forever on his memory. When the day came for him to depart, she kept to her room so that no one would see her weeping.

The zamindar and Balu walked with Hari to the palace gate. The zamindar took the medallion from his own neck and hung it around Hari's, and gave him a sealed message for the rajah. Hari tucked the medallion beneath his tunic and carefully stored the message in his knapsack. Balu pointed out the direction Hari should take and told him of landmarks along the way. The zamindar and Balu gave Hari their blessings and kept watch until he disappeared into the western foothills.

Now he is marked. There is no need to track him every step of his dull journey. Let us play together, delicious one, until the mortal man achieves the rajah's palace.

Play with yourself, tasteless one! I shall mind my own business until the next challenge us upon us.

In due course you will play my tune, Mohini.

I hope never to render such a sour note, Ravana.

Hari did not look back, his thoughts only of the adventures that lay ahead. He rejoiced in the sweeping majesty of the sky, hills, and mountains beyond, and in the many small things that appeared along the path: the bright flash of a bulbul bird scurrying through the brush, the graceful undulations of a caterpillar creeping up a blade of grass, the perfect symmetry of the shiny sloughed-off skin of a snake clinging to a stone, and the wrinkled face that time had carved into the twisted trunk of a long-dead banyan tree.

He saw no other on the path, but Balu had told him the route was not a well-traveled one. The night he spent under the heavens. He slept soundly, lulled by the rhythmical twinkling of the stars playing their silent ragas of eternity. He thought of the stars as the eyes of the universe, eternal witnesses to the events of the night that blinked in wonder at what they saw.

The next day the going was difficult. The path became rocky and the air thinner as the elevation increased. The foothills gave way to stark jagged mountains, their massive faces lined with crevices like somber old men, aloof and unfriendly. With the approach of evening the air grew chilly. Darkness quickly melted down the cliffsides. As Hari was about to settle for a rocky cranny for his bed, he saw a faint light flickering on the face of a bluff just ahead. He walked further up the path to investigate, and saw that the illumination came from a fire burning in a cave low in the cliffside. From the changing shapes of the shadows on the cliff walls, he could tell that the cave was inhabited.

He climbed cautiously to the ledge near the mouth of the cave and was about to peek in when a voice from inside called out: "Come in, come in young man, the fire is warm and the night is cold. No cause to be afraid. There is only one harmless old man here. Ah, yes, quite harmless."

The voice was raspy though gentle and reassuring. Hari peered into the cave and saw sitting before a small fire a wizened old man with a long white beard, garbed in a plain white dhoti and shawl. A teapot sat on the fire, and neatly laid out on a blanket, as if awaiting an expected guest, were two cups and plates.

"Well come in, come in," said the old man, this time with a note of impatience. "The tea is ready and needs to be drunk hot."

Hari entered the cave, gave the traditional hand greeting, and bowed low before the old man. "I thank you, master," he said. "The night is indeed cold, and a hot cup of tea would be welcome."

"Well, sit then," said the old man, pointing to the blanket, "and take some chapatis with your tea. I made them myself only this afternoon. Ah yes, my abode is humble but well provisioned."

"My thanks," said Hari, and he sat down and joined the old man. No one spoke until all the flatbread had been consumed and the third cup of tea poured. Out of politeness, Hari waited until his host spoke first.

"Well go ahead and ask your questions," the old man said finally, the frown on his forehead summoning forth a thousand wrinkles. "I can see that you are curious. Go ahead, but make it brief."

"Old master, I was wondering if you are a guru, for it is said that gurus sometimes live in caves apart from other men."

"Hmm. Some call me guru and some call me pundit. And some call me a crazy old fool. Labels are meaningless. I am Narusimhum. My life is one of solitude and contemplation, although at times I enjoy a little company. There are those who choose to call themselves my followers, and they bring me food and ask a lot of silly questions."

Hari was greatly impressed, for it was clear that his host was indeed a guru. But he refrained from asking any more questions, which the guru would no doubt consider silly.

Hari saw that his host's cup was empty, so he reached out for the teapot, and as he leaned forward the medallion that hung around his neck slipped out of his tunic. A look of amazement came over the guru's face.

Look at what he knows about that talisman!

More than the zamindar does. I hope he does not tell Hari, because the innocent man might be tempted to experiment.

"Young man," said the guru in a tremulous voice, "how came you by that talisman about your neck?" Hari could think of no reason not to answer the question, so he told the guru how he had acquired the medallion and of his promise to return it to the zamindar following his visit with the rajah.

The guru seemed greatly relieved. "Now be sure to guard the medallion well and keep it hidden," he admonished solemnly.

"But, O Guru," said Hari, "you called it a talisman, which is a thing of magic. Tell me, is there something about the charm that is special?"

"Hmm. Well, it is very old and quite unusual. Yes, such things have special value. But enough words have been spoken. It is time for bed. You can sleep by the fire. It will last through the night." The guru then disappeared into the darkness at the back of the cave.

That is a relief.

For you, perhaps. I would be happy to see it kill the fool.

Remember, if he invokes it—

I know, nymph of Indra's heaven, I know. I will not cause it to be invoked.

Hari yawned, tired from his long trek that day. No sooner did he lay his head down on the blanket than he fell into a sound sleep.

He awoke the next morning to the tune of a steaming teapot. A plate of assorted fruit lay on the blanket beside him. The guru sat nearby, frozen in a posture of contemplation, his eyes closed. Hari dared not disturb him and ate some fruit as he waited patiently for the old master to emerge from his trance. But the guru did not move. Finally, feeling the need to be on his way, Hari shrugged, bowed to the guru, and quietly departed.

As he climbed down the cliffside to the path, he suddenly heard the guru's voice ring out: "Should right to left bring peril, remember left to right. Left to right!" He stopped and waited for more of the guru's words, but there was only silence. Strange, he thought, as he set his foot upon the path and continued on his way.

❧ *4* ❧

The She-Demon

Hari whistled as he walked, a simple tune which he composed in his head and elaborated on in endless variations. The path had become level and smoother, though the bluffs were higher now and hemmed him in on either side. The gleaming mountain caps and the sliver of blue sky overhead were the only things of beauty to lighten his heart. The hours passed slowly.

Toward sundown he came upon an empty cave alongside the path. The goddess of fortune still traveled with him, he thought. He gathered some brush that grew among the rocks and with the flint he carried soon had a small fire going.

He watched the reflections from the flickering flames cavort with the shadows on the cave walls as he consumed a meal of figs and mangoes. For water he had only to step outside the cave entrance where numerous rivulets ran down the mountainside from above.

His thoughts turned to the zamindar's medallion. He took it from around his neck and held it up before the fire to examine it. There were Sanskrit letters etched into the metal on both sides, which were faint and worn. There were also symbols on both sides: on one side an eye within a five-pointed star, and on the other a seven-pointed star within a triangle.

Having learned Sanskrit from the village pundit, he tried to read the letters on one side of the medallion. They seemed to form a single long word. He tried pronouncing the word, first one syllable at a time, then by combining them. He tried several times, but some of the letters were so worn he could not be sure he was using the right ones. Finally he said: "Narakasurakanasanjum!"

No sooner had he spoken than the ground began to tremble and small stones fell from the ceiling all about him. And lo! A crack opened up in the center of the cave floor. Swords of flame shot out of the opening and a dense mist billowed forth. The mist churned and condensed and began to shape itself into a human figure.

Ravana! You cheated! You caused him to invoke the amulet!

I did not! I was not even there. I was going to focus on the idiot when he reached the rajah's palace.

Well, the amulet has been invoked, so it is my turn.

The mist solidified, forming into a flesh-and-blood person. And there before Hari stood a beautiful young woman clad in a diaphanous red gown, with cinnamon skin the smoothness of polished gemstones, dark eyes that reached into one's very soul, a cascade of fine black hair that fell to her knees, large full breasts that rose and fell like great ocean swells, and long limbs that tapered to finely etched hands and feet.

Look into his mind. He did it himself.

Because you sneaked the urge into his fancy.

Hari's fear faded into wonder as he beheld the beauteous creature. Surely, he told himself, one so lovely, even though a spirit, could not be evil.

I yield the move under protest. Play it through, and in due course we shall see.

We shall indeed see. I still think you cheated.

"You spoke my name, young master," she said. Her voice was soft and lilting. "By so doing you have released me from my prison within the earth. For that I am most grateful."

"Who—who are you?" Hari stammered. "Where did you come from?"

"I am she whose name you spoke, a name which I myself may never speak. I am a creation of the elder gods who set me upon the earth to dwell among mortal men, to serve them and bring them pleasure."

"Pleasure?"

"Yes. And for many ages I did so, until three centuries ago I was ensorcelled by the great rishi, Baksura, who imprisoned me in a rock deep within the earth. In that prison I have remained until this hour of my deliverance. You spoke my name and set me free."

"But—but why did the rishi imprison you?"

"The rishi is mortal and did not understand my purpose. What mortals do not understand, they sometimes fear and seek to destroy."

"And is your only purpose to bring mankind pleasure?"

"Man, yes. But my pleasure is not for all men. It is reserved for a few great men, the pathbreakers, men of vision and ideas, men who seek to redirect the destiny of nations, men who challenge the very gods themselves. Such are those who have known me, who have partaken of my gift." She peered at him, her lovely brow furrowing. This seemed to make her even more comely, though this was hardly possible. "But I see your next question written in your eyes, my young savior. What of my gift? Well, you shall know it. Because you have liberated me this day, and because I would ask of you one small thing more—and not least because I find you attractive—I will reward you with this, my gift."

Before Hari could utter another word, a light giddy sensation came over him. A shower of tinkling emanations washed over his body, relaxing him, and his mind emptied itself of all questions and reservations. The beautiful lady opened her arms to him, her whole being radiating love and desire. Her gown slipped from her shoulders, revealing her nakedness in all its perfection. Her beauty drew him, impelled him, as surely as a wayward comet is drawn to the heart of the sun.

As he stepped into her enfolding embrace, the walls of the cave faded into invisibility. Softness and warmth enwrapped him in a blanket of ether, the vastness of the universe his bed. His every sense and perception sharpened and refined itself, multiplying and accumulating into tidal waves of pleasure. He felt unbounded freedom.

Deep within his body a turmoil gathered with the strength of a thousand volcanos. Comets of blazing lights and colors flashed all about as if in celebration of some momentous event, enveloping him in a cosmic embrace. The very seams of space seemed to split apart and explode in a blinding radiance. A million stars fragmented and for an instant hung suspended in the firmament before streaming into the limitless void.

He felt himself being lifted in a final shudder of unendurable delight, then the whirling galaxies gradually grew dim and faded away. Darkness gently closed around him, caressing him, lulling him into the sweet oblivion of dreamless sleep.

And I have my second seduction, despite you.

I am by no means sure of that.

He woke to find himself lying on the cave floor next to a crackling fire. At first he could not remember where he was, but as his eyes wandered about the cave he saw the magical lady, and all memory returned.

He did not move or give any sign that he was awake, but watched her secretly. She was kneeling on the cave floor, her back to him, softly chanting some strange words in a harsh guttural language he had never heard before. He wondered if they were magical words and if she was performing a ritual of some kind.

She raised her arms and bowed down as if praying. As her head bent forward, her overflowing tresses parted and fell to either side of her shoulders. And Hari saw that embedded in the back of her head was an eye.

He held his breath, not daring to move a muscle. The eye was open, its pupil black as night, and it looked straight at him, penetrating to his very heart. The lady then lifted her head and her hair fell back into place, covering the terrible eye. She continued her chanting, showing no awareness of being spied upon, so Hari guessed that he had not been seen. Rather, that the eye had seen him but not caught him spying on it. But he knew now that the creature he had conjured up out of the earth was none other than a she-demon.

The creature ceased her chanting and turned toward Hari. He pretended sleep. She gently called to him and he opened his eyes and stretched as though just awakening. He glanced toward the cave entrance and could tell by the receding moonlight that dawn was not far off. Somewhere he had heard that demons were strong by night but weak by day. He hoped that was not a tale told by old wives.

"Come, let us sit together by the fire and talk," said

the she-demon, her voice soft and inviting. Hari obligingly pushed closer to the fire. "Now, young master, I
would ask something of you, a small thing. As it is forbidden that I utter my own name lest I suffer the gravest
of consequences, and not having heard it spoken these
three centuries past until this day, I bid you to speak it
again, twice more, that I may take a measure of pleasure
in hearing it."

Hari knew from stories that demons were deceitful
and not to be trusted, and therefore that he must avoid
saying the she-demon's name again lest some terrible
thing happen.

"O beautiful lady," he replied in an innocent voice, "it
was only by chance that I correctly spoke your name
after many erroneous attempts. And in truth I do not remember the correct pronunciation. So please forgive
my ignorance and inability to comply with your request."

"But you wear the talisman of the Asura king about
your neck. Upon the face of the talisman appears my
name, placed there by the great master himself. Pray
read my name from the disk."

"Oh yes, the medallion. It seems it is more than just
a simple charm. There are signs inscribed on both sides.
Can you enlighten me as to their meaning?"

"The sign which appears above my name is my own.
Its meaning may not be divulged to mortals. Nor is it
wise for you to inquire of the other name and sign. There
is danger in such knowledge. But I ask you again, will you
not read and speak my name?" Her tone revealed growing impatience.

"O lovely lady, I do not think I can say your name correctly, though if it pleases you I will try. But you must be patient with me, for Sanskrit was always my poorest subject."

Hari held up the talisman, shifting his body about to catch the best light. He studied it intently. "You must give me a moment to go over the letters one by one," he said, "for they are faint, and your name is a long and difficult one." He slowly mouthed each letter and formed them into syllables. Then he combined them and said loudly: "Nakasurakasanjum!"

"That is close," said the she-demon, "but you omitted the second and seventh syllables. Try again."

"Hmm. Yes, I see. I shall try once more." He again studied the talisman, slowly forming each letter and syllable with his lips. After as long a delay as he dared, he said: "Narakasirakanasanjum!"

"Almost, almost!" cried the demoness, raising her arms in excitement. "Try once more, just once more. It was the middle letter of the fourth syllable that you misread."

"Ah yes, I see the error. Give me another moment." Again Hari feigned the same ritual, mouthing each letter, this time knitting his brow in concentration. Then he smiled, his face aglow with assurance, and he shouted: "Narakisurakasanjum!"

"No! No!" screamed the she-demon, jumping to her feet in anger and frustration. "Now it is worse than ever! You are a stupid fool!"

Hari sat motionless, his heart racing. He dared not speak. The demoness glared down at him, fire in her eyes, her breasts heaving. Her ravishing form remained, but somehow she no longer looked beautiful so much as dangerous. After a long silence, she became calm and sat down again.

"So, my young lover," she said, her voice now edged with malice, "you play games with me. Let us speak plainly, shall we not?" She pointed her forefinger straight at Hari's nose. "Now, why will you not say my name? I warn you, speak not falsely or it will be at your peril."

Hari gulped down a small lake of spittle that had accumulated in his mouth. "Very well, I will be truthful. But so must you be. I do not think a true love-spirit would threaten her lover—unless you are more than you say."

The she-demon's eyes narrowed. "Very well," she hissed, "telling you my story is a small price to pay.

"Know that I am a princess of the rock demons, created ages ago by the Asura king to seduce mortal men. But, as I told you, my pleasures are not for all men—only those few who would leap the centuries and dare to challenge the tempo of history as preordained by the gods. Such men are grave threats, and so their march must be slowed. Such was my task, and to accomplish it the Asura king bestowed upon me the gifts of immortality, great beauty, and the power to divert men from their purpose. As you have witnessed, my skill is of the flesh, the perennial weakness of man. So it is that I embrace the chosen few as they are about to collide with destiny and alter the path of history. Such pleasures do I bring them that their purpose is forgotten in the oblivion of my embrace. And so that brief receptive moment in history passes by, and mankind continues to stumble through the ages, slowly, step by step, as the gods intended.

"Ten million years I delayed the discovery of fire, five

million the discovery of the wheel, one million years the
bow and arrow, ten thousand years the alphabet, five
thousand years agriculture, three thousand years the
forging of iron, one thousand years geometry, map-
making, the compass. And much more." She paused, re-
flectively, evidently proud of her accomplishments.

"When the rishi, Baksura, imprisoned me in a rock
three centuries past, I cried out to the Asura king for deliverance, but the rishi's powers were great and could not
be easily overcome. And so, with his own hand, the master of demons fashioned a talisman as the means of my
escape. Upon it he etched my name and sign and set it
among mortal men. As you know, the power of the talisman is such that whoever possesses it and speaks my
name sets me free. My name spoken once frees me for
one night, spoken twice, for a century, and spoken
thrice, for a thousand years. You, young master, are my
first deliverer. But you must say my name again before
the sun rises this day, else I will be returned to my prison.

"You have heard my story. The time grows short. So
I once again ask you—say my name. Speak it now. I
know that you can. For your reward I will grant you the
pleasures of my companionship on the first night of each
full moon for all the years of your life."

Hari was horrified by the she-demon's revelation, and
yet he could not help being tempted by her promised reward. Even now, the afterglow of her embrace lingered
and warmed him. But how could he liberate such a creature into the world of men?

He knew that sunrise was not far off. If the she-demon
was history's ageless mistress of delay, he must now be
its master for a few moments longer.

"O demoness," he said, "your story is indeed marvelous. But tell me, what of the sorcerer Baksura, how it is that. . . ."

"There is no more time for questions!" the demoness shouted angrily. "Speak my name now!"

"Very well, I will try." Hari held up the talisman and studied it intently. Out of the corner of his eye he could see the she-demon's expression change from impatience to fury. Suddenly, in an eyeblink, she dissolved into a column of mist. The mist churned and swirled, then began to solidify.

The demoness now stood before him in another guise—that of a hideous monster. A head taller than he, she was covered with warted skin of greenish hue. Three yellow-slitted eyes bulged from a forehead covered with drooping folds of flesh. Her eyes were narrow and pointed, her nose an empty pit, and out of a lipless gash in her face projected double rows of fangs licked by a serpentine tongue. A matted thatch of thick black hair covered her head and pelvis, two pendulous dugs hung limply from a narrow chest, and two attenuated arms extended from stooped shoulders. In place of hands were bony three-fingered claws ending in long curved talons.

The creature spoke, its voice sibilant and menacing. "Speak my name now, or I will rend you limb from limb!"

Hari knew his time had run out. He thought to run, but the she-monster stood between him and the cave exit. His brain whirred. Then, as a bolt from the heavens, he remembered the parting words of the old guru: "Should right to left bring peril, remember left to right." Of course! The she-demon's name was etched on the medallion in ancient Sanskrit which read from right to left. Then left to right must mean to speak the name backward.

The she-monster screeched and raised its claws. Hari backed to the cave wall and with shaking hands held up the talisman. There would be time for only one try. He sucked in his breath and cried: "Mujnasanakarusakaran!"

The creature's talons descended toward Hari's throat, but when only a span away they slammed into an invisible barrier. Again the creature delivered a crushing blow, and again it was blocked by an invisible shield. The she-monster screamed in rage and continued to hammer at the barrier, but to no avail.

The first rays of sunlight peeked over the surrounding circle of mountains and poured down over the crags and crevices. A shaft of sunlight shot into the cave as from a bow and struck the she-monster. A pitiful wail rang out as the creature shuddered and began to turn to mist. The cave trembled and the writhing mist was sucked through the crack in the cave floor. As the last wispy wraiths disappeared, the crack closed and the trembling ceased.

So you influenced the she-demon to let him go.

I did not! It remains my turn.

I deny it. I think you sneaked in a thought. It is now my turn.

By no means. I retain the turn. I protest your challenge.

I protest this entire episode! You are claiming a seduction when you did nothing to promote it.

Our deal specifies seven seductions. It does not say I have to promote them.

We shall have to go to a higher authority to settle this matter, precious.

Yes. I am confident I will prevail, repulsive.

For a long time Hari did not move. When finally his fear subsided, he held out an arm to see if the invisible shield was still there. It was gone. He sighed and gave silent thanks to the goddess Lakshmi for her protection, and asked a special blessing for the old guru whose words had saved his life.

He resumed his journey. The path now sloped downward, and by midday the mountains melted into foothills. His heart gladdened to see the sun again, to feel the fullness of its warmth upon his brow.

5

The Eye of Kali

The land became flatter and turned from green to golden brown. A vast plain stretched out to the horizon, its rippling fur paling and darkening in the breeze. The grass rustled, whispering of dark secrets, and when the breeze quickened, it hissed angrily in warning to the unwary traveler.

Hari trudged through the desolate lowlands for two days without seeing tree or creature, save for an occasional vulture circling high overhead and snakes sunning themselves on the path. Toward evening on the third day he came upon a coppice of coconut palms fed by a spring. The cool water slaked his thirst and revived his spirits, and the fresh coconut meat seemed a feast after days of dried fruit and stale bread.

He has wandered from the proper path.

That is as it may be. Perhaps there will be opportunity for a challenge along this route. Unless you prefer to interfere, to correct his path, and give me the next move?

I shall see what offers here.

As he dined in the shade of a tall palm, a dog suddenly appeared: a small brown mongrel, thin and scruffy, the kind of pathetic creature found on the streets of many villages. The dog wagged its tail and whined, begging for food. Hari tossed it some scraps, which instantly disappeared, and called the dog to him. It approached cautiously, the circumscribed half-wag of its tail advertising its uncertainty. Buttressed by Hari's gentle words and another handout, it allowed itself to be stroked and scratched behind the ear. Hari hoped the presence of the dog meant a village was nearby; his provisions were in need of replenishment and he would welcome a hot meal for a change.

He yawned. His eyelids grew heavy as he watched the sun chariot ride to the edge of the earth and disappear behind a scarlet feathering of clouds. His soul at peace, he was lulled to sleep by the burbling of the spring and the syncopated winking of the stars.

Next morning he took to the road early, the dog running on ahead, barking at any small creature on the path and driving it into the brush. Soon they came to a fork in the path. One branch, no more than a thin trail, veered to the south, and the other wider branch ran north. Not knowing which to take, Hari was inclined toward the wider one, but his companion chose otherwise. The dog ran merrily down the southerly trail, barking for Hari to follow. Thinking the dog might be near its home, he followed its wagging banner, and before long he spied the walls of a village.

The dog ran ahead and disappeared through a chink in the base of the wall. The wall was too high to scale, so Hari walked on in search of an entrance. Soon enough he reached the main village gate, an imposing barrier of solid wood, but it was closed. He rapped on the gate and called out, and soon he heard the grinding of an inner crossbar, and the massive door swung open.

A half-dozen armed guards immediately rushed out

and greeted him with the point of their spears. Without explanation he was hustled into the village and the gate was locked behind him. Though alarmed by the hostile reception, he was even more startled to see that his captors were all young women. None wore the traditional saris, but were clad in dull homespun uniforms, quite in keeping with their stern visages.

As he was marched down the main street of the village, all eyes turned upon him, and he could not help noticing a look of sadness on the faces of the villagers. Too, he saw only men and children in the streets. Other than his guards, there was not a woman to be seen anywhere.

He was led to a large golden-domed temple at the center of the village and through a maze of corridors within. The corridor walls were covered with paintings of the deities, dulled and streaked with age. He saw Vishnu in the proud guise of a lion, and Siva dancing before the figure of a great lingam and yoni. Scalloped eaves were decorated with friezes of fornicating gods, and gilded tableaus from the Hariyana were etched into wooden pillars and baseboards.

Upon entering the central hall of worship, Hari was amazed to see lined up on either side of the room row upon row of women: doubtless here was the entire adult female population of the village. At the far end of the hall, glowering down over the assembly, stood an enormous golden idol, fully five times the height of a man. The giant figure sat crosslegged, a great red ruby protruding from its forehead. The idol's six graceful arms stretched out invitingly; one clutched a sword.

Hari saw that the bare-breasted deity was garlanded

with skulls, and he knew at once that this could only be the great goddess Kali. A shudder ran through him. Kali: the black one, the inaccessible, the patroness of murderers, the goddess of sacrifice and death.

But Kali had other aspects as well, he knew. She was the goddess of fertility, the Divine Mother, the primal female, and as such was worshipped peacefully and lovingly by many of her cult-followers. Finding himself now surrounded solely by women gave him hope that it was the feminine and not the sacrificial aspect of Kali that they worshipped.

A door opened on the right side of the hall and a young woman emerged dressed in an elaborate robe that bespoke her to be the high priestess. She was followed by an entourage of plainly gowned acolytes. As she approached him, Hari saw that her stern demeanor was unable to disguise her striking beauty.

Ignoring Hari's bow of respect, the priestess forthwith accosted him in an angry voice that echoed throughout the chamber. "I am Sumi, tantric priestess of the goddess Kali. Who are you and why did you come to this village?"

"O priestess, my name is Hari. I am but a wandering student traveling in search of truth and wisdom. It was only by chance that I came upon your village. Indeed, I fear that I am lost. The road I seek is that which leads to the city of the rajah. I would be most grateful for your direction that I may continue upon my journey."

"Your journey ends here, intruder, in this village. That much is certain. It is only your fate that is uncertain."

"O priestess, I do not understand. Have I given offense in some way?"

"You are a male. That is offense enough. By the will
of Kali, all men in this village are bound to the service
of women and are governed and ruled by women. No
man who enters this village ever leaves. Your fate will be
decided by Kali herself soon enough. Meanwhile, you
will be given work to do like the other men. And do not
try to escape. The attempt will be fruitless and the punishment severe."

Are you sure you did not interfere to put him in this diffi-
culty?

How could I have? It is a woman who brings him this mischief.
I must admit to liking her attitude.

With that the priestess turned and exited the hall. The
assembly broke up, and Hari was ushered out of the
temple under guard and led down a side street lined with
mud huts. The guard stopped in front of one of the huts
and told Hari to enter and remain there for the night. He
would be given a work assignment in the morning.

Hari sat alone in the semidarkness of the hut wondering at his predicament. Soon a man entered and
greeted him, introducing himself as Balram, a field
worker who lived in the hut.

Balram was of middle years, had an intelligent face,
and seemed quite friendly. He immediately set about
preparing the evening meal, which consisted of maize
cakes, fruit, and milk, which he asked Hari to share.
Hari gratefully accepted, and as they dined Hari told Balram of his experience in the temple and asked how it was
that women ruled over men in the village.

"It is a strange story," Balram said, lowering his voice
to a whisper. "But I will tell it.

"Not two years ago this was a happy village, a good
place to live and raise children. Men were masters of

their own households, as were their fathers and forefa-
thers. And like our ancestors, we worshipped Kali as the
Divine Mother, peacefully and without strife. Kali was
served by both a high priest and a high priestess, who
were equal in importance. Now, it happened that the
high priest, Amar, who was old and ailing, passed on to
another life, and shortly thereafter the high priestess,
Paru, also died. As succession is determined by blood-
line, Sumi, the niece of Paru, was next in line to become
high priestess. Since Amar had no living male in his lineage, it was decided that a new priest would be chosen
by the people at the next Durga Puja festival. I myself,
who was an assistant to Amar in the temple, was a candidate.

"Now Sumi, who was in the full flower of her youth,
did not want to become a virgin priestess. She was in love
with a handsome lad, Anand by name, and waited only
for the day her parents would seal the marriage arrangement. But Anand did not return her love, and instead
thought only of leaving the village and of the adventures
awaiting him in the big cities of the north. So one night
Anand ran away, which broke young Sumi's heart. Her
hurt turned to anger and bitterness toward all men. So
she forsook worldly life and entered into the service of
Kali as her high priestess.

"From that time, things began to change. Sumi
claimed that Kali spoke to her in dreams, that the Divine
Mother wished to glorify and elevate her own kind, and
that women were Kali's chosen instruments and should
cast off the bonds of female servitude which men had
placed upon them. At first such ideas shocked women
and men alike. But then a few widows and unmarried

women took up the cause, convincing many hard-
working wives and mothers that life would be easier for
them if men could be made to do their fair share of the
work. Sumi added fuel to the fire by threatening Kali's
retribution on whoever disobeyed the goddess's pro-
nouncements. Animal sacrifice was instituted, and secret
meetings were held in the temple, from which men were
barred.

"Sumi then announced that Kali had no further need
for male priests and that men would no longer be allowed to worship in the temple. She chose acolytes to
serve her from among the village maidens. The gates of
the village were closed and barred, and no man was allowed to leave. Then Sumi declared that it was the will
of Kali that women and children live apart from men.
And so families were split apart, husband from wife,
and cohabitation was strictly forbidden except for one
day a year, and that only for the purpose of procreation.
A tax was placed on men's labors to support a female
guard, a guard to enforce the will of the goddess—as interpreted by Sumi.

"Many of the men protested, and some even threatened their wives in anger. But the men were beaten by
Sumi's guards, who continually increased in number
and now lurk on every street corner. Any weapon owned
by a man was confiscated, and men were prohibited from
meeting together or congregating into groups. And so a
new order took power, with Sumi at its head.

"It is an unhappy life for men now, and we have been
unable to change things. And I suspect that many of the
women have had second thoughts and yearn for the old
ways. But we are all trapped together. I can only pray that

Kali will open her eyes to what the blasphemer Sumi has done and punish her. The goddess is our only hope. Only by the intervention of the Divine Mother will we once again return to our cherished way of life.

"As to your fate, my friend, I know not. I have heard talk that Kali thirsts for human blood. I do not think Sumi would dare to sacrifice one of the village men. But you are a stranger. So beware and take care." Then he heard something. "Listen! Footsteps outside—the evening post of guards. It is dangerous to talk further. Ah, it is times like these that I am glad I never married. Perhaps the next life will be kinder to us. Good night, now. Try to get some sleep."

Hari lay awake pondering the story Balram had told him and trying to think of a way out of his misfortune. But no ideas offered themselves. His last thought before dropping off to sleep was of an old saying his grandmother had told him as a child: follow a dog and all you will find is a bone.

He seeks truth and wisdom. He has found some he did not need to travel for.

At sunup Hari was led by a guard to the outside of the village temple where he was provided with some rags and a bucket of water and told to wash the frescoes on the temple walls. The guard informed him that this would be his workplace for a few days and that he could go to and from work on his own, though he would be watched. The guard then left. Hari set willingly to his task, for the paintings were quite beautiful and badly needed cleaning.

I shall induce in the priestess a passion for my mortal man, for she is the only one who can free him. Observe her thoughts.

From a small upper window in the temple, Sumi watched the young stranger's every movement. She had arranged his workplace just so she could study him unawares. She had hoped to find bitterness and pettiness in his face to convince herself that any punishment she meted out to him would be justified. But as she gazed down upon him, she could see only kindness, generosity, and an undaunted free spirit behind his shining visage.

How beautiful he is, she thought, and for the first time in two years she felt the pangs of womanly desire rise in her breast. She turned away from the window, a little frightened at the sensations that assailed her.

Would that I could induce similar passion in you, Mohini, for me. For brute power and potent lust.

I suspect you will never understand why those do not suffice. I could be passionate indeed for one I respected.

Hari was busily polishing the brow of the Lord Vishnu when he heard an odd clicking sound. A small hidden door snapped open in the temple wall just in front of him, and one of the white-clad acolytes of Kali popped her head out and signaled for him to enter. He complied and followed her through the low door, which locked shut behind him. The girl led him up a narrow winding flight of stairs to a hallway on the upper floor of the temple, and pointed to a wooden door at the end of a long corridor. She then hastily departed.

Strange, Hari thought. But then everything that had happened to him since he set foot in the village was strange.

He went up to the door and knocked lightly. A female voice from within bade him enter. He did so and found himself facing the high priestess. Unencumbered now by priestly robes, she wore a thin white sari which was tightly wrapped to accent her feminine charms. The room was large and lavishly decorated, and Hari guessed it was her personal quarters.

The priestess seated herself on a sofa and pointed to a pillow on the floor in front of her. "Come, sit down," she said. "I would talk with you." Her voice was pleasant, yet had an undertone of formality. Hari did as he was bidden.

"I am glad to see that you have accepted your situation," she continued. "If you please me, then perhaps there may be more pleasant work. Some compensations. Does that interest you?"

"O priestess, your meaning is not clear to me. What compensations do you speak of?"

"I will explain. There is some discontent among the men of the village, which is unfortunate. There are those who secretly express doubts about the laws that Kali has set down for them. They want a high priest to sit beside me in the temple. That is not possible. But so that they may see that Kali is understanding and compassionate, I am considering allowing a man into the service of the goddess. Not as a priest, but as my personal assistant. It would be a comfortable position for the person selected, and we would work closely together. A male presence in the temple would also serve to pacify the demands of the village malcontents."

She gave him a straight look. "Tell me, Hari. Would such a position interest you?"

"I am honored by your consideration, O priestess, but I am a stranger here. Surely there are others in the village more worthy than I. Nor is it altogether clear what the duties of such a position would be."

"Well, I would expect my assistant to—to assist me in any way that was required. Just as Kali expects loy-alty and unquestioning obedience from her high priest-ess, so her priestess expects the same from those who serve her. There will, of course, be satisfactions—good food and comfortable quarters. And are we not both young?"

"Young?" he asked blankly.

My precious idiot.

Sumi stood up straight, so that her slender symmetry warred with her soft fullness. "Tell me, Hari, do you not find me attractive—even desirable?"

"In truth, I do, priestess."

"Well, I too will confess a certain attraction. Come, let us speak plainly. Although it is Kali's wish that the villagers live in abstinence, her high priestess is permit-ted certain privileges by virtue of her station. So I ask you, Hari, become my consort as well as my assistant, that we may fulfill our destinies in both body and spirit."

And there it is on a silver platter.

But I have confidence in his mortal foolishness.

"O priestess," he replied, "though the desire be strong within me, I can not accept your offer. I could not in good conscience enjoy what others are forbidden. Nor do I believe that the goddess wishes her worshippers in the village to be deprived of such things—or of freedom, family, and friends."

You high-minded fool! Just let her seduce you.

"Silence! That is enough!" Sumi screamed in rage, leaping to her feet. "So you reject my offer! You prefer

to be a righteous and noble philosopher. Very well. You
want justice. Then you shall have it—the justice of Kali!"

That woman has a certain violent appeal.

*Women can be fools too, especially when scorned. What unin-
tended mischief!*

Hari, taken aback by her vehemence, did not know
how to respond. He had supposed his position to be reasonable.

"Hear me well," Sumi continued grimly. "Two days
hence you will be taken before the goddess and asked the
great riddle of Kali. If you fail to answer it correctly, your
life will be forfeit. Let us see if you prefer the arms of
Yama, the death god, to mine. Every man and woman in
the village will be present to bear witness to the trial.
Your sacrifice will be a fitting object lesson to the cow-
ardly troublemakers who whisper and plot in every
alley."

*So your ploy has reversed itself, exquisite spirit. The passion you
incited in this woman's breast will now kill the man without my
intervention.*

"May I ask, O priestess, what if I should correctly answer the riddle?"

"No one has ever answered it correctly. But should
that happen, your life will be spared. More than that, it
is written that if a man correctly answers the riddle, then
all men will be prized in the eyes of Kali. In that event,
the village men will be given their freedom. But I do not
think that will happen, for only Kali herself knows the
answer to her riddle, and only she can say if the reply be
right or wrong. If your answer be correct, the goddess
will give an unmistakable sign. But if she does not give
a sign, if she is silent, then the answer is rejected and you
will suffer the stroke of her dread sword."

Delightful. And you can not interfere, enchanting vision, for it remains my move.

I confess that at times the perversity of women becomes annoying. But perhaps he will manage to answer the riddle.

"Now leave me!" Sumi cried, as lovely in her rage as in her interest. "Guard! Return this ingrate to his labors, only now let them be among the goats!"

That night Hari related to Balram all that had happened with Sumi. "It is worse than I feared," said Balram. "A woman rejected once is bad enough. But twice? She will surely kill you. Ah, my young friend, but you are brave. Your words this day fill my heart with pride and remind me how it was to be a man. I only wish I could help you."

"Tell me, Balram," asked Hari, "what of the riddle of Kali?"

"I have heard speak of it. But no man knows the question, and I think no mortal knows the answer. Some say there are many questions. Others say there are many answers so that Kali or her priestess may deny the one spoken in favor of another unspoken."

"But when I answer, suppose Kali should give a sign for all to see? By thus signaling her acceptance, Kali would at once free both me and the village men, would she not?"

"Yes, that is true. But how can we entice the goddess to speak openly or give a sign?"

Balram and Hari sank into a deep silence. Suddenly Balram's face lit up. "I have it! I have it!" he cried, then quickly lowered his voice. "Remember, I told you I served the goddess many years in the temple. I am one of the few who know of a secret door in the base of the idol. The idol is hollow inside. I kept a ladder there that

I might polish the ruby eye of the goddess, for its glow has a hypnotic effect on the worshipers."

"You mean that the power of the priestess is not derived directly from Kali? That the gem dazzles others into obedience?"

Balram nodded. "In truth, I have never seen a sign unequivocally from the goddess. Always the news is from the priestess, who interprets signs she claims to have seen."

"I find this dismaying. How can we be sure of Kali's true will?"

The man shrugged. "I think we can not, so we had better help ourselves. My plan is this. Tomorrow night I will steal into the temple and hide within the idol. When the time comes the next morning for you to deliver your answer to the riddle, no sooner will you have spoken than the great ruby eye of Kali will come crashing down on the altar, helped on its way by one Balram from within. Such a sign could not be denied, and all will be won. What say you to this plan, Hari?"

"A good and clever plan, Balram. I favor it and will do my part. I pray only that the riddle be such that I am able to give a believable answer—or any answer at all."

And now the man interferes with your success, even as the woman interfered with mine.

"Sobeit. To bed now. We will implement the plan early on the morrow."

We shall see about that.

Hari awoke early on the morning of the ceremony after a fitful night. Balram had stolen out of the hut hours before, and Hari prayed that he had reached his destination unseen.

An hour after dawn four guards came to escort Hari to the temple. The streets were empty, but when Hari arrived at the great hall he saw that all the village men and women had gathered there. Standing before the flower-strewn altar was Sumi, adorned in her priestly robe, her acolytes lined up behind her. The unblinking third eye of the goddess looked down, casting an eerie glow over the assembly.

A faint tinkle of bells sounded. Sumi raised her arms toward the goddess, and the hall grew deadly silent.

"O Kali," she intoned, "Divine Mother, goddess of life and death, your children are gathered here before you to do you homage."

"Kali!" cried the audience in unison.

"This day we ask your judgment on an intruder in our midst, a man who knows not your ways and needs be tested in your eyes. He will be asked your riddle for all to hear. If by your sign he answers correctly, all men will be raised in your eyes. But if he fails to answer correctly, he will suffer the penalty of death upon your altar, a sacrifice to you, O Great Mother, and all men will be shamed."

"Kali!" cried the assembled worshippers, less loudly than before, the voices of the women predominating. The priestess turned toward Hari.

"Prepare yourself, unbeliever. I will say the riddle only once, and only one answer must you give. Harken!

"Three mountains with but two peaks, I see; a smooth sloping plain leading to a forest, and within the forest a cave; the cave is guarded; within the cave a treasure chest, and within the chest the soundless breath of the world!"

She paused, and Hari realized with dismay that she had

completed the presentation of the riddle. It hardly seemed enough.

"Such is the riddle," Sumi proclaimed. "Say now your answer, Brahmin. Upon your reply the great gong will sound, and Kali will make her pronouncement."

Hari closed his eyes and tried to concentrate. The sweet aroma of the altar lamps played with his thoughts, and blazing colors flashed beneath his eyelids. The answers to riddles were always simple, he told himself. It must be something about Kali. His eyes opened and rested on Sumi's attractive body as he struggled to make sense of the riddle. Yet the last thing he needed at the moment was that kind of distraction.

"You must answer now!" cried Sumi. "If not, your silence will condemn you."

Then he had it. "Very well, I will answer," said Hari. "You described a virgin woman. The two mountains with peaks are her breasts. Below is the plain—the body sloping down toward the maiden fleece, the forest. Merging into the forest is the third and lowest mountain, that without a peak, which is woman's graceful curved mound of Venus. The cave is the yoni of woman, the guard signifies virginity, and the treasure chest is the womb. Within the chest, the soundless breath of the world—the unborn child, the future of us all."

The hall was still and breathless. Then a deafening clang reverberated through the chamber as Sumi, hammer in hand, struck the giant gong next to the altar. As the priestess poised to strike again, a cracking noise was heard coming from the head of Kali. All eyes turned upward to see the goddess's great ruby eye shudder, then leap from the idol's brow and fall to the altar below.

There was a stunned silence. Then a screaming and moaning arose from the worshippers. A man cried out, "The answer is correct! Kali has given the sign. We are free!" With that, all the men began shouting and rushing toward the altar. A murderous mob formed around Sumi. Quickly, Hari threw himself in front of her and held up his hands, shouting for silence.

"My friends, please listen! This is a great day. Kali has given you back your freedom. Just as I was tested, so you have been tested these past two years. And Kali found you worthy. Do not be vengeful toward her priestess who but heeded the will of the Divine Mother. Rejoin your families and worship Kali as before, in peace. Now you may choose a high priest of your own."

The assembly cheered, then broke up as wives pulled their husbands away and steered them toward home. The acolytes ran to join their families. Hari turned toward Sumi, who loosened her robe of office and dropped it to the floor. She smiled wanly at Hari, tears of gratitude in her eyes. Hari nodded and smiled warmly, which was more than she could bear, and she ran out of the temple.

Hari heard his name being called, and turned to see Balram staggering out from behind the idol.

"What happened, Balram? he asked. "Are you hurt?"

"Only stunned. I will be all right in a few moments. It is only a bump on the head."

"How came you by this injury?" asked Hari. "Did the guards attack you?"

"No, I fell. I will tell you the story. Last night I made my way into the temple undetected and secluded myself within the idol as we had planned. I waited patiently in the darkness, and at dawn I searched about for the ladder that I might reach and loosen the gemstone in the brow of the goddess. But the ladder was gone. My heart nearly stopped beating. The villagers were beginning to enter the temple, so there was no choice but for me to climb up the inside wall of the idol unaided. That I proceeded to do.

"The feminine contours of Kali provided some footholds, and I gave thanks that our chosen god was a woman. I was about to climb into one of Kali's great breasts when my foot slipped. I can't imagine how it happened; I had thought I was past the worst of the climb. I must have been distracted by the importance of the task, and become careless. I fell to the floor where it seems I struck my head. After that all was blackness. When I awoke, my head was swimming, and I heard your voice as in a dream. You were giving reply to the riddle of Kali. Then the temple gong sounded, and I looked up to see the great eye of Kali tremble in its setting, then leap forward of its own will. What followed we both know.

"I never reached the eye of Kali. But, miracle of miracles, you answered the riddle correctly, and Kali expelled her own eye as a sign of her acceptance. I am ashamed that I had so little faith in the Divine Mother— and in you, my friend."

Hari listened in amazement and wondered if it was the Divine Mother who had saved him.

That afternoon a feast was held in the village. Balram was chosen as the new high priest. Hari, too, was feted, garlanded with flowers, and plied with exotic foods. He politely refused all gifts, but accepted the temporary use of a small house. The villagers implored him to remain among them, but he declined, saying he would remain a few days longer, but then must be on his way.

He looked for Sumi in the gathering, though was not surprised when he did not see her. Balram made a speech about family life, the duties of men and women, and the beneficent side of Kali's nature, and was cheered enthusiastically, though mainly by the men.

At nightfall the celebration ended and Hari returned to his new quarters only to find Sumi waiting for him. Their eyes met in silent understanding and he held out his arms to her. No words were uttered as they embraced and sipped from the cup of a thousand delights. Thereupon, great joy came to them, carefree and uninhibited, and as the swelling tides of pleasure inundated Sumi, she knew she was never meant to be a virgin priestess.

We hardly needed to peek into her mind to grasp that. Now if a certain Apsara would similarly see the light. . . .

Later, as they rested together, a question came to Hari's mind. "Tell me, Sumi," he asked, "do you think my answer to the riddle was correct, and so moved Kali to cast down her eye as a sign?"

"I do not know if your answer was correct, Hari, though it was a clever one. But that is not why the ruby eye of the goddess fell."

"Oh? If you know the cause, Sumi, then pray tell me."

"Very well, but you must keep the secret. It was I who loosened the eye of Kali, such that a slight vibration would dislodge it. The vibration I myself provided by sounding the great gong beside the altar. I—I think you know why I did it."

Hari threw his arms around Sumi, his admiration and affection for her increasing by leaps and bounds.

"But how did you reach the eye?" he asked.

"The idol is hollow and has a secret entrance. With a ladder it was a simple matter to climb to the eye and loosen it. This I did two nights ago."

I did not see that! Had I but known—

You would have known, had you not wasted your time ogling me instead of watching the village activity.

"And did you then remove the ladder from the idol?"

"Yes, but why do you ask that?"

And so your ploy of making Balram's foot slip was wasted. You used up your move for nothing, and now it is my move.

"Just curiosity. Ah, Sumi you are indeed marvelous. I hope you will never regret putting aside your priestly robes."

"No, I will not. The joy of this night alone surpasses a lifetime of rewards as a virgin priestess."

"I am glad you are satisfied. But what will you do now that your power here is gone?"

"Hari, I know you will leave the village soon and I doubt that we shall ever meet again. When you go, I too shall leave. I have an aunt in a distant village, and will go there and try to make another life for myself. But until then, my beloved, stay with me that we may crowd the pleasures of a lifetime into the little time we have remaining."

"Gladly, oh gladly."

Three days later Hari resumed his journey to the palace of the rajah. Along the path he was greeted by the very same mongrel that had led him to the village. The dog jumped happily up and down and ran on ahead, as before, to clear the path. When they reached a fork,

Hari took the northerly branch and the dog took the easterly, this time making no attempt to persuade Hari to follow. Hari waved goodbye, but the dog ignored him as it ran off in pursuit of a butterfly that badly needed chasing.

❧ 6 ❧

Pitali: City of the Rajah

The land shed its smooth brown mantle and became hilly, the vegetation turned greener, and the path widened into a road. Travelers passed Hari by: merchants and mendicants, princes and beggars, priests and wanderers. Most, like himself, traveled on foot, but the more prosperous rode on splendid horses or were carried on tasseled palanquins by dark-skinned Sudras.

The road became crowded. The cries of vendors squatting by the roadway, the squawking of caged birds for sale, and the rattle of bullock carts filled the air in a cacophony of well-ordered confusion. Occasionally a white cow would wander by unattended. It puzzled Hari that these poor creatures were so thin and neglected, and yet so revered that even princes made way for them. But then there were many things he did not understand about the ways of his people.

As he topped the crest of a high hill, the wall of the city hove into view. Mighty it stood, extending as far as the eye could see, shimmering and undulating in the bright sunlight like a giant snake. Beyond the wall there rose a great golden dome surrounded by glittering spires and towers, which could only be the palace of the rajah. Here at last was the great city of Pitali.

Hari passed unnoticed through the city gates amidst

the hustle and bustle of humanity, and followed the main thoroughfare toward the palace. He stopped to admire the handsome multistoried sandstone buildings that lined the roadway, adorned with statues of the gods and scenes from the Hindu epics. Too, he paused at the street of the artisans, fascinated to watch them at their work: weavers and makers of cloth; workers of metal, ivory, stone, and leather; basket makers, potters, and dyers.

Upon reaching the palace gate, he showed one of the guards the seal of the zamindar on the message he carried and was led to a side entrance of the palace. There he was turned over to a servant and ushered through a maze of corridors into the presence of a haughty man of prodigious bulk, who announced himself as the rajah's head housekeeper. Appraising Hari's somewhat bedraggled appearance, the housekeeper shook his head in disgust and ordered the servant to escort the visitor to such-and-such a room at the rear of the palace, which was to be his quarters, and to provide him with water for a bath and a fresh change of clothing.

Hari found the room unpretentious but comfortable, and was pleased to find it overlooked the palace gardens. From his balcony he could see terraced banks of multihued flowers and rows of blossoming bushes that bordered a winding path which led to a graceful half-moon bridge of white stone. Beneath the bridge ran a silver brook fed by a high fountain, the water of which gushed forth out of the upturned mouths of delicate statues of naked maidens perched on the fountain rim. Flowering trees, hanging trumpet vines, and lotus gardens populated with parrots, doves, and peacocks decorated the lawns, and along the walkways were white stone benches guarded by lifesize tigers, leopards, and mythical creatures fashioned out of giant hedges.

No sooner had he bathed and put on fresh clothing than came a knock on the door, and a uniformed officer presented himself to say that the rajah was ready to receive the message of the zamindar. Hari was escorted to the rajah's Hall of Private Audience and told to wait in the back of the room until the rajah had finished with the case he was hearing, which was the last of the day.

At the front of the room Hari could see there were five persons: the rajah, a stately man of middle years seated on an elevated ivory throne; a dewan or advisor standing beside him; and three other people who apparently were the parties in the case being heard. The three were a stout elderly man and a pretty young woman, both richly garbed, and a young man quite plainly dressed. The acoustics of the room were such that Hari could not help overhearing the conversation.

The complainant, the stout man, was an irate father who had caught his daughter in a compromising situation with the humbly dressed young man, whom he now wanted punished. The young man, staring contritely down at the floor, did not deny the accusation, and the tearful daughter conceded that she had not altogether discouraged the young man's advances. The rajah nodded understandingly and assured the father that the lad would be punished, then dismissed father and daughter, saying it would be best if they departed and were spared the unpleasantness of witnessing the punishment about to be administered. When they had left, the rajah sighed and turned to the trembling young man.

"Well, boy, you must learn to be more careful in

choosing your place of trysts. Lovemaking is an art in all of its aspects and must be approached with skill, care, and consideration. You have much to learn. So, for your punishment I sentence you to spend three days in my court library where you will read in their entirety the ancient manuals of love—the *Kama Sutra,* the *Ananga Ranga,* and the *Koka Shastra*—that you may learn something of the skill you obviously lack. Thereafter, stay away from that particular pretty young lady. If you must rove, divide your attentions among the fair maidens, with which this city abounds, whose fathers are not rich and influential merchants. Now begone, and report to my chief librarian on your first day off from your work."

The young man thanked the rajah profusely and scampered out of the hall. The rajah's advisor frowned disapprovingly.

"Lord, was not your punishment a bit lenient?"

"Ah, Amul," the rajah replied, "sometimes I think you were never young. Hmm. Probably you were not. But remember, the young man is an apprentice skilled in metal-making. Each sword he fashions is more important than a thousand of the baskets that yonder merchant peddles in the marketplace. The time may be coming when my army will be in need of swords."

The conversation between the rajah and the advisor quieted to a whisper, and Hari could no longer hear it. But from what he had heard, he liked the rajah already.

While he waited, his eyes wandered around the room and marveled at its beauty and richness of design. The checkered floor was of white ceramic tile, each tile colorfully painted in an intricate geometric design, no two alike. Paintings depicting battle scenes from the *Mahab-*

harata covered the walls. Centermost were the forces of the Pandavas engaging the army of the Kauravas, with Krishna looking on in benevolent approval. The ceiling was leafed in gold save for a large oval above the rajah's throne, within which was painted the artist's conception of the blissful City of the Gods.

"I see that you appreciate good painting, young man," came the voice of the rajah, catching Hari by surprise. "Come forward."

Hari approached the throne and saw that the rajah was indeed a striking figure: tall, slender, sharp of feature, and self-assured, with penetrating eyes that harbored a playful twinkle. Draped in a long richly brocaded robe studded with jewels, he was every inch a king, yet his friendly smile and easy manner belied his high station and dignity of bearing.

In contrast, the advisor, Amul, was older and shorter, with close-set eyes and a bulbous nose, and wore a sullen look that aspired to a scowl. His dress was only slightly less grand than his master's, though his posture was fully as stiff and formal as his demeanor.

"I understand you have a message from my good friend, the zamindar," said the rajah.

"Yes, Lord," Hari replied, handing the message to the rajah. The rajah broke the seal and read the message with an unchanged expression, then folded it and tucked it in his robe.

"So you are Hari," said the rajah. "The zamindar spoke well of you. I am pleased you decided to visit my home. Do you know the contents of the zamindar's message?"

"No, Lord, except that it was to introduce me."

"Well, there is more, but we will talk about that later. Meanwhile, you must be weary from your journey and will want to rest. We will meet at dinner."

Hari thanked the rajah, bowed low, and returned to his room. Tired after days of walking and nights of sleeping on the hard earth, he stretched out on the bed to nap. He did not awaken until he heard a rapping at his door and a servant's voice summoning him to dinner.

The dinner was in the rajah's private quarters, a room decorated solely in green, though of many shades and textures. He was seated between the rajah and Amul. Shortly three young ladies entered the room and seated themselves at the rajah's right. Hari looked from one to the others and was amazed, for not only were they exceedingly comely, but they were identical triplets, alike in every feature and detail. Only the color of their garments differed.

"Hari, may I present my three daughters," said the rajah, "Saras, dressed in white; Suseela, in green; and Sukunya, in red. I insist they wear only these colors, each her own, that I and everyone else may tell them apart." He smiled, obviously well satisfied with the situation and justifiably proud of the beauty of his offspring. There were known to be men who valued only sons, but it seemed that the rajah was generous in this respect also. "My daughters, this is Hari, who comes to us from the palace of our friend, the zamindar."

Hari bowed his head and the young ladies smiled at him, nodding in greeting, but did not speak. Each one seemed prettier than her sisters, with her color setting her off to advantage.

"Although the gods long ago summoned my dear wife," continued the rajah, "they blessed our union with these three jewels. But they are not quite flawless," he added with a chuckle. "I should warn you, Hari, watch out for them. They like to play games, and I sometimes think they take advantage of their father's love."

The dewan allowed an expression of sour agreement to cross his face, and all three ladies flashed merry frowns at him, teasingly emulating his expression. It was plain that there was substantial truth in the rajah's cheerful statement.

And here we have, I think, three potential seductions. They may look the same, but they are three different mortal women. Their tastes should be similar, and I think access will be no more difficult for one than for another.

Perhaps. But you must touch only one at a time, and then it will be my move. I see three potential kills, for I think the rajah's good humor will wear quickly thin if he catches a man molesting any of these jewels.

"Oh Father," interjected Sukunya, "you talk as though we were still children. I am sure our guest would rather hear talk of more interesting things." She glanced brightly around. "I know! Perhaps he can help us answer the puzzle presented to us this day by our tutor. The question is: what is it in all the world that has parts in the greatest number, with no two parts the same? Saras said it was grains of sand, and Suseela said leaves on the trees. But our tutor said no, since some of these may be the same as others. I said people, but our teacher laughed and told me to look upon my sisters." Saras and Suseela giggled as they recalled the incident. "Do not laugh, sisters, for your answers were not accepted either," said Sukunya, cutely pouting. "Does anyone have a better answer?"

Nevertheless, that one strikes me as clever enough to deceive any man, especially her doting father. I will touch her first, with a passion that will not be denied, and we shall see what she makes of it.

"Well," said Amul, clearing his throat to insure that all ears attended him, "there may be some people who are alike in body, but no two souls are alike. Our souls are the mirrors of our deeds, and since no two persons live exactly the same, then no two souls can be the same."

"Oh, wonderful," cried Suseela, and all three girls clapped. Apparently they were not really at odds with the sober advisor, and did not disparage his remarks. "What say you, Hari?" asked Saras.

"The honorable Amul gave a good answer," replied Hari. "It would be difficult to better."

"Make a stab, Hari," encouraged the rajah. "It is only a game."

"Very well, Lord. According to the Great Book of Science which I read in the zamindar's library, no two flakes of snow are identical. Each flake is geometrical in design, the number of possible designs infinite in their difference. Consider, then, the total number of flakes that have accumulated upon the vast range of mountains we know as the Home of the Snow, the Himalayas."

"Hah! A clever answer," piped the rajah amidst the squeals of delight emitted by his daughters. Amul said nothing, his expression dour.

"Father, do you not have an answer?" asked Sukunya.

"Hmm. I thought of the stars. Although I suspect no two stars are the same, the court astronomer does not agree with me, and I have no great book to cite as evidence. But are not numbers themselves different from one another, and do they not march on into endlessness?" Everyone laughed and applauded at this reply.

"But enough of games," said the rajah, "let us give our tongues a rest and enjoy some fine food."

Hari sampled a variety of vegetarian delights, many new to his taste, and as he ate he could not help noticing the rajah's three daughters stealing looks at him, which made him a little uncomfortable.

At the end of the meal the girls excused themselves and left the room, leaving the men to sip a strong drink which the rajah jokingly claimed was extracted from the sacred soma plant and imparted insight and longevity to both men and gods. The conversation turned to questions of religion and government, and whether the one was the ally or the enemy of the other.

"The ruler who seeks Atman achieves a state of benevolent selflessness and wisdom, and so rules wisely," argued Amul. "We can not rely only on intellect, which is but feeble and transitory. We must rise above our pride, our desires, and individual senses, and strive to achieve that which is the silent and formless depth of our being—Atman, the Soul of the World."

"All very well, Amul," said the rajah. "But what will all this purging of the senses and denegration of material things do for us in times of strife? It is their bodies and their property that the people demand to have protected then, not their souls. If a king or soldier becomes preoccupied with the Soul of the World, how well will he skewer his enemy in battle? What say you in this matter, Hari? Speak freely."

"O Rajah, I have been taught that we of the Deccan civilization should seek balance in our lives. Surely we have room for the soul as well as the material world. Yet their importance, one to the other, I think is not constant, but changes with the needs of men. In times of peace and prosperity, a certain amount of asceticism and concern with the afterlife may help to temper the corrupting influences of wealth and materialism. But even while our eyes seek the heavens, our feet should remain earthbound. Recall that the Muslim conquests took place at a time when our people were steeped in the supernatural. When the sultan's armies sacked our villages and killed and enslaved our people, little resistance was offered. Instead, the people took refuge in prayer and spiritual consolation, comforting themselves that the next life would be a better one."

"Let us not be alarmists," countered Amul. "We Madrans can not all carry swords and arm ourselves against phantom enemies. Then our neighbors will become suspicious and arm themselves, and a race will begin that can only end in a conflict that no one wanted in the first place."

"There is much in what you both say," mused the rajah. "But have we not had enough reason to be suspicious of the rana, Chandra, in our neighboring state of Madresh? He has placed troops along our common border, though the Madreshian army officers say they are merely engaged in peaceful camping-out exercises. Perhaps, and perhaps not. What is certain is that we lack good military intelligence."

I grow bored with this prattle.

I agree. Touch him to move it along. You do not lose a turn.

The rajah's expression abruptly changed. "But enough of such talk for one day. Hari, you must excuse me now. There are other matters I must attend to. Come along, Amul, I will need you."

Hari was sorry to see the dialogue end, for he had

been enjoying the exercise of minds. But who was he to decide how the rajah spent his time?

The evening was young, so Hari wandered through the corridors of the palace, perusing its many marvels of art and architecture. As he was looking at a collection of miniature Rajput paintings in an out-of-the-way gallery, a maidservant approached him saying there was a royal command for his presence and would he please follow her. He did so and was led up a narrow stairway, and thence down a dimly lit corridor to a room with a red door. The maidservant bade him enter, then departed.

The door was ajar, so he went in. The room was upholstered in many shades of red, from curtains to tapestries, and it even had pretty pale red sheets on the bed. No sooner had he crossed the threshold than the door swung closed behind him and he heard the click of the lock turning. He turned about, and there leaning against the door facing him was Sukunya, whom he recognized by the red color of her gown.

"I am sorry if I startled you," she said sweetly, "but I did not think I could entice you here any other way. Secrecy is important, for my father would not approve of a man in my room."

But perhaps he will nevertheless learn of it.

"Please forgive me, O Sukunya, for I thought it was your father who summoned me. It is not correct that I should be here, so if you will please excuse me, I will leave."

"But you can not leave, beautiful Hari, for I have locked the door and taken the key. I will not let you go until you have done me a service, and not an unpleasant one I hope." With that, Sukunya stepped over to her bed and began to ease the straps of her gown from her shoulders. The light garment drifted to the floor with mesmerizing slowness, revealing her ivory-smooth nakedness in all its budding glory. If Meena had been the most beautiful of young women, and the she-demon the most striking of supernatural females, this girl in red was surely the loveliest of nubile maidens—except, perhaps, for her sisters.

Though alarmed, Hari could not help being aroused by her loveliness. There was a certain special appeal in her youth and eagerness for experience. But fear rose in his breast, for these daughters of the rajah seemed fickle and untrustworthy. Better he should leave—if he could. He tried the door, but it was securely locked. He saw there was another door at the opposite end of the room which he also tried, but it too was locked. He raised his hand to rap on the door.

"That would be very foolish," said Sukunya. "The guards will hear and come to investigate. Then I will have to say that you forced your way into my bedroom, which I would truly regret. Your punishment would be most unpleasant. Now come here, silly man. You hurt my feelings by ignoring me so."

I was right. She is clever enough to make her snare tight.

Hari saw that he was lost. Were she to lodge a charge against him, the rajah's men would begin by cutting off the anatomy that offended her, and then proceed to less pleasant exercises. There was nothing to be done but to meet the demands of the moment. And so, heroically and unselfishly, he bent to the task at hand, doing his best to fulfill his captor's most ardent desires (for it was his way to accomplish any task set before him to the very best of his ability). Thereupon the twain coupled and clipped, fused and combined, Sukunya clutching and biting her bedcovers to prevent herself from crying out in her frequent peaks of passion lest someone overhear and misunderstand. Or, worse, understand.

When later Hari rose to dress himself, Sukunya grasped his arm and demanded a repeat performance. When he tried to protest inability, she suggested that such inability could readily become permanent, and inhaled as if to scream. Having little choice but to comply, Hari steeled himself and entered once more into the breach. In the end, though exhausted, he emerged victorious, having routed any lingering desires in his partner.

After he had dressed, Sukunya told him it would be safer for him to leave by the rear door, and she bussed him on the cheek as he quietly slipped out. "I would not really have cried the alarm," she confessed contritely. "It was just that I suspected you still had more joy to give." The door snapped shut behind him, and he found himself in a small stairless hallway facing yet another door, only this one was white. He slowly and quietly turned the door handle, but the door was locked. As he pondered whether to knock, he heard the sound of the lock turn and the white door swung open.

And there is no man here for you to touch.

But you may not touch anyone until my turn is done.

I may not need to.

He entered and found himself in another bedroom, which looked identical to the one he had just left, except that it was decorated in white instead of red. As his eyes roamed around the room, noting the white cushions on the floor and white sheets on the bed, the door shut behind him. He whirled about to see the rajah's daughter,

Saras, dressed in a gown of white, in the act of locking the door. She withdrew the key, carried it to her bed, and hid it among the folds. Only then did she greet him, smiling sweetly, bidding him to enter and be at ease.

"Greetings, Saras," he said, not entirely at ease. "I seem to be lost. Please forgive me for intruding on your privacy. If you will show me a ready exit I will be on my way. Perhaps this back door—does it lead to the corridor?" He tried the rear door, but it was locked. "Can you unlock the door for me, O Saras?" he asked pleadingly.

"Surely I can, Hari, and I will. But first you must do me a service." She then dropped her gown to the floor, exposing her nakedness to him, and his heart sank in his breast. "We daughters of the rajah, being identical in every way, insist on identical treatment. That is only fair. If a gift is presented to the one, it must be given also to the others. So, Hari, come and be glad, tarry with me awhile that we may find pleasure in one another's company. Not until the softness has returned to the tips of my breasts will you find egress from this room."

She is truly admirable.

Hari sighed and knew what he must do. Fortunately what might have proved impossible with the same maiden as before became possible with the new one, as was the case with breeding animals; there was potency in novelty. And so the two lay abed and clipped and combined, futtered and fused, and Saras bit her bedcovers to avoid screaming with delight as wave upon wave of pleasure assailed her. Hari, for his part, labored mightily that he might not disgrace his manhood for failing to rise to the challenge.

I am constrained to agree. It shall be similar with you and me, in due course, only more violent.

Perhaps you will find yourself unable to wait for me, and will have to touch a man so that he seduces a mortal maiden for you. Then it will be my move again.

Your humor is of a canine nature.

But Saras, like her sister, demanded a rematch, which Hari was hard put to comply with. But thanks to some special tricks and enticements known to Saras, to Hari's amazement his tired body responded and rose once more to the occasion, fully meeting the requirements placed upon it. When he had spent himself, drained of all strength, Saras kissed him on the cheek and unlocked the back door of her room.

This time, before exiting, Hari carefully looked outside to be sure another blind alley or colored door did not await him. There was a corridor, and he gratefully stepped into it as Saras closed and locked the door behind him. He tiptoed down the corridor, which turned a corner, and lo, it dead-ended into a door of green. Hari groaned and slipped to the floor in utter frustration. Perhaps if he yelled for the guards, he thought, he could invent a plausible explanation. But suppose he was not believed? No, the risk was too great.

Just then a lock clicked and the green door slowly swung open. Hari took a deep breath, hauled himself to his feet, and entered the room. The surroundings were all too familiar, in their new color of green. The walls and floor shared this hue, as did the ornamental plants on the windowsill, and of course the bed dressings. Not surprisingly, a lovely lady in a green gown awaited him. He glanced across the room and saw another door, which he tested halfheartedly, knowing it would be locked.

"Suseela, please open the door," he pleaded. "I wish only to return to my room and partake of a good night's sleep." But she merely shook her head and smiled as she discarded her robe and draped herself over the bed. Hari knew further talk would be useless, so he undressed and, before entering into the fray, paused to perform a few simple yoga exercises that he might invigorate his body and fortify himself for the ordeal ahead. At least this was another new partner, though she looked the same, so that nature provided him with another dollop of potency.

O, delightful!

Thereupon the two commenced to couple and commingle and indulge in many variations of congress as was Suseela's wont, and long were they conjoined, for Hari found it difficult to reach a conclusion despite his partner's caressing undulations. But her accelerated tempo finally coaxed him to a fitting climax, whereupon Suseela shuddered in satisfaction and released the bedcover she had grasped between her teeth to keep from crying out.

Hari nearly fainted from sheer exhaustion. Suseela, having received full satisfaction, since the love match had been of considerable duration owing to Hari's harried condition, sought not to tax his capacity further, for which he was most grateful. He dressed himself with difficulty and wobbled out of the rear door and into the adjoining corridor. He heard the familiar locking of the door as he searched the corridor for a stairway to the floor below.

Now he passes beyond the women's quarters. I have touched a key man. Prepare for the reckoning, sweet flower.

But to his chagrin, the corridor ended in front of yet another door, this one brown in color. Oh well, he thought, as he slowly turned the door handle. At least there were no identical daughters garbed in brown. The door clicked open and he quietly slipped inside.

Perhaps, bitter fruit, perhaps. The night is no longer young.

I know my man remains regardless; I feel his excitement.

The room was in semidarkness and no one seemed about, so Hari began to tiptoe toward another door he could see at the far end of the room. When he was but halfway to his destination, there suddenly came a moaning sound from somewhere in the room. He quickly ducked down only to hear the sound again. It was unquestionably human: he was not alone. The noise seemed to be coming from the corner of the room furthest from him. If he kept on his present course and ducked behind the furniture, he might make it to the door undetected.

There is certainly male excitement.

Crawling on all fours, he slowly made his way across the floor, being careful not to bump into anything. The moaning resumed, now interspersed with occasional grunts and gasps. He was within a few feet of the door now, but there was no more furniture to hide behind. The remaining open territory seemed like a vast plain upon which any moving object would be immediately spotted. He had no choice but to proceed.

Slowly he inched forward. Light was shining through the bottom of the door, which enabled him to see that he was in a bedroom. Just as he reached the door, a loud groan filled the room, and instinctively his head snapped in the direction of the noise. With no objects now blocking his view, he could see across the room to a bed in the far corner.

In the dimness he could make out two men on the bed, both naked and locked together in embrace. One was on all fours, the other mounted behind futtering his companion with great gusto. At that moment the receiving partner jerked up his head in response to a particularly hard thrust and let out a sonorous moan, which joined in counterpoint with that made by his antagonist.

The awful duet nearly terrified Hari into bolting for the door, but he was stopped by the sudden recognition of the undermost of the duo. It was none other than Amul the advisor. The face of the advisor's assailant he could not see, it being hidden in the darkness.

The idiot! He was supposed to intercept your mortal man and convey him to the rajah for keen-bladed justice.

It seems that the long wait allowed him to become distracted. Your move is wasted, again, Ravana.

Were it my move, I would see him futtered by the deepest thrust of a spear! How could the imbecile allow his passion to ruin such an opportunity?

I am sure I do not know. Perhaps he reminds me of you.

Regaining his composure, Hari crept to the door and slowly turned the door handle. The door clicked open and he slipped into the corridor. Apparently he had not been seen. He found a stairway and in a few minutes was safely back in his own room. He plopped down on the bed and immediately sank into a deep slumber. Unfortunately insufficient night remained to give him as much rest as he craved. One thing he knew: it would be some time before he again desired the amorous company of a woman.

The next morning the rajah requested Hari's company at breakfast, which was served out of doors in the garden. Sukunya soon joined them.

"Ah, Sukunya child," said the rajah, "how bright and shiny you are this morning. The warmth of your smile shames Surya, the sun god. But Surya was on time for breakfast. And where are your two sisters? Will they be joining us?"

"No, Father, Saras and Suseela are not here. Last evening after dinner they decided to ride to the lake palace for a moonlight sail. They said they would spend the night there."

In fact, she persuaded them. What passion that child possesses!

"Well, why did you not go too?" asked the rajah. "It was a beautiful evening for sailing, and that was surely better diversion than what was offered here."

Sukunya smiled as if not necessarily agreeing with that. "I was a little tired and retired early to my quarters. My sisters are always so full of energy, it is difficult to keep up with them. Perhaps it is because I am the oldest—old and weary—and tire more easily."

"Hah! Yes, child, that is so, you were the first born—older by all of five minutes. And such an old lady needs her rest."

"Oh Father, you always make joke at me. Besides, by remaining at home alone last night I had the opportunity to visit my sisters' rooms and try on their gowns and test their beds—I was sure they would not mind. You make me wear red all the time, so I wanted to see how it would be to wear white and green for a change."

"And did the new colors open up any new worlds for you, daughter? Beware of vanity, for it shrinketh the soul."

"Oh, I found the experience most rewarding. One's pleasures when tripled are indeed thrice the pleasures of the one." She darted a sidelong glance, smiling mischievously. "Would you not agree, Hari?"

Hari gulped and tried not to choke on the papaya he was eating. "A—a mathematical truth, O Sukunya. I—I can not disagree."

She smiled brilliantly at him, perhaps about to make some seemingly innocent yet painfully pertinent remark. But at that moment Amul appeared and the conversation drifted to other matters, to Hari's great relief.

It had been Sukunya alone who had seduced him the previous night, Hari now realized. He was amazed and could not help but admire her cleverness. But how, he wondered, had she been able to slip so quickly from one room to another? Then he remembered the delays he had encountered in the hallway before each door, and he smiled to himself. She surely had alternate routes to her sisters' rooms. Here was indeed a kindred spirit!

That afternoon he was called into private audience with the rajah where he learned about the contents of the zamindar's message. It seems that at the time of the zamindar's most recent visit with the rajah, the rajah had expressed concern about the camping of Madreshian soldiers on his northern border and whether it might have military implications. The zamindar, having been impressed with Hari's cleverness, had recommended in his message that the rajah consider making use of the young Brahmin's talents by sending him as a spy to the city of the Rana of Madresh.

"It is only because the zamindar thinks well of you that he proposes I send you to Madresh to be my eyes and ears," said the rajah. "I share his estimation of your abilities and believe his idea is a sound one. But the venture is not without danger, so you must decide for yourself. Whatever your decision, I will accept it gladly and without reservation."

"O Rajah," replied Hari, "I am honored that you think me worthy of so important an assignment. I accept most willingly." For one thing, it now seemed that he would get more rest on the road than in the rajah's palace, considering the ruthless cleverness of the rajah's passionate daughter. The odd thing, he now realized, was that yesterday by day she had shown no sign of such interest. Truly the ways of women were beyond the ken of men.

He is learning.

So am I.

"You have my gratitude, Hari. Speak to no one about this, nor will I. And though I will miss you, it will be best if you depart soon. Try to get close to the court of the rana if you can. I will look for your return before the rising of the second new moon. An unpretentious horse will be provided to take you as far as the border. Here is a map of both states. Study it well, and take note of the black area, here. That is the Land of Peril. Stay clear of it, for it is said to be peopled by demons."

Hari accepted the map. "I shall, my lord."

"You are a brave lad. Know that if the gods had given me a son, I would have wanted him to be very much like you. Now you must excuse your rajah, for he must suffer to give audience to the Prince of Punt: a pompous old fool who believes that his frequent flatulencies are the echoes of the gods applauding his non sequiturs."

Hari retreated to the rajah's library where he studied the maps he had been given and sought out books on geography. He was curious about the place the rajah had called the Land of Peril, but could find no reference to it. He inquired of the rajah's librarian, an elderly wisp of a man with knowing eyes. The librarian nodded, and from a locked case withdrew a looseleaf manuscript, which he handed to Hari.

The manuscript was the handwritten diary of an explorer, and told of the author's passage through the Land of Peril and of the terrors within. The region overlapped the borders of Madra and Madresh states and was surrounded by unscalable mountains. Only one means of entry was known, through a narrow pass called Yama's Cut, at the northeastern corner of Madra.

The explorer told of the dreadful Asura who lived beneath terrible twin moons and whose breath hung in a deadly mist over Yama's Cut. By day he was attacked by whirling stone- and flame-demons, and at night by giant sky-demons. Most horrible was the grotesque cloud monster who hovered above Demon Knoll, a hill that must be crossed in order to pass through the fearful land.

That evening there was no summons from any source. Apparently Sukunya required an interval of recuperation also. That was a blessing. An interlude with her would ordinarily have been delightful, were she not the rajah's precious daughter and were she not so enduringly passionate. As it was, she was too much for him, somewhat in the manner of the zamindar's wife.

Perhaps I nudged her too strongly, as I did Meena; I must try to touch the women only as much as is required to do the job.

Touch yourself as hard as you wish, Mohini; I shall surely match your passion.

The next morning by the light of early dawn Hari bid farewell to the rajah and departed the great city of Pitali, leaving it to his host to explain his leavetaking. The rajah would say that wanderlust had beckoned the young traveler, and in that there would be truth.

ᘛ 7 ᘚ

The Rana and the Rani

Hari's path led him through the hills of Uma into Madra's northern forest. Legend told of a secret grove within the forest where trees shed their leaves each morning only to magically regain them again each evening. As a child his grandmother had told him stories of these wonderful trees—the Grand Maharanis, she called them, because they adorned themselves in rich garments each day, much as would a queen.

The forest was friendly and bright, sprinkled with sunlight, though the going was slow. His horse, a lazy old nag, had a will of its own and stopped frequently to nibble at delicacies growing beside the path. Hari tolerated the delays, knowing the futility of trying to reform a creature so late in years. Besides, who could tell? The horse might have been a king in a prior life, or might become one in a later.

At a bend in the trail Hari came upon two sadhus sitting on a rock engaged in heated debate. He dismounted with the intention of seeking direction from the mendicants, but they were so deeply enmeshed in controversy that they did not notice him. He waited patiently for a break in the discussion.

They were arguing the perennial question—the nature of man and woman, and which was the superior sex. Said the one sadhu, a frail stalk of a man, "The female is clearly superior, for she is the source of all life, the great river and creator. By her cleverness and subtle ways she instructs and guides the male, and so directs the affairs of household and state alike. Just as she nurses and cares for the child, so she is the milk of life. It is from her breast that all good things flow."

There is a wise man.

"Phoo!" countered the second sadhu, who was even bonier than his fellow. "Is it not true that the supreme gods are male? Are not kings men? What could be clearer proof that the male is the greater?"

An excellent refutation.

"Bah!" the first sadhu replied. "We are not talking of gods, but of mortals. If men push their faces forward and appear to take control, it is because women permit it. Being wiser, the female uses the male as shield and target. Thus do women control from behind and protect themselves."

How fortunate that mortal men do not listen to such truths; there would be mischief if they recognized reality.

"We can not ignore the gods in this question," insisted the second sadhu, raising his forefinger to the heavens. "It was a god who created man and woman. The Great Book says that Twashtri, the Divine Architect, created man first. He decided to create woman only as an afterthought. He found that he had used up all his materials and so had to fashion her out of odds and ends. So he took the tapering of the elephant's trunk, the clinging of vines, the clustering of bees, the fickleness of the wind, the timidity of the hare, the vanity of the peacock, the hardness of stone, the cruelty of the tiger, the coldness of snow, the chattering of jays, the hypocrisy of the snake, and he combined these things to make woman and gave her to man."

And a sorry gift it was.

Then what is your interest in me, foul spirit? Perhaps you should give up this foolishness and seek some bold ugly freak of a monster like yourself for your romantic notions.

"Ah," fairly sang the first sadhu, "but Twashtri also used other things—the slenderness of the reed, the bloom of flowers, the glances of deer, the gaiety of sunbeams, the softness of down, the sweetness of clover, the warmth of fire, the fidelity of doves, the wisdom of the owl, and the cleverness of the fox."

How well he describes you, Mohini! I tolerate your dainty feminine faults for the sake of your intriguing aspects.

I, having more discretion, do not care to tolerate your enormous masculine faults for the sake of your boring aspects.

"But it is the evil and cruelty that dominates in woman," interjected the second sadhu. "Did not your own wife cast you out of your home, O foolish one? Did you learn nothing from that?"

The defender of your gender has lost the debate, as was inevitable.

He is merely a dull mortal man. Had bright mortal women pursued the discussion, it would have been another matter.

Can we at least agree that it is time to give a neutral nudge to your own dull mortal man?

Agreed, in the interest of accomplishing something.

At those words the first sadhu turned red and was about to deliver a blow to the head of his companion, when Hari politely intervened by bowing low before them such that his body came between theirs. His temerity surprised him; he had acted before he thought of any likely consequence.

"Pray forgive my intrusion, O Gurujis," he said, "I am a traveler new to these parts and wonder if you can direct me to the fabled grove of trees which is said to be hidden somewhere within this forest."

The sadhus looked at Hari in astonishment. Embarrassed to have been caught in a heated argument, for such was not the image that kept food in their bellies, they immediately strove to put their best foot forward. As if by magic, their demeanors transformed into the epitome of tranquility, wisdom, and poverty.

"Yes, O Brahmin," said the first sadhu, solemnly. "We can help you. You are most fortunate to have encountered us, for not many know the secret place of which you speak. You need but continue for a brief while on this path until you reach a place where the fragrance of honeysuckle is strong. Then follow the scent and it will lead you to the grove."

"I thank you," said Hari as he bowed again, deftly depositing a coin in the sadhu's open hand. As he rode off, he could hear their voices rising again in angry debate.

He had not traveled far when the fragrance of honeysuckle reached him. It became stronger as he progressed. At the spot where the smell seemed strongest, he left the path and followed the invisible trail of sweetness into the forest. Soon he reached a large circular clearing. Surrounding the clearing was a ring of tall gaunt trees, completely naked of leaves, and clustered at the center of the clearing was a dense grove of giant honeysuckle bushes covered with brightly colored flowers.

He started across the clearing, but then stopped, startled by a movement in the grove. The honeysuckle bushes began to quiver as if alive. Thousands upon thousands of the blossoms shivered and shimmered such that the whole grove pulsated in waves of colors.

Upon moving closer he saw the cause of the display: the bushes were smothered in a sea of butterflies, millions of fluttering butterflies of every conceivable hue— a sight so incredible and breathtaking that tears came to his eyes. Never had he dreamed there could be so many butterflies in the world. How small is man, he thought, and how great the mystery and majesty of nature.

Long he watched the shimmering panoply in fascination. Unnoticed, the sun arched over the forest and slipped beyond the rim of trees, announcing in red-orange tones the coming of evening.

Of a sudden the grove exploded in a burst of fragmenting colors as the butterflies rose into the air as one, as though at some magic signal. They rose straight up in a variegated tremolo, forming into a giant rotating funnel, rising ever higher. Suddenly they dispersed in all directions. The air was dense with bobbing and fluttering wings, which glittered in the waning sunlight as they flew to the edges of the clearing and settled in the branches of the surrounding trees. Soon the naked branches were crowded with row upon row of the tiny creatures, their wings pulsating and twitching, forming a garment of living color. As darkness settled, all motion ceased, and in the quiet of the dwindling twilight Hari made silent prayer to the All-God for the magnificence of His earthly creations.

All that this nearly perfect scene is lacking is a gentle woman to soothe his brow and slake his recovering groin.

Again we agree. He may think himself alone, but we have each

other's company. If you should desire to soothe my brow and slake my urgent need—

I prefer to be elsewhere. But you are welcome to proceed to your satisfactions without me.

Truly it has been said that the female of the species was invented to torment the male.

Hari slept the night on a carpet of grass within the clearing by a small fire he had built to keep away any curious beasts. He allowed his hobbled horse to graze contentedly in the clearing, for the grass was lush and there was a small stream nearby to abate the animal's thirst.

At dawn he awoke to the music of singing birds. As the first rays of sunlight beamed into the clearing, the circle of trees came alive, first with the slow flickering of wings trying out the new day, then with a rush of motion as row upon row of butterflies peeled off the branches like a trained troupe of aerobatic dancers. They playfully flitted and chased each other in spiraling circles before descending in a cloud on the honeysuckle grove for another day's feasting on sweet nectar.

But one butterfly collided with another and suffered an injury. It spun out of control and landed in the grass.

Hari spied it, and went to pick it up carefully and hold it in his hand. It was a beautiful iridescent little thing, but clearly suffering. "O lovely creature, what am I to do with you?" he exclaimed, saddened to see it in such state.

I must heal that pretty lady butterfly.

If you do, you have expended your move, for its life has interacted with that of the mortal man.

That is not fair! I am not causing a seduction or guarding his life.

But if you heal it, you are affecting his life, for he is saddened

by its plight. Our agreement does not specify how the mortal man's life is affected, only that the intervention of one of us in a way that affects him counts as a move. Unless we agree other- wise—as I do not in this instance.

And you presume I would be fool enough to yield my move, at the risk of losing our contest, for the sake of a passing insect?

This is what I presume, you charming beautiful spirit.

Well, you are correct, you disgusting insensitive lout. I will heal that butterfly, and gladden the mortal man's soul. But you must agree to this: your own next move is limited to the realm of the an- imals, as mine has been.

As you wish. I can do much with a male animal.

I am sure you can. Perhaps you should find yourself a good rut- ting bull and indulge yourself endlessly.

Your wit is less delightful than your appearance.

The butterfly shook its wings, and lo, the damaged wing unkinked and became straight. It had, it seemed, not been broken, merely bent, and was better now. The butterfly flew out of Hari's hand and went to join its fel- lows among the honeysuckles. "O delightful beauty, how you have gladdened my heart!" Hari exclaimed.

Thank you.

As Hari rode out of the clearing, he passed beneath the now drab and naked trees that guarded the grove. How sad they seemed—perhaps because they had lost their beautiful clothes. Or perhaps they missed their happy playful friends. Yes, a home without the bustle of life was indeed a sad place, he thought.

The forest was soon left behind, and by midday he could see the towers of a fort in the distance, a sign that he must be nearing the state border. He released the horse and laughed to see it gallop off toward home at a pace faster than any he had been able to entice from it. To avoid the fort and the border guards, he turned east into some low hills, then gradually circled north. He could see a gathering of tents beyond the fort, which he guessed was the Madreshian camp the rajah had spoken of. Soon he came to a road beyond the border leading northward, and he set his foot upon it with a light and eager heart.

As he passed through village, field, and wood, he saw that the country was rich and bountiful and the people content. There were no signs of unrest that would require the presence of troops, nor any apparent reason why the people would look with envy or desire upon the neighboring land of Madra.

He spent the night in a grassy field, and by midmorning the next day traffic on the road began to increase. A flock of birds flew by and he knew by their size, speed, and the way they flapped their wings that they were homing pigeons, probably in a race. He had had a few racing pigeons himself in his younger years, and had enjoyed racing them against the birds of other boys in the village.

Now comes my turn with a creature of the animal realm. Observe the way of a male with a female.

As the flock flew by, a hawk suddenly appeared and swooped down on the foremost pigeon, knocking it from the sky. The bird fell into a nearby clump of brush, and Hari quickly ran to the spot and retrieved it before the hawk could descend to claim its prey. The circling hawk screeched in anger at having been robbed of its meal.

Hari's fingers searched through the bird's feathers but

could find no injury. Perhaps it had only been stunned. The bird was sleek and well muscled, clearly of high quality, and was banded. Hari carefully tucked the pigeon in his knapsack, hoping it would eventually revive.

What have you accomplished? The mortal man, instead of being dismayed by the pigeon's plight, elected to save it.

Be patient, you delectable trifle; there is some subtlety here.

Subtlety, you odorous organism? That I must observe before I believe.

The outline of buildings appeared on the horizon, and Hari knew his journey was nearing its end. At the city gates he was stopped by guards and searched, as were all incoming travelers. One of the guards found the pigeon in his knapsack and hailed two other guards, telling them to place "the Brahmin thief" under arrest. Without being given the opportunity to ask questions, he was roughly marched through the city streets to the gate of an imposing multiturreted structure, which Hari knew could only be the palace of the rana. There he was turned over to another guard who marched him through the parklike grounds and into the palace, and thence into an audience chamber where he was told to wait.

Thief? What confusion is this?

The natural confusion of arrogant servitors. Your mortal man is doomed.

Not long after, a door opened at the far end of the room and a guard called out: "Make way for the Lord Chandra, Rana of Madresh!"

Hari watched in silence as the rana entered the chamber followed by a dewan. The king was slight, slow of step, and bent, and wore an opulent white beard that peaked on either side of his wrinkled but kindly face. Befitting his station, he was adorned in a red embroidered robe edged in lace and dotted with pearls, and on his head he wore a silk turban bound with a golden circlet encrusted with rubies. The dewan, in contrast, was tall, young, and not unhandsome, with stern eyes and a humorless mouth. Adorned solely in black without ornamentation, his expression was one of self-assurance, almost arrogance.

Hari was pushed forward and ordered to kneel before the rana, which he did in a manner that gave notice of his caste and upbringing. The king, seated upon a raised pavonine divan, gazed intently at the prisoner before him. The guard spoke.

"Lord, this is the thief we found with the rana's pigeon, which still wears the royal band. But the bird is dead." The guard handed the pigeon to the king.

"Tell me what happened, young man," asked the rana in a wavering voice. Hari then explained how he had rescued the bird from the hawk, and of his intention to release it once it revived.

"But the bird is dead," said the rana sadly. "Vega, my favorite hen, the fastest in my lofts—a champion who won many a race for her master. Tell me, what position was she in the race when you saw her?"

"She was well in front of the others, Lord."

"I knew it! A winner to the end. Ah, I shall miss this noble bird."

"Lord, if I may speak. I, too, once raced pigeons and know something of their ills. May I examine it a moment?"

The rana consented, and the guard took the bird and handed it to Hari. Hari knew from experience that sometimes a pigeon could be revived by gently massaging its breasts and blowing into its mouth. This he did, and in a few moments the pigeon regained consciousness and began struggling to be released. Hari let it go and it flew twice round the chamber and then out an open portal high in the wall, heading for its loft.

You touched the bird to make it live again. Now it is my turn.

Your turn, O ill-omened one. But limit yourself to the animal realm, as I did.

"Oh, wonderful, young man!" exclaimed the rana. "My thanks to you for twice saving my favorite bird. I can see that you are an experienced handler. But tell me who you are and what brings you to my city."

"I am Hari, Lord, a wandering student in search of knowledge who heard of the rana's fair city and would see it with my own eyes."

"And that you shall," said the rana, "as my guest. We will talk more about pigeons and I will show you the royal lofts. But now you will want a rest and change of clothes. Dewan Koti will find some comfortable quarters for you and see that you are well cared for."

The dewan made a shallow bow and led Hari to the second floor of the palace where he turned him over to a servant, who in turn ushered him into a colorfully decorated though not opulent room overlooking the city. As he surveyed his new surroundings, Hari wondered at the unexpected turn of events and gave silent thanks to Lakshmi for yet traveling with him.

In the afternoon the rana showed his guest the royal pigeon lofts. Besides racing homers, Hari saw many exotic breeds he had never seen before. There were damascenes from the Middle East sporting white-frosted feathers and black wing-bars; crested frillbacks from

Asia Minor, their backs and wings covered with tight feathery curls; sleek helmets from Persia with colored pates that gave them the look of Christian monks; pouters from the East, tall and stately, strutting about like so many sergeant-majors; trumpeters from Turkestan, their proud faces encircled by large rose-crests; and graceful fantails, with backward-bending necks and spread ribbon tails, prancing about like court ladies.

The rana pointed out his favorite birds, identifying each by name and detailing its lineage. He spoke glowingly of the noble character of pigeons, of their habits of fidelity and mating for life, their love of home and family, and their ways of settling territorial disputes without bloodshed. Hari was moved by the old king's words, which did not sound like those of an aggressor or expansionist.

At the homer loft the rana pointed out Vega, the pigeon that Hari had saved.

"Was the race that Vega was flying a long one?" asked Hari.

"The release was at the border," replied the rana, "so it was less than a half-day's flight. Of late I have been sending all my racers to the border for release."

"And how do you determine their speed, Lord?"

"The birds are delivered to my general at the border camp with instructions to release them precisely at dawn the following day. The time of arrival home is noted for each bird, and the speed in leagues per hour is then calculated. But the speed has been slow in recent weeks, and I am wondering if that accursed general is letting the birds go promptly at sunup."

"Lord, if you wish I will accompany the birds when

next they are sent to their place of deployment and see to their proper release."

"Ah! Will you do that, my boy? Wonderful! You know pigeons, and I can be sure it will be done right. My dewan, Koti, is in charge of military matters. I will inform him that you will accompany the next shipment of pigeons to the border camp. Now come, let us release the rollers and watch them perform their sky tricks. Then we will dine and I will introduce you to the rani."

Dinner was served in a parlor decorated in purple, canopied by an arched ceiling intricately carved in ivory. Hari was surprised at the rani's youth and beauty, a beauty more of the earth than the heavens, he thought. Koti, the dewan, was also present.

"My dear," said the rana to his wife, "Hari here is an expert on pigeons and has generously offered to take charge of the next release of my homers at the border."

"We are in your debt, Hari," said the rani with a smile that seemed practiced rather than genuine. "I hope there will be no difficulty. I understand there has been some trouble around the border of late—Madran rebels harassing travelers."

"There is no need to worry," said Koti. "We have a contingent of soldiers stationed there to keep the peace."

The rana wrinkled his brow. "Is that wise, Koti? It might be taken as a threat by our neighbor, the rajah. Perhaps the border contingent should be recalled."

"But surely we need some soldiers there to discourage further disturbances, my husband," said the rani.

"Indeed, we do," added Koti. "And the border camp is an ideal place to release my lord's pigeons, it is not?"

"Ah, that is true," conceded the rana. "Very well, I leave military matters in your hands, Koti. And the rani seems to agree. Tell me, when is the next shipment of supplies going to the border?"

"Two days hence, Lord."

"Good. My pigeons and their new handler will be ready."

A servant entered the room carrying a glass of green liquid, which was set before the rana. The rana grimaced. "Not that vile stuff again."

"You must drink the potion, my husband," coaxed the rani. "You know it helps you sleep."

This situation grows more interesting.

But this sword is double-edged.

"Better I not sleep," said the rana. "Then I would not have the same nightmare every night. Cursed be that assassin! Though he failed to murder me in my bed, he yet plagues my sleep and poisons my dreams. I pray each night to Lakshmi to reveal him to me that I may dispatch him before I lose my sanity. Each night in my dream he stands over me like a spectre, his face hidden in hooded cowl, and then he strikes—"

The rana clutched his chest and turned pale with terror, and only gradually regained his composure.

"Do not excite yourself, my husband," urged the rani, soothingly, as she held the potion to the rana's lips. He sighed and drank without further complaint.

She deceives him without effort.

Deception comes naturally to the female of the species.

The next morning Hari walked about the city on his own, having refused the offer of an escort, and was much impressed by its beauty and prosperity. In the afternoon he watched the loading of military supplies onto horse-drawn carts in preparation for the trip to the border camp. Koti himself was to lead the caravan. The pigeon cages were loaded onto separate carts, each cage facing outward since the rana believed the birds would become better oriented if they could see landmarks along the way.

The caravan left at dawn. Hari rode on one of the pigeon carts to keep an eye on the birds. The journey was bumpy but uneventful, and the caravan arrived at the border camp at twilight. The carts were promptly unloaded, supplies in one tent and the pigeons in another. Hari placed fresh water and grain in each birdcage, and by the time the task was completed it was late. Tired from the long and uncomfortable journey, he flopped down on a cot next to the pigeons' cages and promptly fell asleep.

Now for another animal ploy.

In the night he was suddenly awakened by a pinching sensation on his right arm, only to discover that he had bedded down in the path of an army of ants who were using his body as a bridge. He brushed them to the ground, being careful not to injure any, and moved the cot to the opposite side of the tent.

From his new location he could hear voices coming from the supply tent nearby. Two men were conversing. One voice he recognized as that of Koti, the dewan, who was speaking.

"I tell you, General, the old fool has no idea that it was I who tried to kill him. My head was covered and he could not see my face. Next time I will not fail."

"And what of the rani? She may be your lover, Dewan, but can you trust her?"

"Yes, unquestionably. She approves of our plan. Kamala is ambitious and would rule over both Madra and

Madresh—as my wife. Soon, my general, your army will be the mightiest on the continent. As soon as the rana is killed, I will dispatch a message to you, and you must attack Madra at once. Surprise will be on our side, and if all goes as planned the city of Pitali will be ours before the rising of the next full moon."

"Do not be overly confident, Koti. The rajah's head does not yet rest on the tip of my lance. Meanwhile, we must take care not to arouse the rana's suspicion. He is much loved and has the ear of the people."

"Fear not, General. The ground has been carefully laid. By indulging the rana's personal whims I have gradually isolated him from the people and the rulers of neighboring states. He is no danger to us."

"And what of the boy you brought with you—how do you know he is not a spy?"

"I think not. He is a Brahmin with a head full of philosophy, nothing more."

"Just the same, it would be wise to keep an eye on him. Now goodnight, Koti."

What a devious ploy, Ravana! Indeed you are capable of brute subtlety. But I shall find a way to abate it.

It will be a pleasure to watch you try.

All became quiet. Hari's heart pounded and his head throbbed. Koti—a traitor. And the rani. Should he escape now, he wondered, and carry the news to the rajah? But what of the rana? He could not leave the old king to be murdered. He must warn him. But how?

The pigeons! He would send a message with Vega, the rana's swiftest bird.

Before dawn Hari arose and readied the pigeons for release. He opened the front flap of the tent so they could fly clear, then passed a rope through all the cage doors so the flock would be liberated at the same time.

The great eye of Surya peeked over the horizon, and just as Hari was about to pull on the release rope, two strong arms grabbed him from behind. A second figure appeared from behind the tent. It was Koti. The dewan walked slowly along the row of cages and stopped before the midmost one. He smiled as his hand reached into the cage and removed a small roll of paper attached to Vega's leg band. The dewan's face was expressionless as he read the message.

"Your suspicions were correct, General," he said calmly. "The boy has large ears and has learned too much. Perhaps he knows more, information that may be of value to us. Do you have something to tell me, my young friend? No? Well, you will. There is a palace jailor in my employ who is skilled in ways of loosening the tongue."

Koti looked around. "Ah, I see the sun is up—time to release the pigeons. Oh, but let us not release them too hastily. Alas, the rana will be so displeased when his birds arrive home even later than last time. And it will be your doing, will it not, my young Brahmin? Yes, it is all clear to me now. Instead of releasing the birds you were trying to steal them. Just think of how disappointed the rana will be when he learns of your treachery."

The false smile and calm expression departed from the dewan's face. Hari read only hate and fury there now.

"Guards!" screamed Koti. "Bind and gag this thief. He returns with us to the city."

The return trip was made in haste, and by late afternoon the caravan pulled up behind the palace. Hari was dragged through an unguarded rear door and down a long, narrow flight of stairs. A guard then removed his bonds and threw him into a dank solitary dungeon.

He is of little interest at the moment. Let us follow the plotters, whose deviousness is most appealing.

Agreed: most revolting.

Koti hastened to the rani and told her all that had occurred.

"You did well in capturing the spy, my love," she said. "But I am not sure it was wise to bring him back here. My overly sentimental husband might hear of his presence and decide to question him. You must go to the rana and tell him that the Brahmin boy escaped across the border after trying to steal his pet bird. Leave it to me to get rid of the spy. I will pretend to be his friend, and even arrange his escape—through the endless caverns. There he will become hopelessly lost and starve to death—a fitting end for a meddler."

"A sound plan," said Koti, slightly unnerved by the rani's cold-bloodedness. "When will you do the deed?"

"This very night. And surely the time has come for you to fulfill your destiny, my love. One thrust of the dagger and a kingdom will be ours. And that will be only the beginning!"

Now will you conceive in her a sudden genuine passion for the prisoner? I think her nature is too jaded to be subject to that, for she loves power more than sex.

True. I shall abide my time. But if she seduces him, it still counts.

You stretch the definitions until their very fabric threatens to tear asunder! But I will allow it, for he will nevertheless die soon enough.

Hari sat huddled on the stone floor of the dungeon,

his head cradled in his arms, and so did not hear the door bolt slide back or the cell door swing quietly open. As in a dream, a voice spoke to him, calling his name. He looked up to see a veiled woman in the open doorway signaling for him to follow her. He obeyed without hesitation.

He was led through a maze of dimly lit corridors, up a winding stairway, and into a dark room somewhere in the upper reaches of the palace. An oil lamp flickered and brightened, and he saw he was in a large and splendid apartment. The mysterious woman removed her veil, and Hari saw that his rescuer was none other than the rani. He bowed low before her in gratitude and wondered if she was really an ally of Koti after all.

"No need for formalities," she said in melodious voice. "These are my private rooms, so please be at ease. Come, let us sit down together. Among friends I am called Kamala."

Hari was not at all sure that she was his friend, but this certainly seemed better than the dungeon cell, so he acquiesced.

"It saddened me when I learned of your imprisonment, Hari," she continued. "I do not believe you are guilty of any serious wrongdoing, but Koti does, so you are in grave danger. If you have any secret information of a political or military nature you must reveal it to me now, and I will try to help you."

"I would gladly, O Rani, but in truth I have none to reveal."

"Well, I believe you, Hari. I will help you in any case. You must escape this very night lest Koti have you tortured or killed on the morrow. I know of an escape route through some hidden caverns nearby. Once through the caverns you will emerge at a place not far from the south-ern border."

"I am most grateful to you, O Rani. You have given me back my life which is yours but to command." But he was not sure why she had decided to help him.

Are you going to instill her passion now?

No need. She already has passion of the flesh, if not of the heart.

"Hmm. Well then, might you be willing to repay that debt here and now?"

"Yes, gladly, if it be within my power."

"Oh, it is that, for it is with your gift of youth and beauty that you may recompense me. Come, O Hari."

The rani took Hari by the hand and led him into her bedroom. Realizing what was expected of him and tak-ing his obligation to heart, being somewhat recovered from his recent depletion, he proceeded to discharge his debt with skill and alacrity. Its sum diminished with in-creasing rapidity, if it was to be measured by the rani's frequent moans of pleasure.

In the next room the rana slept fitfully, tossing and turning in his bed, his face contorted with fear. He was having the same terrible nightmare that plagued him nightly, ever since the unknown assassin had tried to stab him in his bed. He had again prayed to the goddess Lak-shmi, as he did each day, imploring her to reveal the identity of the attacker, but the goddess was ever silent. He was now on the verge of wakefulness, having devel-oped a tolerance for the drafts of sleeping potion the rani gave him.

The rani pulled in her breath as the moment of supreme delight assailed her, and she could not help but cry out in her uncontrolled ecstasy. And whose name would it be most natural for her to call out in her moment of rapture than that of her habitual lover?

"Koti!" she cried. "Oh, Koti!"

The rana's eyes snapped open as a voice came to him out of the darkness. "Koti!" it said.

I did not touch her.

Granted. I was watching closely. But it matters not; your naïve mortal man still will die.

The old king's breath caught and his brain churned. The goddess had spoken to him! The culprit was none other than Koti. Koti! Koti the ambitious. Koti the envious. Koti the plotter. Yes, of course. How could he have been so blind not to have seen it before?

Having extracted a usurious rate of interest on a fictitious debt, the rani, fully satisfied, summoned her personal maidservant and instructed her to take Hari by a secret way to the entrance of the hidden caverns. Hari made obeisance to the rani and departed.

At the cavern entrance the servant gave Hari the oil lamp she carried, saying he would need it in the darkness of the caves. He smiled and thanked her, and was puzzled at the tear that trickled down her cheek.

❧ *8* ❧

The Endless Caverns

In the perennial darkness beneath the earth, time was its own master. No longer under the watchful discipline of sun, moon, and stars, or subject to the control and measurement of human contrivance, time fluxed and flowed, condensed and stretched in strange ways. To one caught in the fickle clutches of the time god, in the aberrations of his secret courses, minutes and hours, night and day, and the many feeble ways mortals measured the tempo of their lives had little meaning.

Hari wandered from cavern to cavern, how long he did not know. The air became stale and his footsteps hollow and distant. Strange obstructions appeared in his path—monolithic rock formations shaped like prehistoric beasts, and great stone icicles growing out of the cave floor.

As he passed through a large cavern, a slow dripping sound reached his ears and he followed it to a clear pool of water. He set the lamp he carried down at the pool's edge and leaned over to drink. As his lips were about to touch the water, a school of small white fish swam by inches from his face. His heart lightened to find life in such a forsaken place. He watched the tiny creatures swim about in endless circles, seemingly content in their isolated world beneath the earth. He saw too that they had no eyes and marveled at the efficiency of nature for withholding from her children what they did not need in their darkened universe.

Despite his hunger and thirst, his vegetarian ways forbade his eating any of the fish or drinking from their pool, so he contented himself with the water he caught in his cupped hands as it dripped from the cavern ceiling.

The oil lamp suddenly flickered out, its fuel exhausted, and lo! the cavern was illuminated in its own light. A luminous blue glow emitted by the rock itself filled the stony chamber. He wondered at the eerie majesty of the vast cavern: such might be the subterranean domain of the Narakasura, king of the netherworld, he thought.

The walls of the great gallery arched upward into the dimness, draped in folding tapestries of stone. Glittering buttresses cut across dark overhanging cliffs, rudely disturbing the vertical symmetry. In the center of the cavern a massive column rose up to the ceiling where it blossomed out into a glistening amphitheater, from which hung stone spears of white, purple, and amber. Rimming the walls were feathery chalk-like ferns, fragile fans and stone flowers, broad shields and veils.

Hari continued on through the caverns, whistling to keep up his spirits, the echoes reverberating in a chorus of many voices. From time to time he scraped an arrow into the floor to mark his way, and when twice he came upon the same marking he knew he was lost.

Passing through a narrow corridor, he tripped and fell, only to discover he had fallen over a human skeleton. The skull-face stared blankly at him, transfixing his gaze, and as he searched its empty eyes, as though await-

ing a message, the lipless jaws moved. He jumped back
only to see a white eyeless salamander crawl from beneath the rotted teeth. It scurried a few feet to a nearby
wall and stopped. There on the wall, Hari saw, was some
writing scratched into the rock: a message no doubt left
by the poor soul whose skull now housed another eyeless creature.

The message read:

> I, Anandrum, died here alone and in my prime. My
> fate is just for my crimes were great. Whoever reads
> this message, pray for me and thee, for neither will
> again behold the light of day in this lifetime.

Now at last the fool catches on.
Yet there is one here who knows the way out.

Continuing on with a heavy heart, he wondered if the
rani was indeed a traitor and had meant to send him to
his death; he intoned the primal word, Om, to give himself courage. Too, he wondered if the salamander was the
reincarnation of the former owner of the skull, and what
terrible crimes must have been committed for a human
to be reduced to such a lowly state.

Weariness soon overcame him, and he lay down on
the stone floor to rest. How ironic, he thought: all his
life he had sought escape from people that he might be
alone with his dreams and fancies. And now he was destined to die alone in this forsaken place without the com-
fort of another human being. Instinctively, his hand
reached up to the amulet which hung about his neck.

Could the amulet save him? he wondered. He recalled
his fearful experience with the she-demon. Who or what
might he conjure up this time if he spoke the name on

the other side of the amulet? Dare he try? No, he decided. He could not risk loosing some terrible creature upon the world. Better he should face Yama with a noble heart.

His eyelids grew heavy, shutting out his fears for a time, and he fell into a peaceful sleep.

Now do I make my move. I hope that my mortal man has the wit to fathom what is necessary.

When he awoke he felt refreshed, although his empty belly complained audibly. A nearby pool of water, this time unpopulated, slaked his thirst and quieted his stomach. It was then that a noise reached his ears—a faint echo. It sounded like a person weeping.

He followed the sobbing sound to a large cavern with shining walls streaked with porphyry. As he entered the chamber the weeping sound ceased. Puzzled, he sat down on a rock and wondered if his ears had played tricks on him or if he was going mad. Then he heard a sniffle, unmistakably human, and he knew he was not alone.

"It is said that the weight of a problem is lessened in the telling," he said, speaking into the emptiness. "Will you not come out of hiding and share your sorrow with me?" The echoes of his voice flitted through distant chambers. There was no reply. "Please, will you not speak to me?" he entreated. "I will not harm you. Perhaps we can help one another."

"You can not help me," came the reply. The voice was feminine and laden with sadness.

"Well, how can you know that?" asked Hari. "Will you not show yourself that we may talk further?"

"Can not the ear hear without the aid of the eye?"

"But why do you hide? Are you afraid?"

"No, I am not afraid, and I do not hide."

"But I can not see you. Are you behind a rock? Please come out."

"I stand before you, but you can not see me, for I am a Bootham in Tri-Sanka Swarga—a spirit of the middle existence between death and rebirth."

Hari was amazed. He had heard of such spirits but had never thought to encounter one.

"Forgive me, O Spirit," he said in an apologetic tone. "I did not mean to disturb you, but I thought I heard someone weeping. Was it you?"

"Yes."

"It seems, then, that we both have reason to be troubled. I am lost. Pray tell me of your plight, O Spirit."

The weeping commenced again. It was so heartrending that Hari could not help but feel sympathy.

"Please do not cry, Spirit. Perhaps if you tell me what distresses you, you will feel better." The sobbing diminished to an occasional whimper. "Do you have a name? Mine is Hari."

"My name is Pudmini."

"A lovely name. Now, Pudmini, tell me what troubles you."

"Very well," the spirit replied. "Not two years past I was alive and mortal and living happily in my village not far from the city of the rana. I was soon to be married and was blessed in that the match was made with one whom I dearly loved. His name was Arjun.

"In the months prior to our marriage Arjun and I would meet secretly in the fields, though we restrained ourselves from intimacy and breaking the rule of troth. But our passions grew strong within us, and when on the day before our marriage vows we met one last time in the fields, we could no longer restrain our love. And so we revealed our nakedness to one another and would have there consummated our love but for the interjection of cruel fate. We were being spied upon, and as we kissed, cries and shouts rose up around us, and a horde of villagers surrounded us.

"Arjun became afraid and ran, and as the sin of love before marriage is less for the man than the woman, the villagers let him escape. But a rain of stones descended upon me and did not cease until my body lay limp and lifeless in the field. Thus it was I departed life before my allotted time.

"As it is for those whose death is premature, I became a Bootham—a spirit imprisoned in the middle existence, who must linger in this state half a lifetime more until the time comes that would have been my normal span upon the earth. Only then will I escape this prison, will my soul be released and reborn into another life. Such is my curse and my sorrow."

Hari sighed, feeling great pity for Pudmini. A grave wrong had been done her. Yet he knew the laws governing the cycle of life, death, and rebirth were sacred and immutable. But surely the gods were not blind to injustice, he thought. Perhaps there was a chink in the armor of divine law that might be pried open if the occasion merited and the need was great. His eyes stared into space as he contemplated the problem.

"Tell me, Pudmini," he asked finally, "while living as a spirit, have you ever received any supernatural message or sign of any kind?"

"No, not a message. But as I was passing from mortal life into spirit life, I remember hearing a voice, as if in a dream. I do not know why, but I thought it was the voice of the Lord Krishna. But it could not have been."

"Pudmini, tell me, what did the voice say?"

"It made no sense. The voice said: 'Though spirit be not flesh, so spirit flesh will be not spirit. When love denied is love fulfilled by a mortal heart that is pure, so will the soul of the innocent be unbound.' I have pondered those words long, and dwelt upon them much, for I have little to do here but weep and think, but their meaning escapes me."

Hari pondered the words. What could they mean? How could the flesh of a spirit who had no flesh not be a spirit? That could not be possible—unless a spirit did have flesh. But how could an invisible noncorporeal being have flesh?

"Pudmini," he asked, "are you standing close to me?"

"Yes, just in front of you. Why do you ask?"

"Please do as I ask, Pudmini, I beg of you. You must trust me. I am going to hold out my hand to you. Please take it in your own hand."

"But—" She seemed to shrug. "Oh, very well."

Hari stretched out his hand and waited, his heart thumping. Then he felt the soft touch of a hand upon his own.

"Pudmini, I can feel your hand!" he cried with delight.

"And I yours, Hari."

"Now I understand the meaning of the words you heard. Surely it was a message from Krishna. You see, Pudmini, you are both spirit and flesh. You can not be seen, but your body can be touched and felt like that of any mortal. And you can feel me in turn. Pudmini, the Lord Krishna in his mercy left you a means of escape. Your soul can be freed!"

"Oh Hari, is it true? Pray, tell me how!" Hari could feel Pudmini's hand trembling with excitement.

"By Krishna's own words, your soul will be released when you complete that final act of love—which you were denied and unjustly punished for as a mortal— with a mortal man who is pure of heart."

He did fathom it!

In that situation I would have fathomed it faster.

But you are not eligible, for you are neither mortal nor pure of heart.

I have desire enough to make up for both, as I will demonstrate if you will simply hold still for the denouement.

But you must be accustomed to singular outcomes—or should I say climaxes. Go perform a solo.

As the echoes of Hari's words died away, an utter stillness filled the chamber. When finally Pudmini spoke, her voice was soft and hesitant.

"A mortal man? But—but there is only you, Hari. You have been kind and understanding, but I can not ask this of you. I have no right."

"Oh Pudmini, you do not need to ask. I want to help you. But Krishna's words say that he who would free your soul must be pure of heart. I do not think I qualify."

"Do not say that, Hari. That is the least of my doubts. Thought I have known you but a brief time, I know that your heart is pure."

As it is, for he is perpetually naïve.

"Well, there does seem to be a dearth of candidates. But if you are willing to risk my heart's uncertain condition, I gladly offer my unworthy self to you, Pudmini. You need not decide now. Think on it awhile."

"There is no cause for delay, Hari. Long have I suffered imprisoned within these walls. My soul craves freedom. You discovered the means of my salvation. Now

I beg you to liberate me forthwith. Do this, and my heart and my gratitude will be yours forever."

"If you are truly decided," he said, discovering the notion to be increasingly appealing, because of the merit of the cause.

"I am ready, Hari."

Hari spread out his tunic over a smooth plateau of rock to use as a bed—the best he could do. He held out both his hands and she placed her hands in his. Her trembling fingers spoke of shyness and hesitation, which he understood, and he was gentle and patient with her.

His fingers were his eyes. He ran them through her hair, thick and silken-soft, over her face, her satin-smooth skin, and high cheekbones, over her long lashes, which fluttered to the touch, over her large deepset eyes, straight narrow nose, and soft full lips that parted and shivered ever so slightly, down her slender neck and small rounded shoulders, over her firm full breasts, which rose to the touch, across her narrow waist and generous hips, and down to her trembling thighs. He marveled that such beauty could be revealed by the mere touch of a hand.

He set his lips to hers, which ceased to tremble and answered with willingness and warmth. Her breath quickened and her hands explored his body, searching out places of secret pleasure and lingering there when his body responded. His hands and lips and tongue also found her secrets, and when she arched her back in a sudden shock of delight, he did not let her fall back but led her on to ever-greater heights.

She did not cry out as a searing sweetness filled her being; her body rose eagerly to meet its tormentor, rising and ebbing, the sweetness building, ever building, finally exploding in a spasm of joyous rapture: a brief moment of eternity suspended in time and space.

Oh, I wish I were doing that!

I have been trying to make you play the role, ravishing nymphid.

Not with you, hideous oaf. With him.

Somehow I had suspected that. But soon enough I will win the contest, and your plaintive desires will have no relevance. It is now my turn.

As they lay resting in one another's arms, an image came into Hari's mind, and he smiled to himself, amused. He pictured himself in the act of making love to Pudmini, an invisible woman—how ridiculous he looked!

Suddenly Pudmini pulled herself from his embrace.

"Hari, something is happening to me," she cried.

Hari leapt to his feet. In the empty space before his eyes a shadowy figure appeared. It gradually increased in density, darkening and solidifying, until lo! standing there before him was a maiden of such startling beauty that his breath caught. His eyes recognized the features that only his hands had known; but, oh, his hands had been such poor judges, he thought. A sweet pain pierced his heart.

"Hari, it has happened!" Tears of happiness filled Pudmini's eyes. "My soul is free! But, oh, I can not stay. Another life beckons me even now. Thank you, Hari, for my release. My heart is yours. Perhaps we will meet again in another life. Now you must save yourself. Follow the trail of the amber spears of stone, and seek out nourishment in the dark corners of the caves of black rock. Farewell, Hari. Farewell."

Hari watched in joy and sadness as Pudmini faded away, the faint echoes of her voice yet lingering in distant chambers. Sobs joined with the far-off echoes, and he realized they were his own.

He wondered what new body her soul now resided in. Her soul was noble, he knew, and he chose to think of her cradled in the arms of a queen, child to a king, a princess with a destiny.

Pangs of hunger returned him to the harsh reality of his own predicament. He sought out the caves of black rock where he found edible mushrooms growing in abundance. He consumed them with avidity, and they seemed a princely meal indeed. Then returning to the corridor from which hung the amber spears, he set about following their trail as Pudmini had advised.

And I have achieved another seduction, and the mortal man has another escape from death.

There is more to this than the caverns.

Hari guessed that many days must have passed, and at last the stone floor began to slope upward. High-pitched cries reached his ears and seemed to be coming from somewhere in front of him. They became louder, and as he entered a large cavern an amazing sight greeted him. The roof of the cavern was covered in a living mass of wriggling brown bats. Countless in number, their furry snouts and membranous wings twitched constantly, and their tiny clawed thumbs seemed to be pointing directly at him.

Suddenly, as though on cue, the tiny creatures took wing, forming a dense cloud of flapping monsters in miniature. They darted and wheeled in a graceful ballet, circling the great gallery in close formation, miraculously avoiding colliding with one another. The whirling circle then broke and the formation began leaving the cavern. Hari saw that the bats too followed the trail of the amber spears, and he hurried on after them.

See. Winged fingers point the way.

The upward incline of the floor became steeper and the walls gradually narrowed. Hari's heart leapt when he saw that the cave opening was just ahead.

"God is good!" he cried, as he dashed out into the cool night air. But then he looked about and gasped, for the face of god was not smiling.

It was as though he had stepped into an alien world. The curvature of the sky was bent and broken, and blinding colors flashed and swished across the firmament. Luminous streamers streaked by overhead, arching sky-curtains of flaming violet fluttered eerily, and elliptical rings of yellow light darted through the heavens.

Above the tumultuous maelstrom in the sky's cup there glowed two spectral moons, terrifying in their magnificence. Recalling the description in the explorer's diary, Hari now knew where he was: the Land of Peril.

He shuddered and looked back toward the safety of the cave. "No!" he screamed. "I will not go back." He shook his fist at the turbulent heavens. "I will fight your demons!"

Yes, I counted on that foolishness.

Clenching his jaw, he set his step toward the dark hill that loomed below the southern horizon, which he knew could only be Demon Knoll, domain of the fearful cloud monster.

The eyes of the twin moons followed him and took on a pale penumbral glow. The perimeter of the easternmost moon brightened and expanded, then broke free and drifted outward to form a brilliant ring around the now paling central disk. The encircling corona began to pulsate, and with each pulsation contracted toward the inner orb, hugging it ever tighter. Upon reaching the outer edge of the moon, the ring continued to shrink, consuming the very moon itself.

Hari tried not to look and felt trickles of sweat running down his back.

The remaining moon brightened and cast off its encircling red mantle, which floated upward and formed a shimmering double moonbow. The heavens hissed in disapproval, and spear-like bolts flashed across the twisting firmament. Great pillars, vertical shafts of red light, shot up from the horizon and across the face of the moon as though to hold up the wavering superstructure. Out of the distant space a ragged ball of green fire appeared and rolled across the heavens, growing ever larger until it dwarfed the moon itself. Straight it sped toward the monstrous pillars of light, colliding with them in an explosion of eye-searing color, threatening to split the very sky asunder.

Hari threw himself to the ground, covering his head with his arms. Was the end of the world at hand? he wondered. But when next he looked up, as if by magic the sky was clear and serene, save for a few dancing beads of light that zigged and zagged about playfully. The heavens seemed to glow in mock contentment, or perhaps amusement.

Suddenly tired, he stretched out on a bed of moss beneath an overhanging rock. Though intending only to rest for a moment, he fell into a sound sleep.

He awoke to see the face of Surya greeting him as it pushed its way up over the eastern hills. The sun fluttered a moment, and then it suddenly disappeared. Hari jumped to his feet, alarmed, only to see Surya once again rising up proudly in the same place it had risen a moment before. He realized then that the sun he had first seen had been only a reflection, an early image of the real sun mirrored against the sky.

He continued on toward Demon Knoll and had not gone far when a hot dry wind came up and dark low-lying clouds rolled in over the hills. Flashes of forked lightning cracked horizontally through the air, followed by roaring peals of thunder. The air became mysteriously alive, tingling his skin. Invisible currents pushed and tugged at him, and miniature atmospheric whirlpools whipped at the earth. Ahead he could see strange glowing balls rolling along the ground at great speed, and when they struck a boulder or outcropping they exploded violently. One was heading straight at him, and he dived aside to avoid being struck. The fiery ball exploded against some rocks behind him and shattered into myriad tufts of flame, which danced about in ghostly fashion before flickering out.

He will not always be so fortunate. Soon—soon.

Whirling columns of air followed in the lightning's wake. Like omnivorous devil-demons, the spinning wind-eddies raced along the ground, sucking up dirt and stones, which they hurled about wildly. Hari hugged the earth to avoid being struck. Then as suddenly as it started, the turmoil ceased and the air grew calm again.

When finally he reached the base of Demon Knoll, it was nearly evening. The humpback rise loomed vacant and foreboding over the surrounding land, silently declaring its mastery over all. A stationary cloudbank surrounded by mist hung over its crest. Determined to pass over the hill before dark, he began the ascent without delay.

The incline was not steep and there were few obstructions in his path. Much to his surprise, he reached the summit quickly and without difficulty.

The top of the hill was flat, and looking about, he could see no sign of danger. Then he looked up and his heart leapt to his throat. There, staring down at him from the low-lying cloudbank, was a giant demon face. Trembling, he gaped in frozen silence at the monstrous visage. It floated just above him in the cloud shadows, its features ugly and distorted, altering constantly into myriad grotesque shapes. Unable to move or tear his eyes away, Hari waited for death to strike him.

But nothing happened. His wits returned to him, and he wondered if the cloud demon might not be harmful after all. Then a bizarre thought came to him. Could it be?

In a sudden leap he dived backward to a position just below the top of the hill. He crouched down so that his body would not be visible to the gaze of the demon. He waited several minutes, then slowly raised his head just far enough to get a clear view of the hovering cloudbank. The monster was gone! He had guessed right.

To confirm his theory, he stood once more upon the hilltop, only to find that the monster had also returned— as he had expected. He stepped to the left and the demon moved with him. He jumped to the right and the demon mimicked him again. He clapped his hands and laughed out loud, and the demon seemed almost to smile. He was right: the monster was nothing more than an apparition, a phenomenon of nature. The explanation was simple. The sun was low on the horizon, and so looked up at the crest upon which he stood. Like a great projector, it cast his shadow onto the cloudbank, as it would anyone's who stood upon the hill. The distortions were created by the convoluting movements of the clouds themselves.

He grimaced and shook his head from side to side, which the shadow-image faithfully imitated, and it was

not until darkness threatened that he gave up the game
and made his way down the far side of the hill.

He found a shallow crevice to rest in for the night.
Though hardly comfortable, it shielded him for the turmoil of the heavenly fireworks. As he munched on a
mushroom, he thought about home, especially his
mother's wonderful cooking and his own soft bed, and
he wondered if he would ever escape this unfriendly land.

The next day he made good headway. The land became flat and sandy and the surrounding mountains
closer. His eyes ached from the bright sand, which shimmered in waves of yellow-gold like a great phantom lake.
In the distance a dark band appeared in the sand, stretch-
ing the full width of the land from mountain to mountain. He wondered what it could be. When he reached
the darkened area his heart sank. A great chasm split the
land, impossible to cross, as though some angry god had
run a finger across the earth and cut it open. He fell to
his knees, too benumbed to cry out or weep.

Long he gazed at the brooding chasm, even as the blazing eye of Surya, ever watching, inched past its zenith.
As though in sympathy, or perhaps defiance, the dark
band also crept forward like some great black lizard.
Hari shook his head to clear his vision. The chasm
moved again. He jumped to his feet and ran toward the
opening, but it as quickly moved away from him. He
stopped and it stopped. Finding a stone, he hurled it into
the center of the dark band, only to see a splash of sand
leap up where the stone had struck.

He has fathomed its bluff. You hoped he would kill himself by
reacting to fancies, but he has not.

He has been lucky. But luck can turn both ways. He has not yet
escaped the Land of Peril.

How foolish he felt. There was no chasm. It was only a mirage, a trick of sun and sand. Would he never learn? Oh well, he thought, perhaps next the sun will fall out of the sky and roll at my feet. If so, he would pay no attention.

He passed through the sandy wilderness without further incident and by midafternoon reached the base of the mountains. The towering giants arose abruptly out of the earth to form a walled barrier. He knew that somewhere in the fortress was a breach, the pass which the explorer had called Yama's Cut.

As he walked eastward along the base of the mountains, he caught a faint whiff of fragrance in the air. The odor gradually became stronger, and he saw ahead a large purple cloud hanging low in the air, hugging the cliffside. Through the dense mist he could make out an opening in the mountain wall, doubtless the pass he sought. He remembered the explorer's diary telling of the deadly mist that hung over Yama's Cut—the breath of demons—and wondered if it was poisonous. No matter, the pass was his only means of escape and he had to take it.

He entered the cloud. Its sweet pungency was sickening and burned his eyes. He groped his way to the gap in the mountain wall, and within its narrow confines the purple mist was even denser. His head began to spin and he fell to his knees. But closer now to the ground, he found that the air was clearer. His breathing became easier. Surely the goddess Lakshmi still traveled with him, he thought.

As his eyes cleared he saw he was in a passage that cut straight through the mountains. He also saw the source of the pungent mist: champak bushes, row upon row of champak bushes growing all along the passage. He laughed as he surveyed the thousands of lovely purple starlike blossoms. Champaks: he knew they loved the shade and craved protection, and here was the perfect arboretum for them. The cloud of perfume that filled the air was nothing more than the pollen emitted from the dense clusters of flowers.

He continued on through the pass crawling on his hands and knees. The going was slow, though in places the champaks thinned out and he was able to walk. Finally, to his great relief, he found himself on the far side of the mountains.

So he has escaped it despite you.

But I did not intervene. The move remains mine.

He emerged beneath a still blue sky, the great vault of Indra, and spread out before him was a scene to gladden the heart: an expanse of rolling green hills dotted with silk-cotton, mango, and gova trees; gold-tipped fields sprinkled with yellow carnations, primroses, and daisies, guarded by great flowering rhododendrons and proud bougainvilleas. Lapwings and kites darted about the lea, and overhead a flock of crimson-billed kingfishers flew toward the westering sun. A lone crow shook its wings in a nearby neem tree, disturbing its delicate lacework leaves, and squawked in raucous counterpoint to the sweet melody of the lark.

The burden Hari carried became lighter as he breathed in the serene beauty of his new surroundings. He would have liked to languish here awhile, to do nothing but sit upon a hill and gaze out upon the majesty of nature, the great gift of Brahma. But he had a task to perform, and so, with a sigh, he turned his step southward toward the city of the rajah.

❦ 9 ❦

The Loan

Hari spent a peaceful night beneath the protective branches of a tamarind and was awakened in the morning by the cooing of a dove among its russet pods. He rose and stretched, shaking off his weariness, even as the eastern sky shed its mantle of white and struck fire from the golden pearls of dew upon the grass. A faint fragrance of the champak came to him, and he smiled, for bits of its pollen still clung to his tunic.

As he walked along munching on a mango, a brightly banded caterpillar crept out of the grass onto the path. He stopped, watched its graceful undulations, and waited until it crossed the open path and reached the safety of the grass beyond. He had noticed that his were not the only eyes that followed the slow-crawling creature. From a nearby tree a jaybird squawked in protest at the human's intervention, which had allowed its breakfast to escape.

By way of compensation Hari broke off a piece of the mango he was eating and tossed it on the ground for the ruffled bird. Without a note of appreciation, the jay promptly descended on the juicy fruit and proceeded to consume it greedily. Oh well, thought Hari, perhaps a thank-you was not called for. No doubt the jay's culinary preferences ran more toward caterpillars than mangoes.

Ordinarily he would not have interfered in nature's ways, but of late he had he seen the footprints of Yama on the path before him, and he would put them behind him if he could. Besides, the caterpillar was quite lovely, and as a vegetarian he knew there were alternatives to flesh-eating.

But suppose, he asked himself, that the jaybird depended upon a diet of caterpillars to survive. How could he then in good conscience deprive the bird of necessary sustenance? Morally and logically, the answer was clear: he could not. All his life he had been brought up on morality and logic; it had been drummed into his head daily by the village pundit. But now, somehow, such reason seemed cold and distant. Perhaps some irrationality had crept into his character, a flaw that his teacher and, indeed, any self-respecting Brahmin, would find appalling. But he was glad he had saved the caterpillar.

Toward evening he came upon a small village, a welcome sight. After many days of solitary wandering he looked forward to the company of other human beings.

As he entered the village, he saw there was a crowd gathered in front of one of the clay houses that lined the main street. The assembly was subdued, the people talking in hushed voices; some of the women were weeping. He asked a man standing at the perimeter of the group the reason for the gathering, thinking that perhaps an important personage had died. He was told that the house was that of the village guru, an elderly and much venerated teacher in the community, who was ill. It was feared the guru might die soon, so the villagers had come to the old master's house to pay him homage.

Hari also learned from the bystander that it was a custom in the village for all newcomers to appear before the guru, and as he was a stranger, he was encouraged to join the gathering of devotees who were beginning to file into the house. Not to respect such a custom, he knew, would be an offense. Also, he would be unlikely to obtain a free meal and a roof over his head if he did not comply.

He joined the end of the queue as it filed into the house and waited patiently as it wove its way slowly from room to room. Upon entering a large parlor, he could see there were three people seated yoga-style on the floor receiving the visitors. The first was a frail elderly man, bearded and wearing the simple white gown of a master-teacher—doubtless the guru. Each of the visitors bowed low before the old man and exchanged a few polite words, the more worshipful kneeling to touch his feet and then their eyes. The guru did his best to discourage this act of supreme reverence, thereby revealing his own humility. His gentle eyes blinked with pleasure each time he recognized a familiar face, and Hari could see the old teacher was loved by all.

Seated next to the guru were two attractive young women, both garbed in the robes of disciples. They in their turn greeted the visitors with a polite nod and clasped upturned hands. The visitors then passed out of the house through a door at the far end of the parlor, some leaving small gifts on the mat at the exit.

The line gradually dwindled until only Hari remained. He approached the guru and bowed before him. The guru smiled, his old eyes twinkling as he studied the newcomer's face.

"Ah, it seems we have a special visitor tonight, Sharmila, a young Brahmin no less," declared the guru. "Welcome to this humble house, young man. We are pleased to have you. It is not often we have the pleasure of welcoming strangers to our village—we are so far off the beaten track. But forgive me, I must present you to these lovely ladies. To my right is my wife, Sharmila, my most devoted disciple and the flower of my life. And next to Sharmila is her equally lovely sister, Shanta, also a devoted disciple, and a dedicated teacher to the children of the village—although I fear we may soon lose her to the university at Agrapoor. As for myself, I am Sundar, also a teacher, and like yourself a victim of Brahminical heritage—a condition that can be overcome, I assure you."

The old man chuckled at his own joke, but then began a fit of coughing. It was several minutes before he was able to continue.

"Forgive me. My body seems to have reached its limit somewhat ahead of my spirit. But now tell us who you are, young man, and what brings you to our humble village."

"My name is Hari, O Guruji, a student from a village in the northeast of Madra. In my wanderings it was by accident that I happened upon your village. I regret I have no gift to offer, but accept my prayers for your health and my humble thanks for your kind welcome."

"That is more than gift enough, young Hari," said the guru. "You are as well-spoken as you are well-mannered. Sharmila and I insist you stay with us this night that we may have the pleasure of your company. Do we not, Sharmila?"

"Yes, my husband, assuredly. We would be most pleased and honored."

O, were it but my move, one of these two beauteous young women would be the seventh seduction!

Yes, I knew you would come up with some such, if I failed to gain and hold the move.

How lovely and feminine she is, thought Hari as he bowed in appreciation of the invitation.

"Good, then it is settled," declared the guru. "While Sharmila sees to the preparation of our evening meal, we will retire to the library to chat further. Shanta, I hope you will stay and dine with us."

Look into his mind! See what he contemplates!

Your luck is obscene!

As is your character, so we are even.

"I thank you and beg your forgiveness, Master," Shanta replied, "but I can not. This evening I am expecting a visit from the head pundit—the Mahomahopadyaya—of Agrapoor University. Whether I am successful in obtaining the teaching appointment I have applied for may well depend on my interview this night. Although the pundit is visiting me to assess my character and learning, I thought to provide an encouraging environment by setting out a good meal before him."

"Most wise, Shanta," said the guru. "But your character is saintly and your scholarship superb, so if the pundit is not a fool I am sure you will be found acceptable—even if your chapatis are overcooked."

As Shanta rose from her sitting position on the floor, she bumped her head on a protruding wall shelf. Hari heard not one but two "ouches" uttered at the same time, one from Shanta and the other from Sharmila in the adjoining kitchen. Sharmila poked her head around the door, looked at Shanta, and when she saw that her sister was not injured, she giggled, as did Shanta. The guru did not notice the incident as he struggled to gain his feet. Hari helped the old man up and supported him as he walked on unsteady legs to the small library next to the parlor. Shanta voiced a final farewell as she left the house, and Sharmila resumed her preparations for the evening meal.

Hari deposited the guru in a comfortable chair in the library and accepted another for himself at the guru's invitation. The old teacher stroked his beard for several minutes before speaking.

"Hari, I would say something to you, something that is important to me. And then I would ask you a question—a somewhat unusual question. It is a personal matter, and for that I beg your indulgence. I believe you to be a man of virtue and good character, a person of discretion and judgment. And as you are an educated Brahmin, I am sure you will appreciate the subtleties and complexities of the matter I am about to explain in an appropriately detached manner. When I am finished, you may even be agreeable to performing a small service for an old man not long for this life."

It was clear that something of serious consequence was afoot. "I shall be glad to help in any way I may," Hari said. For this was an essential part of his search for truth and wisdom: he wished to learn how best to help others, especially those most deserving. Whatever service the guru wished would surely be instructive as well as beneficial.

"Let me begin by telling you of my marriage to Sharmila. We were wed two years ago, at the time my health began to fail. She was one of my most devoted disciples, and she unselfishly insisted on looking after me in my waning years. Rightly or wrongly, I married her, although she was young enough to be my granddaughter. At the time, other than her sister, she had only a father, who has since died, and he cared only for the reflected honor of his daughter's marriage to the village guru and thought not of the life she would lead. And in truth, I did not fully consider the matter either, although I have thought about it many times since." The old man allowed a small sigh of regret to escape him.

After a moment he resumed his narration. "She cared for me well, and I grew to love her dearly. Because of declining health, I could not provide her with the normal corporeal enjoyments of married life. Yet she never complained, although I know she must have suffered because of it. She remained faithful always, the model of a self-sacrificing and virtuous wife.

"I hoped and prayed my health and body might revive, if only for a little while, that I might give to Sharmila at least some measure of the pleasure that is the right of any spouse. But the depreciation of time would not relent, and my condition gradually worsened. Now the shadow of Yama is upon me, and my Sharmila will soon be alone. She can not marry again, for custom forbids it. Nor would she wish to. Rather, I believe she is intent on remaining here the rest of her life that she may impart my teachings to the children of the village. Ah, how this old heart breaks when I consider that my beloved Sharmila, yet in the flower of her youth, must live out her life unfulfilled, without ever knowing the joys of physical love.

"So you see, Hari, why my heart is heavy. How often

have I wished there was a moment of youth I might steal and share with Sharmila. Such are the foolish fancies of an addled old man. But it was that idle wish that set me to thinking—not of stealing, but of borrowing a moment of youth. The idea, I know, sounds absurd, but it is not. Let me explain."

Hari's surprise must have shown on his face, for the old guru smiled as he continued. "If you look around this room, you will see books on many subjects, not a few on the art and practice of Hatha-Yoga. My teacher was an eminent practitioner of Hatha-Yoga, and it was from him that I learned and eventually mastered the difficult art of spiritual transmigration. Only a few experts have successfully accomplished spirit transfer. I have done so on two occasions, both times in my younger years under the tutelage of my master-teacher. Though I have not performed a spiritual transfer in a long time, it is a skill that once learned is not forgotten.

"This brings me to the question I wish to ask you, Hari. It is not a question that is easy to ask, even by an old guru who has spent his life asking more questions than he has been able to answer. It is a boon I seek of you. Though your acquiescence will mean much to me, know that if you refuse, I will understand—indeed, I might well refuse myself if I were in your place. So do not feel obligated where no obligation exists. Whatever answer you give, I will accept, and we will enjoy our dinner all the same.

"What I wish to ask of you is the loan of your body for one night that I may lie with my wife. You can understand that I could not ask this of anyone in the village where everyone knows one another. Also, Sharmila,

I am sure, would not be comfortable if I wore the body of someone she knew in another capacity, and there could be no assurance that sooner or later the lender of the body might not misspeak and reveal the incident. You, being a stranger who will soon be leaving the village, are an ideal candidate. Of course, Sharmila would have to agree, but I am confident I can convince her.

"Well, I have said enough. Perhaps too much. I would not blame you if you conclude that you are in the company of a crazy old man. Perhaps I am. But what I have said is true, and I am confident that I can perform a spiritual transfer without any harm to your body or your spirit. The decision is yours."

A long silence ensued as Hari sifted through the confusion of thoughts that filled his head.

"O Master," he said finally, "I would ask a question. What happens to my spirit when yours has entered my body? And what of your body when it has lost its spirit?"

"Your spirit, Hari, will remain in your own body, even as my spirit enters your body to take possession of your thoughts and movements. You will not be wholly unaware of my spiritual presence, nor will you lose all bodily control. I can achieve dominant control, but only if your spirit permits it. Your spirit and your will must assume a passive role during the brief period of the possession. As for my own body, it will remain alive and simply lie at rest, dormant, until I transfer my spirit back into it."

But it will count as a seduction, for his body will have congress with another woman.

And if he gets killed in this village, it counts too.

Another long silence followed as Hari considered the

matter further. He felt genuine sorrow and compassion for the ailing guru. Too, as a student and a Brahmin, he was respectful of the revered status of the master-teacher, and it was in the Brahminical tradition that he should obligingly render service to others. And the experience would do him no harm.

"Master, I will gladly make my humble body available to you for a night's employ. Tell me what I must do."

"My thanks to you, O Hari," said the guru with an equanimity and humility that belied the joy in his heart. Only the trembling in his fingers betrayed the emotion of the moment.

"There is nothing to be done just yet. First I must discuss the matter privately with Sharmila so that she will understand and be agreeable. She already knows that I have the ability to perform spiritual transfer, and so will not be disbelieving of the arrangement we have made. I am confident she will comply, for she will think the experience to be a pleasing thing for me, and she strives to please me in every way she can. I will go speak with her now. Make yourself at home in my absence and browse through my collection of books if you like. I will return presently."

The old guru pulled himself to his feet and shuffled out of the room.

Hari surveyed the shelves of books and selected one entitled: *Strange Phenomena of Nature*. He thought perhaps to find within its pages some clues to the strange happenings he had observed while traveling through the Land of Peril.

When the guru returned to the library, he was pleased to find his guest deeply engrossed in a book.

"Ah, yes. Your choice is a good one," said the guru. "A most revealing tome, and well documented. But now it is time for dinner. Come along. And if Sharmila seems a bit shy, I am sure you will understand. She consented to our arrangement as I knew she would, and I will perform the transfer after dinner." He sniffed the air appreciatively. "Ah, this old nose is not dead yet—I can smell the curry and pickles from here. Prepare yourself for some fine food, my boy, for Sharmila is a magical cook."

At the dinner table Sharmila busied herself with arranging the dishes just so, and occupied herself with a myriad of minor details so as to avoid looking into Hari's eyes. Hari understood and did his best not to contribute to her unease, so he concentrated on sampling the many savory dishes and listening to the guru lightheartedly expound upon the subject of reincarnation.

"It is written that the rebirth of a human into the form of an animal is retrogressive—a punishment for a life of sin," said the guru. "But I have my doubts. Why is an animal necessarily a lower form? Animals do not sin. They are born innocent and remain so. If they kill it is usually to survive; they act on instinct. But man? Ah, how well he has taught himself the fine art of inhumanity. Even the gods seem not to value the human form over that of creatures. Consider the great number of godly incarnations that take the form of animals."

"But," asked Hari, "among the creatures, are not some higher than others, just as among humans?"

"Perhaps so," replied the guru. "But higher in what way? The noble eagle soars majestically on the wind currents and then descends from on high to rend and consume the small ground squirrel. Yet the eagle is revered and the squirrel is scorned. But the squirrel kills not and eats not of the flesh. He eats as we do, of fruits, nuts, and vegetables. He does not kill but is killed, victim to the strong and powerful. Therefore, I ask you, would it not be better to be reborn as a ground squirrel than as an eagle—or a man?" The guru chuckled, pleased at the inevitability of his logic.

"O my husband," chimed in Sharmila, "if you will permit an observation. Before you begin burrowing holes in your next life, perhaps you would do well to consider what might be in store for the ground squirrel in its next life."

The guru and Hari laughed at these words, and Hari saw that Sharmila was as clever as she was beautiful. But he also wondered how serious the guru might be, for very few men, if given the choice, would choose to be a squirrel rather than an eagle. It almost seemed that the guru believed that he did have such a choice. That spoke well for his sincerity, for it was easy to advocate a humble reincarnation when there was no prospect of it. Just as it was easy for a poor man to renounce the trappings of wealth, and difficult for a rich man to do the same.

After dinner the guru showed Hari to a guest bedroom and there explained the next step in preparing for the spiritual transfer. "Are you ready, then, Hari?"

"Yes, I am ready."

"Good. Now lie down on the bed and relax yourself. Assume a comfortable position. You need only shut your eyes and empty your mind. Intoning the primal word will help you do this. I will go now to the vacant room adjacent to my bedroom. From there I will perform the transfer. It is not necessary that I be in the same room with you to detach and transfer my spirit, and you can understand that the ritual is secret and can not be seen by another. Remain passive and I will take control of thought and movement. My spirit will direct your body to leave this room, whereupon I will take it to my own bedroom where Sharmila awaits.

"Later in the night I will return your body to this bed and release my spirit, which will return to its own body. Then all will be as before."

With that the guru bowed and left the room. Hari lay quietly on the bed, his eyes closed, and inwardly sounded the primal word as he awaited the coming of the guru's spirit.

But let us see what the sister is up to.

That innocent is boring. Still, who knows?

Upon leaving the house of the guru, Shanta made her way toward her own dwelling down the road. The sting from having bumped her head against the shelf in the guru's parlor was all but gone, and she smiled to herself as she recalled that she and Sharmila had cried "ouch" at the same time. When they were children, she remembered, they had suffered pain together then too, and experienced the same pleasures as well, though their lives had not been so exciting that bodily pleasure or pain had visited them very often.

Everyone in the village knew that she and Sharmila were twins, although not identical. But among the living only the two sisters knew that they had been born joined together at the shoulder and had been skillfully separated at birth without injury to either by the village midwife, who had since died. Only the slightest of scars remained.

And no one but they knew that since their birth each experienced the same physical sensations of the other.

If Shanta ate a spicy dish, Sharmila also experienced the taste, and if Sharmila sniffed a fragrant flower, Shanta too enjoyed the smell. And if Shanta cut her finger, Sharmila's finger, though it would not bleed, would feel the same pain. Indeed, each had become so accustomed to experiencing the ordinary daily sensations of the other that sometimes neither was sure who was the initiator and who the recipient of their common feelings. It was only that rare and unexpected event that caused them to be aware of their unusual talent as well. If their empathy did not extend to seeing and hearing, for that they were grateful. All their lives they had kept their secret to themselves lest they be thought of as freaks. Sharmila had not even told her husband.

Shanta arrived home and set about putting the finishing touches on the evening meal. She wanted the dinner to be perfect and dearly hoped it would be to the liking of the pundit. More than anything in her life she wanted the university appointment. Everything was in order. The parlor and dining room were neat to a fault, her meager library was prominently displayed, and she had on her best sari.

A loud rapping sounded at the door as might be delivered by an angry woodpecker. Shanta nervously brushed away the imaginary wrinkles in her sari, took a deep breath, and opened the door. There stood her guest for the evening.

"Pundit Rajagopala, how good to see you again, and how kind of you to come," said Shanta effusively, her palms pressed tightly together. "Please come in."

"Harumph, well yes, yes," sputtered the pundit in a

haughty tone, his puffy red face screwing itself up disdainfully as he looked around in undisguised disapproval. He was short and portly with close-set blinking eyes and thick lips, entirely bald, and moved about in much the same manner as an overweight duck.

"Please make yourself at home, Master. This is the most comfortable chair. Will you take some tea?"

"Tea? Yes. Plain and not too strong. Yes, properly served, tea should not be too strong. Harumph."

But we must not neglect the guru's activity.

You watch the seduction; I will watch the pundit's meal. Neither aspect of this episode should be missed. I shall assuage my boredom with thoughts of future conquests.

Agreed. Here is my report.

Hari lay still in his bed awaiting the coming of the guru's spirit. Sharmila too lay in her bed, expectant and apprehensive, her eyes fastened on the door, waiting for her husband to enter in the body of Hari. She did not know exactly what to expect from the experience, for her husband had not been very specific about the details.

Hari felt a tingling sensation, which soon dissipated, and he became aware of the presence of the guru's spirit within him. He marveled at its richness, serenity, and gentle nobility. Relaxing his will, he let the guru take control of his body, which then rose from the bed and left the room. Although his brain no longer instructed his movements, he could sense the excitement and anticipation that emanated from the guru's spirit.

Sharmila watched in wide-eyed fascination as the body of Hari entered the room and sat down on the bed next to her. If the voice that spoke to her was young and strong, the words and gestures were familiar, and she felt assured that it was her husband who now attended her. She gradually relaxed, and when the firm young body pressed gently against her, she did not protest.

As the lovemaking intensified, Hari did his best to submerge his spirit and remove himself from the sensual emanations that assailed his body so as not to trespass upon the privacy of the guru and his young wife. But this became increasingly difficult as the waves of emotion heightened and splashed upon the shores of his senses. He could sense Sharmila's wonderment at the new emotions she was experiencing, nor could he help feeling her firm young breasts press against his body and the pulsing warmth deep within her.

Then, inexplicably, his body faltered, and in his mind he heard the voice of the guru calling to him. "Help me, Hari," it said. "I need your youthful spirit to assist me. My spirit is too weak to accomplish the task alone. Please help me. She will not know."

Hari could feel the guru's spirit weakening, and he obligingly tried to reinforce it with his own. He did not want to dominate or even become a full partner in the lovemaking, so he participated only enough to reinvigorate the flagging activity and restore it to its former pitch. By exercising due restraint he succeeded in playing the minor role of accompanist to the now fast-moving duet, rather than become a soloist or third performer in a whirling trio. In his best altruistic fashion, he bravely endured the many pleasures and delights that intruded upon his being.

When finally the guru's spirit relaxed, its task complete, Hari willed that his own spirit retreat so that the guru and his wife might be alone together. It was not until late in the night that he became aware of his body returning to its bed and the guru's spirit departing. Tired from the night's labor, he soon fell asleep.

And here is my report.

The wry expression on the pundit's face as he sipped tea gave way to a look of lofty indulgence as he turned his attention to Shanta.

"I assume," he squeaked, "that your knowledge of the Vedas is thorough and complete?"

"Oh yes, Master," replied Shanta eagerly.

"And that you are proficient in the Indian system of logic?"

"Oh yes, indeed."

"And that you are fluent in the major languages of the south and also three of the Indic languages of the north?"

"I am fluent in Bengali, Master. But I did not know of the requirement of three northern languages."

"Hmm. Three. Yes, three. Well, I must tell you, there are several candidates for the faculty opening, and the language requirement is important. Yes, quite important."

Shanta's heart sank at these words, but she bravely maintained her poise.

"You must surely be hungry by now, Shriman Rajagopala. May I serve you some curried eggplant and chutney? And please have some roti and chapatis."

"Ah, yes, by all means. As the sage so wisely said, there is a time for all things, and all things in their time. The body is the vessel of the soul and must have its due."

It was as Shanta was serving her guest a second helping of eggplant that she felt a warm caressing sensation in her breasts, which so surprised her that she nearly dumped the dish on the pundit's lap.

"Oh, please forgive my clumsiness," she exclaimed.

"Harumph. Yes, of course."

The caressing sensation in Shanta's breasts suddenly increased in intensity and was now accompanied by a disturbing hotness in her lips. She sucked in her breath audibly and instinctively clapped her hands to her breasts in surprise and disbelief. This action so startled the pundit that he ceased masticating and stared open-mouthed at the amazing scene of Shanta holding her ample breasts in her cupped hands.

"Oh!—Oh, forgive me, Master, just a touch of—of indigestion," she said with forced calmness. "Please, have some more dhal."

Shanta bit her lip to avoid showing any reaction to the strangely pleasant sensation that newly assaulted her anatomy, this time in a distinctly more private place. Her thighs shuddered beneath her sari and feelings of overwhelming delight coursed through her body. She began to writhe in her chair and breathe heavily, and she involuntarily uttered little cries of "oh" and "ah," her eyes the while lighting up like fiery stars. The pundit dropped a half-eaten chapati from his gaping mouth, his eyes fairly popping out of his head. If he was flabbergasted at Shanta's incredible behavior, he was also keenly aware of the erotic nature of the display, such that he became excited and his lingam rose.

Shanta strained to gain control of herself, and in a supreme effort aided by unmitigated but well-disguised panic, she managed to reduce her writhing to a slow rhythmic undulation. But the seductive swaying of her hips only served to excite the pundit the more. Could it be, he wondered, that this lovely young woman was erotically attracted to him?

"I sometimes have an allergic reaction to chutney, O Master," she said, trying to explain her reactions. She realized now that her sister must be having an affair. Her partner certainly knew what he was doing! "It causes an itch, and—oh!—ah!—oooh!" Shanta gasped and sucked in her breath, her eyelids fluttered wildly, her lips opening and closing of their own volition. Her billowing breasts pushed hard against her sari, threatening the security of the fabric, and her arms and legs shuddered visibly. Finally she let out a long low rapturous moan the like of which her astonished guest had never heard nor dreamed of, but which his anatomy comprehended all too well, for it pulsated and emitted a moist response, much to the pundit's dismay. The pundit gulped audibly as bits of drool gathered on his lower lip, his hands surreptitiously moving to cover the widening stain on the leg of his dhoti.

But the woman was paying almost no attention to him. Shanta's breathing slowed, and she cleared her throat as she gradually regained her composure.

"These allergy attacks are infrequent, but they can be most annoying," she said in a tone of mock impatience, her voice cracking slightly. She avoided looking directly into her guest's eyes.

"Um, yes. I have no concern. Yes, not at all. I understand," stammered the pundit. "Chutney will do that. Yes." But he was not at all sure that the cause of the remarkable performance was indeed the chutney. Other intriguing possibilities raced through his mind, suggesting fantastic opportunities for the future. His now languid lingam twitched, as if to urge him to consider the potential advantages of having such a talented teacher at the university, isolated as it was, and of which he was the undisputed commander, not to mention the counselor to new members of the faculty with whom he often found it necessary to work quite closely.

"Will you have some rice pudding for dessert?" asked Shanta nervously.

"Ah, pudding. Yes. That is, no. Uh, did you say you can write as well as read Bengali?"

"Oh yes, Master."

"Well then, in that case the requirement is satisfied. You are qualified and may consider yourself hired."

"Oh! Thank you, Master," exclaimed Shanta. "Thank you. How can I ever repay you for this most singular opportunity?"

"Ah, well. Harumph. Who can tell. Yes. You can report to the university whenever you wish, but no later than two months from now. Housing and servants will be provided, of course. We can meet and work out your teaching schedule together when you arrive. Yes. Now I must be on my way. A fine meal. Good night."

Shanta did not notice that the pundit held his satchel over his left leg as he waddled toward the exit, for her head was in the clouds. She had feared that she had botched the meal and interview, but it seemed that she had after all made a favorable impression.

As she cleaned up the dishes, she sang to herself and could hardly wait until the morning to tell Sharmila and the guru the good news. She must also remember to ask her sister about the odd sensations she had felt at dinner. The experience had not been at all unpleasant, except for the time and place, and if her body insisted on misbehaving again in the same way, she would willingly tolerate it, but hopefully there would be some advance warning so she could retreat to the privacy of her bedroom and not inflict any discomfort on others. If this was the way of love between a man and woman, she would not be averse to experiencing it directly at some near stage in her life.

Now do I strike. I shall put the realization into the pundit's mind that his hostess was suffering the effect of her twin sister's activity—and he will soon conclude that such goings-on cannot be the result of the ancient guru's passion. He will believe that adultery has been committed.

But the guru will explain that this was not the case, if there is any challenge.

I think not, for the guru is dying.

Hari awoke the next morning to the sound of wailing and weeping coming from somewhere in the house. Alarmed by the commotion, he jumped out of bed, hurriedly dressed, and went to investigate. A group of villagers was assembled in the parlor, the men in a clot whispering and shaking their heads, the women weeping and moaning and rocking to and fro. He squeezed through the crowd and followed a procession of village elders into one of the bedrooms. There he saw to his great shock the body of the guru, pale and lifeless, lying on the bed, a bouquet of flowers upon his breast. Sharmila was kneeling beside the body, shivering and weeping. At that moment Shanta came rushing into the room. She uttered an agonized cry and fell to her knees beside her sister.

Tears trickled down Hari's face. He felt to be very much an outsider in this moment of intimacy, and he quietly returned to the guest room. He guessed the cause of the guru's death and knew he had played a part in it. The old man's spirit had not been strong enough to endure the excitement of the previous evening. If only he had refused the guru's request to borrow his body, perhaps the old master might still be alive.

There was a knock on the door and Sharmila entered. She managed a wan smile.

"Hari, I know that you are saddened by my husband's death. But his last hours were happy ones because of you. He was very grateful, and so am I. His time was near at hand, and with your help he lived his final moments as he wished to. Now his spirit lives in another life. But he has not left us, for there remain his deeds, his mark upon this village, and our memories."

"Surely so," Hari agreed. "Yet I feel a share of responsibility."

"Have no such concern. He spoke of you before he died, saying that he would repay your favor in his next life, if not in this life." She wiped her tearful eyes. "The funeral pyre is being prepared. I hope you will attend the ceremony."

"I will come," said Hari. "And I thank you for your kind words. Yes, I too will long remember him."

The guru's body was placed upon a platform of logs and fagots in a meadow at the edge of the village. The villagers assembled in a half circle around the pyre, Sharmila and Shanta foremost among a small group of disciples. Hari stood by himself at the outer perimeter of the gathering. He had attended cremation ceremonies before in his own village and had found the experience distasteful, though he knew it was a deeply rooted custom.

Attendants poured ghee over the fagots, which would help spread the flames. A carven urn was brought forth to house the ashes of the deceased. A Vedic priest chanted devotional prayers for the departed spirit of the guru and to the glory of the puissant pantheon of gods. As custom required, Sharmila walked thrice around the pyre, touched the feet of her husband and then her own eyes, broke her bangles upon the wood of the pyre, and wiped the beauty spot from her forehead. She then rejoined the group of disciples. Since the guru had no son, the priest assumed the task of setting the sacred torch to the pyre. As the spears of flame leapt up, as though to the bosom of Agni, their master, so a great wail rose up from the assembled villagers.

Then a squat gross man approached, whom Hari guessed must be the pundit Shanta had entertained. "There is something that must be said," he declared. "I have reason to believe that there is scandal here that must be dealt with."

"Can't you see that this is a funeral?" the priest demanded, irritated. "Whatever your business is, it can surely wait until we have done proper honor to our beloved guru."

"But it is his honor I am concerned with. I have cause to believe that his wife had congress with a man not her husband, on the eve of his demise. There must be punishment of both adulteress and lover!"

Hari was shocked by this interpretation of the night's events. But if the people believed it—

You made your move. Here is my countermove.

From where he stood Hari could not see Sharmila in the crowd, or that some of the widows and elderly women of the village had gathered around her, perhaps responsive to the suggestion of scandal the pundit was trying to make. They were whispering and hissing, repeating a single word over and over again: suttee—suttee—suttee. Only too late did he see her as she ran to the flaming pyre and flung herself upon it. Nor did he hear Shanta cry out or see her faint as she shared her sister's brief moment of searing pain. But he did see the pundit, his prime witness suddenly lost, throw up his hands in disgust. There was no longer a case to be made, for if there had been a crime, its prime witness was gone, and a sinner had been punished.

Hari stood frozen, shocked and dismayed. When finally his wits returned, he heard cries of praise from the villagers for Sharmila's noble sacrifice. A deep hatred welled up within him, hatred for the barbaric ways of his people, and he felt himself not one of them. Indeed, had he ever been?

The wind shifted and brought to him the odor of burning flesh. He turned and ran.

❧ *10* ❧

The Sack of Grain

And now I have accomplished seven seductions, and if you are unable to kill the handsome mortal man with your next move, I will have won the contest and will be free of you for a full century, not one moment less. I delight in the very notion.

By no means so hasty, creature. Remember that I challenged the seduction involving the she-demon, because neither of us had any part in that; it happened without our influence.

It was a fair seduction! And anyway, you cheated.

I notified a higher authority. Now I believe it is time to ask for that decision.

What higher authority?

Yama, the god of death, as death is my object. Will you accept his decision?

I shall have to.

O Yama, you know the issue and the facts of the case. What do you say?

A dense bank of clouds hung low in the sky, blocking out the waxing sun, casting a pallid shadow over the land. The countryside was bleak and colorless. For a moment the bank seemed to intensify, and to become truly terrible.

The she-demon seduction is null.

The narrow path upon which Hari traveled cut straight across open fields, gradually tapering to a thin line in the distance, terminating in a small black dot where it touched the horizon. Hari had only the grasshoppers to keep him company, which flitted through the air all about him. One landed on his forearm. The insect rubbed its legs together and flicked its antennae as it surveyed its strange perch. In a sign of approval, or perhaps disgust, Hari could not tell, the fearless creature opened its mandibles and deposited a drop of sticky brown substance on his arm, then flew away.

There you are. You have only six seductions—and it remains my move.

I think it would have been another decision, had I taken it to a more romantic god.

Now will I make that move.

The sky brightened, melting away the cloud shadows, and ahead Hari saw there was a path from the west which joined the one he was on. Through the glare Hari could make out the blurred outline of a lone figure on the path walking in his direction. The two travelers arrived at the fork at the same time.

But all you did was motivate that harmless low-caste wanderer to intercept our mortal man.

That is enough, I think.

Hari saw that the other was a young man about his own age, though clearly poor and of low caste. He was barebreasted and without sandals and wore only a tattered half-dhoti; his dense black hair was matted and unkempt and his thin dark-skinned body unwashed. Yellowed teeth poked out of a slack half-opened mouth set too low in a face that was scarred and pockmarked. His ears stuck out comically, belying the dark deepset eyes that peered out furtively beneath unbroken eyebrows.

Our man will simply dismiss him, and think no more of it, for he is of far higher station.

You underestimate his folly. He has been singularly lucky, but now he shall become singularly unlucky.

Wiping his nose with the back of his hand, the young man stepped back and bowed to Hari, waiting for the Brahmin to pass by first. Fortunately the sun did not cast his unclean shadow upon the high-caste traveler—he yet carried scars for not having been attentive to such carelessness in the past.

Hari spoke: "Good afternoon. It seems we are the only travelers on this lonely road, and as we seem to be going in the same direction, why do not we travel along together? It will relieve the monotony. My name is Hari. What is yours?"

Ugh! This could mean trouble.

The young man was startled at Hari's cordiality, for he was accustomed to being at best ignored and usually scorned by persons of higher caste.

"O Swami, my name is Suka. I would be very honored to walk with you. Thank you, thank you," he replied, his voice timid and subservient.

"Very well, Suka. Then come, let us be on our way."

The two walked along, Suka keeping slightly to the side and a little behind Hari and not daring to speak unless spoken to first.

"Are you from this region, Suka?"

"Oh no, Swami, I am from farther north."

"And where is it that you are traveling to?"

"Oh, anywhere. It does not matter. It is the same everywhere. Anyplace is better than my village."

"Ah, you are a wanderer in search of knowledge and adventure, then?"

"Oh no, Swami, I am just running away. I lived with my uncle and he always beat me. So I pushed him into a dung pile and ran away."

"You have no other family, then?"

"My father and mother and youngest sister are dead. I have no brothers. My other sisters are married—their husbands do not want me. Before she died, my youngest sister liked me. Her name was Ambika. My uncle arranged her marriage, but her husband beat her. Ambika wanted to return to my uncle's house. We could have taken care of each other. But my uncle would not take her back, and her mother-in-law wanted more dowry to be paid. My uncle would not pay more, and so Ambika's husband and mother-in-law burned her alive. They killed Ambika, but my uncle did not care. He only kept me so I could work for him. He is a gatherer of wood and dung-cakes. He said I did not find enough wood and was lazy. So every day he beat me. I am glad I ran away."

"What will you do now, Suka? What of your future? Can you read or write?"

"Oh no, Swami. No one in my family can do that. There are no teachers for the low-castes in my village. Future? I do not know that word, Swami."

"Well, today you are traveling with me. What will you do next month? Or next year?"

"I have never thought of that. I know only today. Yes, the weight of each day is enough. It would be too heavy if I added tomorrow's weight to today's."

"Hmm. Yes, there is something to be said for traveling light."

"Ah, yes! That is so, Swami," exclaimed Suka, suddenly beaming. "Light and free, with no cares." Suka
then realized that he had spoken to a Brahmin without
having first been asked a question. Fearfully, he dropped
back a few paces, unsure of what to expect. When nothing terrible happened, he resumed his former position
but remained wary. He knew from bitter experience that
one could never tell about the moods of the upper castes.

Toward evening a farmhouse came into view.

"Well, Suka, shall we stop at that farm ahead and see
if we can find a bed for the night and perhaps a bite to
eat?"

"Yes, Swami, a good idea. Let us try. But please,
Swami, it will be better if you talk."

Hari laughed. "Very well, Suka."

As they neared the farmhouse, they saw a farmer
weeding in a field near the road. The farmer saw them
and approached. He was a large man with graying hair
and stern demeanor. Judging from the deep furrows in
his brow that made a permanent frown, Hari was unsure
of the reception that awaited.

"Blessings upon you, good sir," said Hari. "We seek the
owner of this fine farm to ask for shelter for the night."

Seeing that Hari was a Brahmin, like it or not, the
farmer well knew his obligation. "I am the owner. I suppose I can find room for you in the house. But as for that
one," pointing to Suka, "if he is not your servant he can
move on."

"No, he is a traveler like myself," said Hari, his voice
yet civil though he felt a surge of anger. "He also seeks
shelter for the night. Surely you can provide shelter for
my companion too and thereby earn credit in the next
life."

The farmer hesitated, eyeing Suka suspiciously. Con-
descending to address the low-caste directly, he said in
a surly tone: "Well, worthless one, you will have to
work for your keep. There are still two hours of light left.
You can thrash the millet stalks piled up by the barn.
And you can sleep in the stalls."

Turning to Hari, the farmer's tone became more
amiable. "You may go to the house if you like. My wife
will give you some cool water. Dinner will be at sundown."

"I thank you," said Hari. "But a little exercise before
eating will do me good. I will join Suka here in thrashing the stalks. And as I do not wish to intrude, I too will
sleep in the stalls."

Suka stared in disbelief at Hari, thinking him quite
mad. Who can understand a Brahmin? he wondered.

The farmer shrugged. "As you like," he replied curtly,
and returned to his work, muttering the while and wondering what kind of Brahmin would keep the company
of a low-caste, let alone speak up for one. A poor farmer,
he was not far above the level of a low-caste himself. If
a Brahmin put himself on the same level as a low-caste
good-for-nothing, where did that leave him? Social order
depended on strict obedience to the rules of class structure; otherwise how was one to know who one was?
How dare this young Brahmin break the sacred code,
curse him!

As Hari and Suka walked past the farmhouse on the
way to the barn, the farmer's wife and a young woman,
doubtless the farmer's daughter, appeared at the door.
Hari nodded politely to them and gave the hand sign of
greeting. The farmer's wife returned the salutation while
the young woman simply stared.

At the side of the barn they found a stack of stalks and set to flailing them against the barn wall. The shed seeds they swept into a pile to be later winnowed. Suka worked in fits and starts, stopping frequently to gaze idly about. Hari worked steadily, and though annoyed at Suka's loafing, said nothing.

Now I initiate my final seduction. I can hardly wait to be free of you.

It was not long before the farmer's daughter appeared carrying a cup of cool well water for each of the young workers. Hari thanked her and saw that she was robust and quite attractive, and especially well endowed. She wore a coquettish look that she made no effort to conceal and swiveled her torso provocatively, her long black tresses swishing to and fro, as she watched the boys drink. Her eyes twinkled mischievously as she first studied the one and then the other.

And observe my counter, now that I have established a male in the presence of the subject.

Hari smiled, thanked her again for the drink, then returned to his work without paying her further heed. But Suka leered at her boldly, looking her up and down, which she ostentatiously pretended not to notice, thus advertising to Suka her vainglorious pleasure. Suka knew that her caste was not far above his own, so that a conquest was not beyond the hopes of one even such as he.

"I wonder what there is around here to do for fun," said Suka to no one in particular.

"Are you addressing me?" inquired the young lady in a pompous voice.

"Who else would I be talking to?" shot back Suka in a slightly rude tone.

"Some people just do not have manners," the young lady exclaimed, studying Hari out of the corner of her eye to see if he showed any signs of interest in the conversation. Hari kept to his work.

"You will find the thrashing easier if you hold the stalks further back," she said to Hari in a friendly yet flirtatious tone, swinging her hips as she spoke.

"I thank you for that advice," said Hari as he lengthened his grasp. "Yes, it is easier that way."

"You are being of great help to my father. Perhaps you can remain awhile. Farm life can be fun as well as work, you know."

You have motivated the low-caste man to desire the woman, but I had already motivated her to desire the Brahmin. She will not be dissuaded. See, she is giving him every chance.

Hari glanced at her and smiled. "Oh, I am sure it can. But I must be on my way in the morning. I thank you for the thought."

A fool and his seduction are soon parted.

"Tell me what kind of fun you mean," interjected Suka in a suggestive voice.

"I am sure you would like to know," she answered sarcastically, whereupon she wheeled about in mock anger and headed for the house. After a few steps she stopped suddenly and turned, exclaiming in a pretentious singsong voice: "My name is Nalini!" She then continued on her way.

Suka called after her in an exaggerated imitation of her singsong voice: "Goodbye, Nalini!" Hari was embarrassed by Suka's behavior, but said nothing. After all, he told himself, Suka was only having fun in his own way.

Suka resumed his daydreaming until he saw that the farmer was approaching, whereupon he snatched up the last bunch of stalks and energetically began pounding them against the barn wall. The farmer surveyed the work that had been done and seemed satisfied.

"The winnowing can wait," said the farmer. "It grows dark, so you two can stop work. There is a well by the stalls to wash. You will find some food on a bench near the back door of the house." With that the farmer walked off, his manner toward Hari distinctly less cordial than before.

As Hari washed at the well, he saw that Suka barely sprinkled a few drops of water on his hands and face and grimaced at that. Suka muttered to himself, for he would not have made even that small pretense at washing were it not for the Brahmin's elaborate display of cleansing the body.

Behind the farmhouse, as the farmer had promised, they found their dinner: a bowl of vegetable curry, some sambar, a platter of rice, a bowl of milk, and two mangoes. Suka waited for Hari to take his share of the food first, and dearly hoped there would be a decent portion left over for him. He could hardly believe his ears when Hari invited him to help himself first, which convinced him that this was a crazy Brahmin indeed.

Suka reached into the curry bowl with his left hand and plunged his right into the rice, emerging with the lion's share of both. He proceeded to stuff both his hands into his mouth at the same time, gulping down the food in great quantities, bits of it dribbling down his face. Hari took some sambar, milk, and a mango before they too became polluted, and left the rest to Suka, who, from his eager display and accompanying sound effects, was probably hungrier anyway.

When the food was gone, Suka wiped his mouth with the back of his hand, burped loudly, broke wind, and uttered a grunt of satisfaction. He and Hari then headed for the stalls, which were located beyond the barn, to find a place to bed for the night.

The stalls were in a small outbuilding which contained two compartments separated by a wooden partition. One of the compartments housed several sacks of grain, which lay side by side on the floor. The other was empty, except for a heavy floor-covering of hay.

"It seems we can each have a private room to ourselves, Suka. Do you have any preference? We can take some of the hay from this stall and put it in the other so we will both be comfortable."

"Oh no, Swami, you take the hay. I am used to hardness for my sleep. Hay is too soft for me. I will sleep on the bags of grain."

"Very well, Suka, if you prefer. Good night, then. Until morning and the call of Surya."

Suka bowed. "Good night, Swami."

Hari closed only the bottom half of the swinging door at the front of the stall, leaving the top open so that he could see the stars. There was also a small rear window which he opened to let the night breeze pass through. Lying on his back he inhaled deeply of the cool sweet air which mingled with the fragrance of freshly cut hay. He yawned. Taking the book the guru had given him from beneath his tunic, he placed it under his head to use as a pillow. Through half-shut eyes he watched the twinkling stars—were they perhaps the beautiful nymphs of

Indra's heaven winking at him?—and listened to the soft chirping of the crickets echoing in the vast silence beyond. A small lizard clung to the wall, and the light of a moon sparkled in its unblinking eyes, reflecting a ray of peace into Hari's soul.

But his tranquility was short-lived, for from the next stall there suddenly arose a raucous noise not unlike the snorts of a chained bullock that had winded a cow in heat. Suka! He was snoring. Hari sighed at his karma and turned over on his side. But to no avail. The snoring grew louder, taking on a dissonant, irregular sonority that crescendoed and exploded into a staccato-like sputtering, culminating in a horrendous sneeze. Thereafter, for a time, the snoring was quieter and assumed a rhythmical regularity, punctuated only occasionally by a hissing wheeze or multitonal nasal whistle. For that, Hari was grateful.

It was during one of Suka's less turbulent intervals that Hari heard footsteps coming down the path toward the stalls. The footsteps got closer, then stopped quite close by. Hari pretended to be asleep, but kept his eyes open a slit. In the moonlight he saw a head slowly rising above the edge of the stall door, and when it reached full ascendance he saw that it was Nalini. "Brahmin!" she whispered. "I have come to show you what we do for fun."

Hari could no longer feign ignorance. "I thank you, but I am weary and prefer to sleep."

The utter dimwit!

"You reject me?" she demanded, rapidly developing a fury.

Hari had encountered such a reaction before, so was

wary. "By no means. I merely feel that such a liaison is inappropriate in this, ah, circumstance, and beg you to return to your home."

She made an exclamation of disgust. Then the head quickly lowered itself and disappeared. The footsteps resumed and seemed to be heading for the next stall.

Why do you not touch her again, and make her seek your man more ardently?

Because as you know it is a lost cause, when he refuses her. I shall save my move to save his life, if he blunders worse.

Suka, fast asleep, did not hear the stall door open. Only when he felt a smart pinch on his buttocks did he jump up, his hand automatically clapping itself against the offending part of his anatomy, for, having frequently been bitten by insects in the night, he was quite adept at taking instant revenge.

Lo: there standing before him was none other than Nalini, and she was wearing nothing but a thin nightcloth around her body and a smirk on her face. Suka instantly guessed the reason for her nocturnal visit.

"The Brahmin is in the next stall," he said derisively. "You came to the wrong place."

"I know where the Brahmin sleeps," she replied haughtily, being careful not to speak too loudly, yet at the same time loudly enough to be sure that Hari overheard. "I came to the right place. It is you I want." With that, Nalini slipped out of her nightgown and stood unclothed before Suka, naked except for the gold chain she wore around her neck.

Suka could hardly believe his good fortune and fairly drooled at her voluptuousness. Having lived a life of want where grasping at every opportunity without hesitation often meant the difference between feast and famine, he delayed not to appease his escalating appetite. Grabbing Nalini roughly by the arm, he pulled her down onto the sacks of grain and proceeded to assault her without further ado. And as it happened, perhaps not surprisingly, this economical approach pleased Nalini immensely, and she quickly rose to a blissful pitch of intensity that matched and even surpassed her partner's.

You see, all I needed to do was provide an object to focus your mortal man's foolishness, and he ruins your ploy himself. This is better than gambling on single moves that you can then counter.

There are other women.

If he does not blunder himself into death before he accepts them.

Hari, in the next stall, could not help but hear the conversation and ensuing sound effects through the partition. Nalini's choice of a lover at first amazed him and even pinched his ego. But on reflection he realized their basic compatibility. Nalini wanted immediate physical gratification and was not interested in lofty conversation or the subtleties of foreplay. And perhaps she wanted more than just one night's companionship. Perhaps she wanted a permanent relationship—something a Brahmin could not give her, but a homeless low-caste just might, with the proper incentive.

Hari's musings were interrupted by a scratching sound accompanied by an occasional clucking, and he could see through the moonlit space beneath the stall door that a chicken was picking around on the ground outside. He watched as the chicken's feet made their way along the outside wall of the stall in the direction of the grain compartment before disappearing from sight beyond the edge of the door.

The chicken, upon a well-trodden mission, spotted the familiar space beneath the door of the grain stall and easily squeezed through. Once inside it commenced to search out bits of grain that were inevitably scattered on the floor, emitting a contented cluck whenever a choice morsel presented itself. Engrossed in its culinary quest, the fowl ignored the strange motions and even stranger sounds of the two humans lying astride the sacks. However, it was not long before the floor was picked clean, and the chicken discovered a good reason to abandon its indifference to strange motions of the humans.

There was a small hole in one of the grain sacks upon which the two humans lay, and whenever the uppermost delivered a particularly hard thrust to the undermost, the resulting shock to the sack caused a few grains to pop out onto the floor. The chicken was delighted at discovering this new source of supply, which seemed a veritable cornucopia. It now stood watching the kinetic exhibition with awakened interest, waiting patiently for that special thrust that would deliver up its next ration of grain.

The clucks of pleasure from the chicken mingled with the grunts and groans of the human activators, and although Hari next door was oblivious to the casual links in the chain that led to the chicken's stomach, he fairly grimaced at the rudely imposed cacophony of the unlikely trio of Suka, Nalini, and their unwitting accompanist.

Suddenly the trio became a quartet as above the din Hari heard the sound of the farmer's voice in the distance. "Come, chick! Come chick!" the farmer was calling. Hari leapt up and peered through a crack in the door. Walking slowly toward the stalls he could see the farmer, lantern in hand, searching about and calling the recalcitrant chicken.

"Come chick! Come chick!" the farmer cried. "Bish! Bish! Bish! Back to your coop."

Hari guessed the farmer knew the chicken's favorite haunts and would look for it in the grain stall. The thought of Suka and Nalini being caught unawares in naked embrace by the farmer filled Hari with terror. The consequences could be devastating, too horrible even to contemplate. He must warn them. No, that would be dangerous. What if Nalini or Suka should panic and do something foolish and bring down disaster on them both? Better that the chicken should be moved elsewhere and used to lure the farmer away from the stalls.

Quickly and quietly Hari crept on all fours out of his stall and into the grain compartment, opening both doors just enough to squeeze through. Keeping to the shadows, he snuck up on the unsuspecting chicken from behind and grabbed it, clapping one hand over its beak to prevent an outcry. Suka and Nalini, yet in the throes of passion, were oblivious to their surroundings and so did not see him—to his great relief. Clasping the struggling chicken to his breast, he crept out of the stall and into the cover of the tall grass that lined the path. Slowly and with difficulty, scratching his legs and arms in the rough grass, he crawled toward the farmhouse. Upon reaching a position behind the farmer and well toward the house, he released his hand from the chicken's beak and gave the creature a good squeeze, whereupon to his relief it uttered a resounding squawk. He peered through the grass and saw the farmer, now only yards from the stalls, stop and turn around. "Chick! Chick!" the farmer called. "Where are you, you feathered offspring of a demon?"

Hari crawled several yards closer to the farmhouse and again gave the chicken a healthy squeeze. But by this time the fowl had become quite exasperated, and instead of sounding off it chose to grasp Hari's nose in its beak. Hari muffled a cry, cursed the fickle fowl beneath his breath, and realized he would have to assume the task of baiting the farmer himself. Taking a deep breath he pursed his mouth and let out a magnificent squawk, which was apparently sufficiently authentic for the farmer to start walking back toward the house. The chicken too was evidently impressed, and without further encouragement began to sound off of its own accord, perhaps choosing not to be outdone by the strange human's clumsy imitation.

At a turn in the path Hari dashed out of the grass and made his way unseen to the chicken coop, a small structure that stood alone not far from the farmhouse. Upon seeing its home, the chicken set up a loud ruckus which ceased only when Hari thrust the unruly bird through the door of the coop. Looking back, Hari saw that the farmer was fast approaching. He was in the open now, and there was not enough time to run for cover without being seen. There was no help for it—he must join the chicken.

Into the coop he scrambled, barely squeezing through the door on all fours. Luckily, the pen was solidly built and well enclosed, and would serve to conceal him as long as the farmer did not peer in through the door.

The farmer came up to the coop and called out: "Chick! Chick! Are you in there?"

The chicken, settled comfortably on a roost just above Hari's head, chose not to answer. Hari worried that if the farmer did not hear from the chicken forthwith, he might look in through the doorway. He knew that if he was discovered there would be no explaining the situation. And the shock might well be injurious to the farmer. There was nothing else to do but for him to take the part of the chicken and reply to the farmer's call.

Hari inhaled deeply, shut his eyes, and emitted what turned out to be a reasonable facsimile of a satisfied chicken squawk. But just as he did so the fowl also decided to speak out. However, the chicken's cry was at a decidedly higher pitch than his roommate's, and Hari prayed silently to the goddess Lakshmi that the farmer had heard only one combined squawk and not two. The goddess was compassionate, and the farmer, satisfied that the chicken was safely back in its pen, closed the coop door and returned to the farmhouse.

Hari breathed a deep sigh of relief, though the chicken apparently did not share the Brahmin's feelings. Having failed to expose the intruder in its house, the fowl issued a final and decisive protest in the form of a prodigious dropping which it deposited squarely atop Hari's head. Hari clenched his teeth in utter frustration, and reminded himself that he was a vegetarian and bound not to harm any of nature's innocent creatures.

Having determined it was now safe to leave the coop, Hari backed up against the door, only to discover to his horror that it would not open. Turning himself around, not without difficulty, and thereby further decorating his anatomy with excrement, he saw that the door had been latched from the outside. He pushed his forefinger through a wire opening in the door, but could not reach the latch. He sighed and settled back to ponder the matter.

An hour passed before a solution suggested itself. He could use the chain holding the medallion which hung around his neck to lift up the latch. But, alas, the chain was not quite long enough. Looking about he found some moulted chicken quills on the floor of the coop. These he braided together and onto the chain to increase its length, and lo, he was then able to reach and lift the latch handle.

Exhausted, Hari made his way back to the stall and flopped down on his bed of hay. He could hear Suka snoring next door, and guessed that Nalini had long since returned to the house. Sleep fell upon him like a leaden weight.

Nalini arose at sunrise as was the custom on the farm. She was in a cheerful mood and hummed softly as she helped her mother prepare the breakfast table. Her father, accustomed to silence at that hour of the morning, grumbled and cast a disapproving glance at his daughter. His brows knitted.

"Nalini, come here," he ordered in a gruff tone. Nalini did as she was bade. "Where is your gold chain?" he asked. He had given the chain to her when she was a child, and she had never taken it from her neck. It had been his mother's and was the only piece of jewelry the family possessed.

"Oh! He must have taken it last night!" Nalini blurted out without thinking.

"Who took it?" Her father shouted angrily as he grabbed her by the wrist. Nalini was terrified.

"It was—" She realized that the truth would be utterly

disastrous, so shaded it somewhat. "It was the Brahmin!"

Ah! Now it comes!

"So! You were cavorting with the Brahmin in the stalls, were you? And he stole your chain, did he?" With that the farmer smacked Nalini across the face and sent her sprawling, whereupon she commenced wailing at the top of her lungs.

The farmer stormed out of the house in a rage and headed for the stalls. On his way he picked up a stout stick from the ground, which he swished through the air a few times to test its feel.

Jolted from his sleep by a sharp pain on his back, Hari leapt to his feet. There before him stood the farmer, red-faced and shaking with rage, clutching an upraised stick. The stick descended swiftly and caught Hari in the side. Taken by surprise, Hari could only gape at the enraged farmer in utter bewilderment. Before he could speak the stick descended again, this time hard across his shoulders. Quickly reaching for his book, he held it up just in time to shield himself from a blow across the face. He realized this was not a time for rational inquiry, but rather one for running. But the heavy bulk of the farmer blocked the doorway. So with a leap and a bound Hari hurled himself through the open rear window, and as he sailed through the air he felt the stick slash across his buttocks.

His landing was a soft one, if not wholly aesthetic. He dropped head first into a pile of cow dung. Trying desperately to gain his feet, he fell back repeatedly in the slippery muck, thereby spreading the sticky feculence liberally over his body. It was hardly a consolation that the offal salved the pulsating welt on his buttocks. That he was involuntarily merdiverous he was sure did not technically violate vegetarian rules.

He escaped the mire only by crawling out on his hands and knees. Fortunately his book had been thrown clear of the dung heap. He picked it up just as the farmer rounded the corner, rushing at him stick in hand and yelling something about a chain. Without stay or delay Hari took to his feet and galloped off through the fields toward the main path, leaving a trail of dung in his wake. He could hear the farmer shouting at him as he ran, and he did not slow his pace until the farm was far behind him.

Panting, he sat down on a rock by the path to catch his breath, only to be greeted by the fetid odor he carried about with him. Too, his feet were sore and he realized that he must have left his sandals behind in the farmer's stall. Flies gathered around him in swarms, covering every part of his body, and he repeatedly had to remind himself of his Brahminical heritage which forbade him from swatting the bothersome insects. So he took to his feet; at least when he kept moving most of the flies left his body. He prayed he would soon find water that he might wash himself.

He wondered why the farmer had beaten him and what had happened to Suka. He hoped that the poor low-caste had escaped unharmed.

The land became greener as low rolling hills replaced the flat open fields. He came upon a stream where he washed his body and clothing, then sat beneath a banyan tree to read while he waited for his tunic to dry in the sun.

Further along the path he came upon a grove of coconut palms, and there lying beneath one of the trees fast asleep and snoring loudly, a half-eaten coconut on his lap, was Suka. Wrapped around Suka's arm was a golden chain, and on his feet were Hari's sandals. Hari shook his head and sighed, then carefully eased the sandals off the sleeper's feet, slipped them on his own, and continued on his journey.

Well, it seems our man is still alive and well.

If I failed, so did you. The game is not over.

✤ 11 ✤

The Lake Palace

From the summit of a cloud-capped hill Hari could make
out the spires of the rajah's palace glistening in the distance. The city of Pitali at last.

It began to drizzle and he quickened his pace. The
deaths of the guru and Sharmila lay heavy upon him
and, too, he was worried about the old rana. How
strange, he thought: only a short while ago his life had
been simple and carefree, blind to the serpents of misfortune that now seemed to lurk beneath every rock. He
had left home in search of adventure, to consume the
pleasures of the moment, only to find that pleasure had
a cost, a cost measured in sorrow and pain. He understood now the wisdom of his village teacher, the need for
mortals to escape the reality of the senses, to close out
the world and merge with the universal soul. Time wore
a new face, and in its unblinking eyes he saw reflected
the ceaseless tides of past and future sweeping all before,
tossing up scraps of mortal souls like so much drift upon
the sea.

Upon arriving at the city gates, he was allowed to pass
through after only a cursory search. The streets were
bustling with activity and everything appeared quite normal. The chief guard at the palace gate remembered him
and personally escorted him to a receiving room in the

main building. Before long the rajah's advisor, the dewan Amul, arrived and greeted him, courteously if coolly. The advisor explained that the rajah was at the moment presiding at a state meeting but would see him shortly. Amul then summoned a servant and ordered that Hari be shown to the same room in the palace he had occupied previously.

It was not long before a guard knocked on Hari's door, saying that the rajah was ready to receive him. He was led to a private audience chamber and in a few moments the rajah arrived. Hari could not help noticing that the rajah seemed tired and careworn.

"Ah, I am glad to see you again, my young friend," he said, embracing Hari warmly. "And all in one piece. Good. We missed you.

"I want to hear your report, but first I have news for you. Much has happened since we last spoke. To begin with, not five days ago I had a state visit from the Rana of Madresh himself. I can see you are surprised. I was myself. Until now he had been quite aloof and, indeed, suspect. Hence the reason I sent you to Madresh. But that matter is now cleared up, with good result I am happy to say. The rana told me an interesting story.

"It seems there was a plot within his own palace to assassinate him and usurp the throne. The perpetrator and pretender was none other than his own dewan, one Koti, who was joined in the treachery by the rani herself and a handful of others—an army general and several well-placed officers. It was they who had isolated the rana and discouraged him from any contact with neighboring chiefs of state. Fortunately, for the rana as well as for us, the old fox somehow learned of the plot. His palace guard was still loyal, and in a single night the rana captured or killed the leaders of the cabal—that is, all but the two main devils. The dewan and the rani escaped. The rana learned that they rode north to ally with the Mogul king, Akbar.

"The rana also mentioned a young traveler, a Brahmin, who he believed was unjustly victimized by this Koti, and perhaps killed. The Brahmin's disappearance seemed to be of great concern to the king. I guessed it was you."

"Yes, Lord, it was," said Hari, relieved to learn that the rana was alive and well.

"Well, I will send the rana a message letting him know that you have been rediscovered. He left a cartful of homing pigeons with me for the very purpose of expediting messages, and I also gave him some birds from my palace loft.

"But it is this Akbar that has me worried now. Not much is known about him. He is said to have Turkish blood in his veins and to have beheaded a Hindu with one stroke of his scimitar at the age of fourteen. Some say he is an illiterate barbarian, and others say he is a man of culture—a philosopher no less. But more to the point, he is said to have an army numbering in the tens of thousands. If so, he would be a formidable foe indeed. As a protective measure I have been trying to convince the other provincial kings of the south to join with me in an alliance for our common defense.

"Yes, for all his might, it may be that this Akbar is mad. It is said he seeks to combine and unite under one roof all the religions and cultures on the continent. What insanity! With such ideas perhaps he will defeat himself.

"As for the rani and the dewan, Koti, I am sure Akbar

welcomed them with open arms. Now he has a queen of the south to show off as a supplicant. According to intelligence the rana has received, Akbar has given Koti a high rank in his army. Hmm. The Mogul had better watch his back.

"Now I must tell you some sad news, Hari. Our friend the zamindar is dead. I just received the report, and am massing my troops to occupy the area and wreak vengeance if they can, though I fear it is already too late. Apparently a surprise attack was made on his palace. His troops were badly outnumbered. I am sure he and his men fought valiantly, but the raiders used flame-arrows and set the palace afire. No one survived. A tragic event—one that will not happen again if I can help it. We do not know who the attackers were. They may have been a roving band of outlaws, or mercenaries, or a raiding party from the north. It may be that Akbar is behind it, but there is no proof. I have had reports of spies dressed in black riding about the hills by night, and we have been trying to capture one of them to learn what we can. But they have evaded us thus far."

But that is not true! The zamindar was never attacked.

It was a false report, made by a spy the rajah does not suspect. The intent is to cause him to organize for a fancied threat in the wrong direction, so that he will be ill prepared for the real threat when it comes. His enemy is cunning.

But this affects my mortal man, for he has the zamindar's amulet, and now may fail to return it.

That is no concern of ours, as we did not cause this report to be made. In a few days the truth will be ascertained—by which time there may be another false report from another direction, putting the rajah farther off balance. Mortal politics can be pretty to watch.

I suppose so, for monsters. Meanwhile, we shall complete our contest. You shall not deny me my final seduction.

Nor do I wish to deny you your effort, for then the move will be mine, and I will kill him and win your favors for the coming century.

The mere thought appalls me.

The mere thought of your being appalled delights me. I shall encourage you to scream with revulsion as I endlessly smite your lusciousness.

Never!

"And now tell me of your exploits in Madresh," said the rajah. "Did you learn anything that might be of value in dealing with this new threat from the north?"

Hari only half heard the rajah's question. He was thinking of the zamindar, recalling his infectious laugh, the merry twinkle in his eye, and his many kindnesses to him. And he thought of Balu, too. And Meena, lovely Meena. He choked back a sob. It was surely his fault, for he had deprived the zamindar of his protection: the talisman.

"Was there nothing, then, Hari?" asked the rajah.

"Oh, please forgive me, Lord. I was distracted by the unfortunate news, for the zamindar was a fine man. Yes, there is something that might be of value."

But he has no suspicion of the truth: that it is a lovely lie.

Because he is a good mortal man, who is not of a suspicious nature. I like him well for that.

Naïvete must be hard to come by, for a creature like you. Yet you know you can never touch him directly, whereas I am freely available.

I enjoy his embrace when I enter a mortal woman he clasps; I feel her feelings, and I shall do that often once I am rid of you.

"Suspecting that I was a spy, the Rani of Madresh sent me into a vast underground cavern to die. The cavern extends for many leagues from a point near the rana's palace to the northern edge of the Land of Peril. I discovered the southern exit to the caverns and thereby entered and passed safely through the Land of Peril into Madra. I am sure that no one knows of this secret route which leads to the north. Perhaps it could be of some importance in the future. The secret of passing through the underground caverns is to follow the way of the amber spears which grow from the ceiling. As for the strange phenomena in the Land of Peril, they are all natural—freak events of nature. They are fearful to behold, but it is mostly one's own imaginary terrors that are dangerous, not the region itself. Once warned and instructed, an army could pass northward through the Land of Peril and the caverns safe and unseen."

The oaf has a better grasp of military relevance than I supposed.

"Also, in the southern part of the caverns I saw rich deposits of iron ore and a vast supply of saltpeter. There are also great quantities of bat guano, enough to fertilize many fields for many years."

And of commerce and agriculture.

"Ah, Hari, these are valuable discoveries indeed!" exclaimed the rajah. "Amazing, quite amazing. You have done a great service to your country and your ruler. For such knowledge, you have earned a reward. Name it and I will grant it. What is your wish?"

"I thank you, my rajah. But to be able to help is enough. I have only one wish at the moment and that is to return home. It has been long since I have seen my family, and I miss them."

Yet he remains a fool. He could have had an appointment to the zamindar's position.

Except that that position is not open. In any event, he is a seeker of grace, not of power, and I respect that.

Respect it? You are falling in love with the simpleton.

"I understand your feelings, Hari. Very well, but I will be sorry to see you go. Know that the doors of my palace will always be open to you. But before you depart I pray you will visit a few days with me at my lake palace which is but a few leagues to the south. The rest will do you good."

Hari bowed in acceptance.

"Good! My daughters are already there and will be glad to see you again. Sukunya has asked about you often. Since no one knows about your secret mission to Madresh, she thinks you have been off wandering through the countryside making merry. So you may be in for some teasing."

Hari returned to his room, bathed, and donned fresh clothing. He was then led by a servant to the royal stables where the rajah awaited him.

"We will travel by horse," said the rajah. "It will be fast and also fun. Pick out a steed that suits you."

Hari looked over the many magnificent horses and chose a speckled Arabian that was slightly smaller but perkier than the rajah's black stallion. In one of the stalls he saw his friend who had earlier carried him to Madresh, and he patted the old fellow on the neck. The horse nodded and snorted, although whether in happy recognition or disapproval at his choice of steeds, Hari could not tell.

"The old boy may not be much to look at or very fast," said the rajah, "but he is faithful and reliable nonetheless. And since he performed his duty so well in delivering you to the border, he has earned the right to loll around and enjoy his oats."

The rajah and Hari mounted their steeds, both resplendent in jewel-encrusted saddles and red tassels, and followed their equestrian escort through the city streets and into the southern hills. The afternoon was bright and they moved along at a steady canter.

It was not long before the lake palace came into view. The rajah leaned forward and whispered something to his stallion. Then in a burst of speed the horse charged ahead, outrunning the entire party, the rajah urging him on. Chagrined at the rajah's behavior, the captain of the escort, whose duty it was to remain close to and protect his master, immediately took off in pursuit, galloping at full speed and signaling the rest of the troop to follow. Hari joined in the chase. His Arabian was fast and soon passed the guards and came abreast of the rajah.

"A race!" shouted the rajah. "First to the palace gate!"

Hari nodded and urged his steed forward. The Arabian gradually pulled ahead, but the black had greater stamina. In the last half-league the speckled tired and slowed, and the rajah arrived at the palace gate several lengths ahead. Hari bowed to the victor and they both laughed heartily. The captain, red-faced, pulled up behind them and barked orders for his men to fall into formation and escort the rajah into the palace grounds. The rajah suppressed his merriment so as not to further embarrass the captain, satisfying himself with an exchange of amused smiles with Hari.

Hari marveled at the beauty of the palace. Constructed of white marble, it stretched in a long, graceful semicircle around the contour of a shimmering blue lake. Slender turrets rose from each corner, and running between were scalloped portals inlaid with semiprecious stones and laced screens intricately carved from stone. Etched in the marble walls were elaborate floral designs, graceful arabesques, and figures of the gods at love and play. Walled gardens and cascading fountains lined the walkways, beyond which stately rows of cypresses hovered along the water's edge. White swans glided beneath the overhanging branches, which bowed to them in the breeze.

Within the palace the walls were of polished marble of many hues, their edges accented with agate and jasper engraved in floral designs. The inner hallway was painted with panoramic scenes from the *Ramayana* and *Mahabharata*; its domed ceiling sparkled with inset jewels to simulate the stars and planets by night and the sun and sky by day.

Hari was shown to a room overlooking the lake, and from his balcony he watched the rajah's majestic sailboat gliding into dock. The triplets were aboard and waved to him excitedly. He watched them as they disappeared into the palace, Sukunya hindmost. Seeing her reminded him that he had better check the lock on his door. Much to his relief he found that the door had no lock, which he presumed was the case in all the rooms. He did not want to be trapped again by the crafty Sukunya and have to pay an outrageous price to be released. It did not occur to him that a door lock also served another purpose—to keep people out.

At dinner Suseela and Saras plied him with questions about his travels, and they listened in fascination and feigned terror as he told them about the terrible cloud monster and the poisonous purple mist. They applauded and breathed a great sigh of relief when he explained the scientific reasons for these phenomena. Sukunya, though, was more interested in hearing about his romantic adventures, but he cleverly avoided answering her questions directly so that she pouted and wrinkled her brow.

Now I make my move. I touch Suseela with passion for the handsome quest.

But Sukunya's passion has not yet worn off. Perhaps it is deceit as much as coupling that she enjoys.

Hari has little remaining interest in Sukunya, however; she made him work too hard before. He seeks to avoid her. So Suseela will have the advantage in snaring him.

After dinner Suseela and Saras insisted on taking Hari for a moonlight sail, though Sukunya showed little interest. Finding it impossible to refuse the invitation, accompanied as it was by not a little arm pulling, especially by Suseela, he consented, although he would rather have retired early to catch up on his sleep. But the sail proved enjoyable and he was glad he went. The view of the palace and the starlit heavens reflected in the lake was breathtaking, and the cool breeze that blew in his face and filled the sails relaxed his mind and soothed his soul. Too, he enjoyed watching the fish jump beside the boat, their silver bodies glittering in the moonlight; Suseela attracted great schools of them by tossing bits of bread overboard, and he could not help noticing that in her distraction she displayed rather more flesh than was proper. Naturally he did not speak of that, and neither did he embarrass her by becoming obvious in his attention. Ducks swam alongside quacking for a handout and performed funny antics as they chased about trying to steal one another's piece of bread.

"Perhaps it is time to return to the palace," Saras remarked after a time.

"Oh, are you tired, my sister?" Suseela inquired solicitously. "I remain full of energy." She darted a glance at Hari. "And I am sure our honored guest wishes to see all of what the lake has to offer. Why don't you return, and I will undertake to show him what he may not suspect?"

"I could not do that," Saras protested. "For it is well known that appearance is as important as reality, and some might insinuate that a princess who sailed alone with a visitor was compromised by the mere fact of it. I would not want my selfishness to bring any such hint of a taint to your reputation. I shall remain."

"It is good to have a sister who is so solicitous of my reputation," Suseela said, though somehow her appreciation seemed less than wholehearted.

They showed him the remaining wonders of the lake, and Suseela especially seemed eager to make his excursion comfortable. But she remained somewhat careless about her dress and posture, so that though Hari would never be so crass as to remark on it to any person, he was satisfied that her feminine endowments were in every respect the match for those of her sister Sukunya. In fact he could not help wondering what her body might feel like, were he able to explore it more closely. He almost wished that Saras had elected to go to shore early, though of course that thought was unfair to Suseela's reputation.

It was late when the boat docked, and after bidding the girls good night, aware of an uncommonly long glance from Suseela as she returned his courtesy, Hari went directly to bed.

As he crawled beneath the blankets his leg bumped into something. He lifted a corner of the blanket to see what it was, only to discover a strange leg. He raised the blanket higher and saw that the leg had a mate and was attached to a quite naked and lovely female torso.

What is this?

Delicious deceit.

"Oh!" came a voice from under the blanket. Hari saw a hand appear above the covers. The hand pulled the blanket down to reveal none other than the face of—of whom? It was one of the triplets, but which one?

"Hari! What are you doing in my bed?" the young lady asked in an astonished voice. "You woke me up. Why are you here?"

"Ah—ah—" stammered Hari nervously. "Who—which sister are you?"

"Which do you suppose I am?" she returned archly.

Hari, ashamed of himself, replied with the name of the one he wanted her to be. "Suseela."

"Suseela!" She sounded outraged, but he did not understand that at first. He took her tone for agreement. "What makes you say that?"

"I noted the care with which you attended me on the boat, and I must confess that I was intrigued by your form. But I apologize for intruding on you, and I shall immediately withdraw. The doors look alike, and I must have come to the wrong room."

"On the boat? How did you interact with me there?"

"I am sure it was merely your distraction," he said, concerned that he not give further offense. "At times your limbs inadvertently showed, and I could not help appreciating their rondure and symmetry."

"My accidental exposure," she said thoughtfully. "I begin to understand. It seems that what one sister likes, so does another."

Hari began to suffer doubt. "You *are* Suseela? I did not hear you deny it, but neither did I hear you accede to it."

She came to a decision. "You guessed at the one who seemed to show interest in you today. Were you to guess again, whom would you choose?"

He realized that there was potential awkwardness here. But all he could do was name the next one he would like her to be. Familiarity was better than outraged innocence. "Sukunya."

"This time you are correct."

He was not sure of that, because of the deviousness of her attitude. He had been deceived about their identities before. "You are——"

"Sukunya, of course."

"How—how do I know you are Sukunya?"

"Well, if it were anyone else but me, you would be hearing screams, not questions. Have we not been in similar circumstances before?"

Hari now believed it was Sukunya, and for that much he was grateful.

"I—I thought this was my bedroom," he explained. "Please forgive me. I will go now."

"Just a moment," snapped Sukunya in an angry tone as she grasped Hari by the arm. "You enter my room and bed uninvited, you wake me up, you look upon my unclothed body, and then you rudely dismiss me. Am I so ugly that you should insult me that way?"

"Shh—shh, Sukunya, please do not raise your voice," whispered Hari in near panic. "Someone will hear. I did not mean to insult you, please believe me. Of course you are beautiful. You are very beautiful. But—but I did not mean to disturb your sleep—it was an accident. I am only leaving so you can continue with your sleep."

Sukunya kept her grasp on his arm. "But since you woke me, I am no longer sleepy. You will have to make me sleepy again."

"How can I do that? Do you want me to tell you a story?"

"O Hari! You say that I am beautiful, but then you insult me again!"

"Shh— Please, Sukunya, you are raising your voice. Please talk softly, I beg of you."

"I will talk softly if you do not insult me."

"But I was not insulting you, I was only—"

"You were!"

"But how?"

"Well, if you are so blind, let us take it step by step. You said I was beautiful, did you not?"

"I did—and you are."

"And is a beautiful woman desirable or undesirable to a man?"

"Well, desirable, of course, but—"

"Good! Then is it fair to conclude that you, Hari, desire me?"

"Well—well, yes, but there is a proper time and place for the satisfaction of desires."

"Such as being in bed at night alone with the woman of your desire?"

"Uh—no. I mean yes!" Hari felt a sinking sensation in the pit of his stomach.

"And are we not now so situated?" she asked.

"Well, yes—but the woman must also be desirous of the man, which she surely would not be if she had been disturbed and upset by someone, would she?"

"Oh, but I do desire you, Hari. Now, you see, you have proved both to yourself and to me that there can be only one conclusion. Do you know what that is?"

"Yes," said Hari, his tone now one of total resignation and surrender. "I must want to make love to you."

"Oh Hari, do you?" asked Sukunya lovingly.

Hari bowed to the inevitable and commenced to make love to Sukunya, albeit with only half a heart—at least at first. Sukunya's prodigious lovemaking skills were such that he could not help but rise to the occasion, and so they coupled and clipped with exceeding passion until there came unto them that moment of supreme delight which is the gift of Kama, the god of love.

Upon completing the exercise, Hari was about to rise from the bed when Sukunya stopped him.

"Where are you going, my lover?" Sukunya asked, her voice a soft purr.

"Back to my own bedroom," he replied, dreading her next demand.

"That will not be necessary," she said as she hopped from the bed and slipped into a red robe which she had earlier hidden under the bed. "This is your bedroom, my love. My room is down the hall. Did you not see that the decor is not in my color? Good night!" With that Sukunya quietly ducked out of the room and closed the door behind her.

Hari sat on his bed with his mouth open. "How stupid I am!" he blurted as he clapped his hand to his brow. "She tricked me again!"

He jumped out of bed and dragged a heavy chair over to the door and propped it against the door handle. He then went out on the balcony to be sure there was no possible way anyone might enter from outside. Satisfied that his quarters were secure, he returned to bed. Oh well, he thought, and he smiled. It had not really been so terrible an experience after all, but he was grateful that Sukunya's sisters did not have her appetite or her cleverness.

Perhaps it was just as well that he did not hear the light footsteps that approached his door thereafter, or the quiet knock at the door, or the cautious testing of it. The door was securely blocked, and he was fatigued. After a time the footsteps departed.

And so your seventh seduction is balked by the wiles of your third seduction. The same woman twice does not count double. She was not on the boat, so was able to reach his bedroom first, and use him up before your choice arrived. Seldom have I enjoyed watching mortal schemes more. Now it is my move.

May your luck be as ill as mine!

That night Hari dreamed he was lost in a strange city. He ran from street to street asking people where he was and the way out of the city, but no one paid him any attention. He saw many familiar faces—Meena, Sumi, Pudmini, Sharmila, Kamala, and Sukunya—but none of them recognized him or would speak to him. Suddenly the city melted away and he was running in a dark forest. He called out but no one answered. The ground opened beneath him and he fell into a deep hole which became brighter and brighter as he fell. A great cloud of butterflies appeared, attached themselves to his clothing, and lifted him out of the hole. They carried him high over the forest and the ocean toward his home, but a flock of birds descended and ate the butterflies, and he fell into the sea.

The days that followed were enjoyable. Hari swam, sailed, went horseback riding with the rajah, and in the evening took long walks by himself around the lake. He kept his door firmly barricaded and slept well. One morning Suseela found a helpless bluebird beneath a tree and came running to Hari with tears in her eyes. The bird had somehow gotten sticky tree-sap on its wing feathers and was unable to fly.

Together they cleaned the poor bird, Hari holding its wings outstretched while Suseela patiently dabbed at it with a damp cloth. When its wings were dry, Suseela placed the bird gently on the ground, whereupon it fluffed up its feathers and flew off amidst a twitter of complaints. They both laughed at the happy conclusion of their efforts, and Hari saw that Suseela had a good heart and shared his love for nature's creatures. She also liked his company, but of course he was careful not to presume on that, and did not compromise her reputation by allowing himself to be seen alone with her too long. If at times she seemed saddened or frustrated, he felt sure that he was not the cause.

The utter ninny!

A perceptive judgment.

On the evening of his fifth day at the lake palace, Hari announced at dinner that he would be leaving in the morning. He declined the rajah's offer of an armed escort, nor would he accept the gift of a horse, explaining his desire to walk. The rajah understood and restrained his daughters' protests and entreaties for him to remain. Sukunya was more reticent than her sisters if only because she was the most disappointed, though Suseela seemed almost as troubled. Hari saw the hurt look in their eyes and smiled at them warmly to let them know that he would miss them too, in his own way. But he was careful not to reveal in his smile or his eyes any message that might be interpreted as a nocturnal invitation, for this night as usual a chair would be firmly propped against his door.

What am I to do with you, you noble idiot?

It seems really too bad that you will never have the chance to seduce him in your own right, as it is clear that you have fallen in love with him.

I confess it, the more fool I.

That night as he stood on his balcony watching the ripples on the lake wash over the reflection of the moon, his thoughts turned to the talisman. He could no longer return it to the zamindar, and it was not something he wished to keep himself. Nor did he think it wise to give it to the rajah. Although the rajah was benevolent and farsighted, he was not experienced in the ways of magic. In times of war or other great need, he might be tempted to draw upon the powers of the talisman and so fall into the clutches of the terrible she-demon. No, the risk was too great.

Hari could think of only one person who understood the powers of the talisman and could be trusted with its care: the guru, Narusimhum. On his journey home he would stop at the guru's mountain cave and give him the amulet.

The rajah arose early in the morning to see Hari off. Suseela and Saras, still half asleep and in their night-gowns, waved to him from their balconies. Saras was decorous, but Suseela, ever the careless one, accidentally leaned too far forward and showed more of her well-formed bosom than was seemly for a princess. It was perhaps fortunate that he was leaving, for otherwise he might have been sorely tempted by untoward thoughts. Sukunya was nowhere to be seen.

"Hari, since you will not accept a boon from me," said the rajah, "I have taken the liberty of having a small gift sewn into the lining of your tunic."

"Thank you, Lord," Hari replied, and he bowed low to show his respect and appreciation. Under the circumstances, he could not refuse.

"Farewell, then, Hari. I feel certain we shall meet again. May Lakshmi travel with you. And be careful."

Once outside the palace grounds, Hari stopped a moment to look back. He saw a lonely figure in a cupola atop the palace and knew it was Sukunya. He waved, but she did not return the wave. He turned and continued on his way. It was not until he had reached the distant hills and was lost from sight that the watching figure left the cupola.

ᘯ❧ *12* ᘯ❧

The Rider in Black

Hari chose the least trodden paths that he might see more of nature and less of people. Once he saw a tigress and her two cubs in the brush devouring a doe. Another time he witnessed in a rocky crevass the strange mating ritual of the king cobra, and nearby he saw the hooded serpent's bridal gift: a paralyzed snake-bitten rat that also watched the love ritual, its glazed terror-stricken eyes only too aware of its fate.

What, are you not going to cause that male cobra to attack our mortal man?

No. While he carries that talisman he remains somewhat charmed, and threats tend to turn aside. I shall wait until he divests himself of it. Then he will be most vulnerable. As I think you know.

Yes. I think it has also charmed him somewhat to my cost, helping him to avoid additional seductions he thinks he does not want. So if you do not kill him, I shall certainly seduce him.

Atop a hill Hari surprised a flock of feral rollers basking in the sun, their turquoise wings outspread to catch the warmth, and they exploded in a rainbow of color, loosing clouds of feathers into the air. He watched the feathers slowly seesaw downward, some catching in his hair; their iridescence shimmered in the bright sunlight, decorating the grass like so many velvet jewels. Amidst the grassy treasure he found the limp body of one of the rollers, its neck broken from having struck an overhead branch in its panicked flight. If only he had not frightened them, he thought.

Further along he nearly trod upon a fledgling dove that had fallen from its nest. Though not yet able to fly, it was quite able to run and gave him a merry chase through the grass until he finally cornered it. Gently he picked up the angry ball of feathers, which peeped in protest. He knew it would have to be returned to its nest lest it become a snack for a passing snake. He spotted the nest in a nearby tree and began the climb, though not without difficulty, for he had to pull himself up with one hand while carefully holding the bird in the other. The scratches and scrapes he earned for his trouble, he silently endured.

Upon reaching the nest, he discovered that another problem presented itself: the brooding mother dove, all puffed up and glowering, refused to budge an inch to make room for her fallen baby. There was nothing to be done but simply stuff the fledgling under the obstinate hen, which set off a tumult of peeping from yet another chick that was buried somewhere beneath its mother. The returned birdling, happy to be home, joined its sibling in a frantic duet, while the angry mother bird delivered the human intruder a nip on the finger. Though not painful, the bite caused its startled recipient to topple from the tree.

Oh, not for only passion have I lost my heart to a mortal.

Hari lay sprawled on the grass, unhurt save for a knee scrape. A moment later the hatchling he had rescued fell to the ground next to him. It had been rejected by its

mother and pecked to death. Hari wept unashamedly
and raised his fist to the heavens.

He did not understand why the gods heaped such suffering on the innocent creatures of the earth and on the
mortals who sought to preserve and protect them. The
injustice of it angered and frustrated him. He knew what
his village teacher would say, who was always able to explain away any dilemma. It is a matter of balance in the
universe, he would say. The discomfort received is in
proportion to the pleasure obtained. A mortal able to
embrace and enjoy Brahma's creations can not help but
be sensitive to their destruction and rebirth. Others
blind to Brahma's wonders may suffer less, but their
souls are the poorer for it. One must experience pleasure
and pain in order to defeat and rise above them.

In the early afternoon, as he was passing through a narrow valley, he saw a flash of movement behind a distant
stand of trees. He thought it was a horse, but could not
be sure, for it could have been a deer or the sunlight playing tricks with his eyes as it filtered through trees and
clouds.

The hills grew smaller, dwindling to hillocks, and finally crept beneath the flat skin of the earth and disappeared. By late afternoon he reached a brown grassland,
a dreary expanse completely vacant of green, broken
only by craggy ridges and stony outcroppings. The forbidding scene gave him pause, but to look for another
route now would mean backtracking and the waste of
many hours. Better to spend the night where he was, he
decided, and continue on through the grassland in the
morning.

He slept fitfully, unable to dispel the feeling that he

was being watched. At first light he set out. The path gradually narrowed and was eventually swallowed up in matted grass and heavy weeds. Unseen holes and broken roots tripped his feet, bogs and mires sucked at his legs, thorns and brambles stabbed at his flesh. The air became stifling, and reeked with the odor of rotting vegetation. A foul mist rose up to form a dense canopy overhead, all but blotting out the sunlight.

Weirdly shaped shelves of stone appeared out of the gloom, forming a great circle. Like ghostly markers, they pointed to a large moss-covered mound at their center. The humpbacked rise looked to Hari like an ancient burial place, and he trod not upon its dim shadow that fell upon hollow beds of long-dead reeds and husks of withered pods.

By afternoon the land hardened and its breast rose up out of the mire. Matted weeds gave way to coarse reeds and patches of ragged brush, and clumps of rough green grass struggled through the dust and stones. The wan orb of the sun reappeared, revealing the lost path, and a cool breeze arose. A cricket crawled from beneath a rock seeking the sunlight, but the dry reeds hissed and frightened it back into the shadows.

Soon jagged ridges and ramparts appeared, and in the distance, sketched against the still gray sky, loomed the outline of snowcapped mountains. Wispy bands of dark clouds hung about the lofty summits and barren ridges, casting eerie shadows on the lower cliffsides. However forbidding, the sight lightened Hari's heart, for he knew that deep within the mountain fastness was his destination—the cave of the guru.

As he started the climb through the rocky foothills,

he heard the neighing of a horse, but looking about, saw
no sign of man or beast. He proceeded warily, keeping
to the shadows of the outcroppings that lined the trail.
A chill wind swept down from the snowy heights and
whipped at him, slowing his progress. At a narrow turn
in the path a barrage of stones tumbled down the cliffside, which he barely evaded, and he wondered if the
demons of the mountains were trying to prevent him
from delivering the talisman to the guru. In the dim
heights above he could make out eddies of snow whirling
about the jagged caps like so many demented ghosts,
and in the distance a low rumbling told of an avalanche
somewhere deep in the mountains—or was it the mountains whispering angrily of an alien in their midst?

The mountains' shadows deepened, calling down the
night, and on a cliffside ahead he saw a pale light flickering like a solitary firefly lost in the fastness: the cave
of the guru at last. As he climbed the rocky slope to the
cave entrance, the weight of the talisman around his neck
seemed to grow lighter, and he wondered that he had not
been aware of its heaviness before.

"Come in, come in, my friend," came the familiar
voice of the guru Narusimhum from inside the cave.
"The night air is chilly and I have prepared some hot re-
freshments for us."

Hari pulled himself up to the cave entrance and saw
within the smiling old guru sitting crosslegged on a blanket before a small fire. On the fire was a steaming teakettle, and set out on a mat were two cups and a plate of
chapatis. Everything looked exactly the same as when he
last visited, as though time had somehow overlooked the
guru and his small corner of the universe.

Hari bowed low before the old master.

"Ah, I am glad to see you again, my young friend," said the guru cheerily. "Come, sit down and help yourself to some tea and a bite to eat."

"I thank you for your kind hospitality, Master."

Hari was cold and hungry, and the meager repast seemed a veritable feast.

"You were indeed fortunate to escape the she-demon," said the guru. "And you were wise always to keep the talisman with you."

A look of surprise came over Hari's face.

"Master, I do not know how you came by the knowledge of my encounter with the she-demon, but had it not been for you the creature would surely have killed me. It was your words that saved me, and for that I am most grateful."

"Well, you were clever to divine the meaning of my words. For many, the press of necessity closes rather than opens the mind. But you should not have called up the demoness—that was dangerous and foolish. Perhaps I should have given you more warning, but I did not think you would be able to invoke her even if you tried."

"I was fortunate—or unfortunate. I happened to pronounce her name correctly. Still—" He peered questioningly at the guru.

"Yes, my young friend, I have followed your exploits with interest from within these very walls. This old man has his ways. Mmm."

"O Master, then you must know the fate of the zamindar."

"Yes. I learned about the news that messenger brought, though my informant hinted that all was not as it seemed. Very sad. Dark clouds from the north are spreading over the southern lands, though I can not tell whether it be for good or ill."

"If you mean war, how can that be good?"

"War is never desirable, my friend. It was its aftermath I was wondering about. It could bring a new age. Oh, but there are more immediate matters that concern us. I speak of the talisman. What will you do with it now?"

"It is a weight I wish to shed. I came here to deliver it into your hands. You know best what to do with it."

"I am glad you have so decided. There is little I do not know about the talisman and its history. I will keep it safe and see that it does not fall into the wrong hands."

Hari lifted the amulet from around his neck and handed it to the guru. The old master examined it carefully, nodding to himself, and placed it around his own neck.

"O Guruji," said Hari, "I have been curious about the letters etched on the other side of the talisman. Can you tell me something of their meaning?"

The guru smiled, then rose and retreated into the darkness at the back of the cave. He returned carrying a rolled parchment. Hari could see that it was worn and very old. The guru reseated himself and carefully set the parchment down on the blanket beside him.

"There will be no harm in enlightening you, but you must never reveal what you are about to learn, just as you must never again speak of the talisman. Do you swear?"

"I swear, Master."

"Good. Now, the talisman is very old, made by the

hand of the Asura king himself, master of demons. He fashioned it as a means of releasing the love-demoness from a rock beneath the earth where she had been imprisoned by the good rishi, Baksura. But the laws of good and evil require balance, so when the Asura king etched the name of the she-demon on one side of the talisman, he was obliged to engrave yet another name on the opposite side—that of a benevolent demon. Without that balance the magic of the talisman would be ineffective. But the Asura king was cunning, and he carved on the talisman the name of a demon whose powers were limited. He chose an old air demon of ancient times whose only magic power was in seeing the present and the past. Of course, that is by no means a trivial power, but it is less than what most demons are capable of.

"I am sorry to say that the air demon was unable to help you when you released the she-demon. But he has been of great value at other times. Indeed, only by his vigilance has the talisman been kept safe these past three hundred years—with the one exception. And he is very wise in the ways of the world. Ah, many are the wondrous tales to be told of how the old fellow thwarted the plans of ambitious rishis and magicians who desperately sought the talisman. By his powers of sight the machinations of the evil power-seekers were observed. And by being forewarned, the noble ancestors of the zamindar were able to protect the talisman.

"This parchment I hold is an ancient tantra which tells the origin of the talisman and the secret names inscribed thereon. It is useless to speak the name of the she-demon without having possession of the talisman. But not so for the air demon. He can be summoned without the talisman because of an oversight of the Asura king. This tantra holds the secret of summoning him. One need only hold the parchment and utter his name written therein and he will appear. Of course, he may also be invoked by the possessor of the talisman, in the same manner as you called up the demoness."

Hari smiled to himself, remembering the many times he had imagined the terrible monster he might loose upon the world if he dared utter the mysterious word upon the back of the amulet.

"Many times I have used the parchment to call forth the air demon," continued the guru. "And through his eyes I have observed many things—including your exploits, my young friend. But, to my knowledge, the talisman itself has never been used to call up the air demon. So why do not we give it a test? I think you will like the old gentleman. He and I have become quite friendly over the years and have spent many days together debating the habits of gods and mortals. But first I must be sure that his name on the talisman is identical to that in the mantra. Hmm. Yes, it is.

"Now do not be frightened if the demon arrives with a little fanfare. The old rascal enjoys putting on a show."

The guru cleared his throat and held the talisman up to his eyes. Hari watched closely to be sure the guru was peering at the right side of the amulet lest the unthinkable occur.

"*Arunakachandumunshasa!*" cried the guru.

For a few moments nothing happened. Then a low rumbling sounded and the ground began to tremble, which rattled the teakettle and loosed a few small stones from the ceiling. A thick jet of green smoke shot up from the floor and billowed outward, threatening to fill the cave. The guru and Hari held their breath and fanned the air to keep from choking.

The sound of coughing came from somewhere within the cloud, and as the air began to clear Hari saw, sitting yoga-style on the ground before him, an old man waving his arms about trying to keep the smoke out of his face. Hari suppressed a grin. Garbed in a stained white robe and a scarlet turban that sat askew his wrinkled brow, the old demon was red-faced and slightly plump and sported a luxurious snow-white beard that badly needed combing. His dark eyes blinked in surprise, as though he did not know where he was or how he had gotten there. Altogether, Hari thought he looked like someone's kindly old grandfather.

"Phoo!" exclaimed the demon. "I thought to try green smoke this time to celebrate my first calling by the talisman, but something seems to have gone wrong. Too much smoke. Phoo!"

"Welcome, my old friend," said the guru. "The green smoke was a fine idea. Very colorful. I hope I did not interrupt you in the midst of anything important."

"I was napping—which is not unimportant at my age. But as King Solomon used to say, a week's nap is enough for any demon, so it is just as well you awakened me."

"May I offer you some tea and chapatis?" asked the guru.

"Hmm. Perhaps a bite." The demon helped himself to a chapati and began munching it around the edges.

"May I present a young Brahmin to you, Hari by name," said the guru. "His affairs, er, travels are already quite familiar to you."

Hari bowed to the demon.

"Ah yes! Yes indeed! My boy, following your adventures makes me wish I were young again. I am pleased to see you in the flesh—in person. And I am glad you were not harmed by the she-demon. You are a brave young man." The demon's face brightened. "And now that the courtesan princess of the rock-demons has been returned to her prison, perhaps I can take that heavenly vacation in Indraloka I have promised myself these past two hundred years. Ah, the gods know how to live well."

"By all means, do so," insisted the guru. "I have disturbed you much too often of late. I can see no need to call on you again soon. When you return, perhaps we can talk about certain developments in the north."

The demon waved a hand in the air. "Ah, my friend, you never disturb me. I enjoy our visits. And if I do not hear from you before long, I will come to see you anyway."

"Well said, old friend, well said," exclaimed the guru. "You are always welcome. Hari, do you have something you would like to ask our esteemed visitor before he leaves? Something about the past or present? Or perhaps something that may be troubling you? I know there are many questions on your mind, but now you may ask only one of them. Neither wisdom nor magic must be abused."

Hari thought a moment. He realized that this was an exceedingly rare opportunity that would probably never come again, so he needed to make the best possible use of it. As it happened, there was something he wished to know about. When he had traveled here from the palace of the rajah, he thought he was being followed, and he wondered who it was. Should he ask such a question? If he did, the guru might be saddened that he had wasted his question on so trivial a matter.

And indeed the guru knew that Hari was troubled by more serious questions, for he was wise in the ways of such things. The guru read the suffering in Hari's eyes, and guessed that in his travels his young friend had experienced life in ways that he had not expected or wanted, that he had heard the world's heartbeat and found it to be fickle. And so he might want to ask a question the answer to which would lighten the weight he carried.

So Hari decided not to ask the simple question. Instead he would ask a significant one. But what could that be? He knew better than to inquire about the meaning of life, for that would surely entail a prolonged discussion and was probably a matter of interpretation anyway. He should ask something practical yet ultimately meaningful. But what could that be?

Then a question came to him. "What is it that I must do, to be of the greatest service to myself and those whose friendships I value, that I would not think of myself?"

The demon nodded. "I had thought you were about to ask something selfishly trivial, such as whether you were being followed from the palace, and if so, by whom and for what reason. And my friend the guru would have been rightly disgusted at such a waste of opportunity."

"I confess, that was my first inclination," Hari said, abashed. "Only the realization that such a question would disappoint the guru dissuaded me. I sought a more significant question, so that I would not be exposed as the shallow ignoramus I am."

The guru laughed. "It is a wise supplicant who sees his triviality coming, and avoids it. All of us have consequential and inconsequential aspects warring for attention, but few of us exert some control over their expression." He turned to the demon. "But I am curious, my friend: what would you have said, had he asked that question?"

"Yes, my young Brahmin," replied the demon, assuming a pose, "you were being followed from the time you left the rajah's lake palace. It was the captain of the rajah's guard who was tracking you on the instruction of the rajah himself. When you refused an escort, the rajah ordered his captain to follow and watch over you until you reached the safety of the mountains."

Hari nodded, not surprised, and in his heart he felt a warm affection for the kindly rajah, despite his surreptitious act.

"I thank you," he said to the demon. "You have put to rest at least one of my cares."

"A small service for one who so nobly sparred with the immortal enchantress and won," replied the demon. "Now, however, I shall address your actual question, whose answer is simple but has perhaps surprising ramifications. You must take back the talisman."

"What?" Hari and the guru asked together, equally startled.

What?

He is aware of us!

The demon smiled. "It seems that you both have a sudden problem with your ears. I said—"

"I heard what you said!" the guru said. "But why did you say it?"

"I am glad you were the one to ask that question, my friend, for I could not have answered it had Hari asked it, being limited to a single answer for him. For you I will answer, and if he happens to overhear, that is his good fortune. The reason he must take back the talisman is that he has not completed his commitment with respect to it."

"But his commitment was to return it to its owner, and he is unable to do that."

"Why do you say that?"

"Because the zamindar is dead!"

"And the blame is surely mine," Hari said with grief. "For I should not have deprived him of its protection, thus leaving him vulnerable to disaster."

"Now that is a curious statement, considering that the zamindar and all his retinue remain alive and healthy."

"Alive!" the guru and Hari said together. Then the guru continued "But you told me—"

"That news of his violent death had been received. That was true. But the message was false, rendered by a spy whose purpose was to cause the rajah to make a tactical error. A fell ploy, but effective."

"But why did you not clarify that for me at the time?"

The demon shrugged. "It is, as you know, my custom to address only the questions I am asked. You did not ask."

The guru looked almost as chagrined as Hari felt. Then, without a word, he removed the amulet from his neck and gave it to Hari. It seemed that he had inadvertently received a lesson in humility.

"I thank you most sincerely for the information that

my friend the zamindar is alive," Hari said to the demon. "I never thought to question the news."

"Therefore you would not have thought to ask for the amulet back," the demon said. "That was a condition of your question, and a remarkably clever one. But I might mention, strictly as an incidental, that the need for cleverness has by no means passed, and the outcome of your larger quest is by no means determined. I might also hint, were I inclined, that there are factors closely affecting you about which you have no slightest inkling."

That's sufficient, demon! You may not inform him of us.

Agreed. Divert yourself in some other manner hereafter.

The guru and the demon then became involved in a philosophical debate about the sex of the Supreme God, whether it was indeed neutral, and whether it was possible for Brahma to have created the universe by laying it as an egg. The discussion continued on for hours, and eventually Hari drifted off to sleep. But he remained grateful for the amazing information the demon had so unexpectedly provided. A certain joy had replaced a certain sadness.

When he awoke the sun was shining brightly through the cave entrance, and the guru and the demon were still deeply engaged in debate. He nibbled on a cold chapati as he waited for the conversation to end, or at least to falter, so that he might make his farewells. Considering the intensity of the debate and the status of its participants, he dared not interrupt. Finally, seeing no break in sight, for the discussion had not yet advanced beyond the first of ten logical principles relating to the egg-laying propensity of a neuter god, he decided he would depart.

He faced the debaters and bowed low before them, and in so doing did not notice the brief trace of a smile pass across the guru's face.

This time as he climbed down from the cliffside to the path, he heard no parting words of wisdom from the guru, and he wondered whether the silence boded good or ill.

The chariot of Surya arched toward its zenith, igniting heaven's cup, even as Hari passed out of the mountains into a broad green valley. The sight of grass, hill, and tree beneath the bright blue sky soothed his heart, and he plucked a ripe mango to taste its sweetness. Having yet a long way to go, he decided to leave the beaten path that wound through the hills and head straight northwest toward his village.

Now do I make my move, though I am annoyed that the demon interfered, leaving the mortal man with the talisman.

Hari had not gone far when there appeared on a hill ahead a lone horseman garbed in black mounted on a jet stallion. Both rider and horse stood motionless, like an ebon statue against a wall of light-blue sky. A silk scarf covered the bottom half of the rider's face, hiding his features. But his dark staring eyes Hari saw, and he felt them burning into him. He remembered the rajah telling of roaming spies dressed in black, and he wondered if this might be one of them. It was surely not the rajah's captain, who should have gone home by now.

Suddenly the rider came to life. He lashed his mount, which whinnied and pounded at the earth, then shot forward with lowered head. Hari watched in helpless fascination as the ebon steed galloped down the slope toward him. He saw the rider reach down and unsheath a graceful curved scimitar, such as were used in the north;

its shiny blade glittered hynotically in the bright sunlight. In a swift movement the rider swung the weapon high, as though to pierce the heavens, and leaned forward into the wind, somber and unyielding.

O Ravana, he can not escape that cruel warrior!

With a calmness that surprised him—perhaps there had not been enough time to prepare his thoughts— Hari realized that he was about to be killed. Well, at least he would face Yama with dignity. But another voice within him, less accepting, screamed out and set him on alert. His body became taut and he quickly looked right and left, searching for something, anything, that might provide some cover. But there was nothing—he was out in the open and helpless.

What is your point, Mohini?

As rider and steed bore down upon him, he could see the white froth spewing from the horse's mouth, the beast's flaring nostrils and dark frantic eyes, eyes that betrayed fear and desperation and seemed to say: am I not also a victim like yourself, but another spoke in the wheel of life, death, and rebirth? And reflected deep within those wild eyes he saw the terrible third eye of the she-demon, which became the glaring jeweled eye of Kali and the searing flame of Sharmila's pyre; and, too, he saw the thousand eyes of the gods mocking him in their indifference.

Spare him, and I will yield to your desire.

But in the eye of the rider he saw naught but hate. Why such hatred? he wondered. It saddened him. As if in reply to his question, the wind quickened and blew the rider's scarf to one side. And Hari saw that the attacker was none other than Koti. Koti, the advisor to the rana of Madresh, whose affair with the rana's young wife, Kamala, Hari had inadvertently exposed. Now the reason for the man's hatred was clear, though perhaps he should have blamed himself for his treachery, rather than Hari for exposing it.

I shall have my desire in a moment anyway, as your mortal man dies.

I will give you two centuries!

But your awareness will always be on him, because you will love him as long as he lives. I want your full attention, whether positive or negative. I want you to know throughout who is having at you. Your mortal man is doomed.

O Hari—I love you, but I can not save you.

Even as the graceful blade arced downward—perhaps there was a murmur somewhere in the heavens—a ground squirrel popped out of a nearby hole and darted across the grass in the path of the galloping steed. Frightened by the flash of the small animal, the horse jolted to a stop, hurling its rider forward through the air. Koti, sword in hand, sailed over Hari's head and came down in a heap upon the grass. The terrified horse ran off through the hills.

You interfered!

Hari stood frozen, his heart pounding, watching to see if Koti would stir. But the body lay still. Carefully he approached the prone figure, which was lying on its face. Grasping one arm, he pulled the body over. Koti's head lolled to one side: his neck was broken and he was quite dead.

I did not. It is my move, but there were no female creatures near enough to use. That squirrel is male.

Hari stared at the lifeless body. The questions that assailed him he tried to push from his mind. He knew now there were questions beyond logic, at least the logic he had been taught and understood. There were some things he would just have to accept. Or else escape from.

That squirrel interfered deliberately! If not one of us, who motivated it?

Perhaps he should become the disciple of a sannyasi, he thought. The life of an ascetic had much to offer. Not least he would learn how to conquer the torment of the senses, to deaden life's pain.

Almost, I recognize it. There is a familiar aura.

He had no tools to bury Koti's body or materials to prepare a cremation. He would have to leave it untended. That the corpse would be consumed by vultures or other creatures did not disgust him, for it seemed a more humane way of leaving this life than simply going up in a puff of funereal smoke which benefited no one.

Yes, I have seen that aura before. But who?

The ground squirrel suddenly reappeared and came running over to him and stood up on its haunches. He broke off a weed pod and gave it some seeds, a meager offering, he thought, considering that the small creature had saved his life. The squirrel chattered its appreciation and munched on the seeds contentedly.

The guru whose young wife he serviced in Hari's body!

As he gazed into the creatures dark eyes, Hari remembered something the old guru, Sundar, had told him: "Would it not be better to be reborn as a ground squirrel than as an eagle—or a man?" Hari wondered: Could it be?

Disgusting. To be deprived of a century of brutal delight by a mere mortal reincarnation!

The squirrel finished its meal, washed its face thoroughly with its tiny paws, elaborately groomed its tail, then uttered a series of small squeaks before running off into the grass. Hari smiled.

✢ 13 ✢

The Zamindar

Hari reached the zamindar's palace in due course, having suffered no further mishaps along the way. He was glad that he would be able to return the talisman and honor his word, yet also saddened to realize that he had not achieved the worldly knowledge and personal enlightenment he sought. He had seen many marvelous things, and experienced a number of straits and emotions, but somehow remained dissatisfied.

Now it was time to return to his village, as he had promised his mother and sister, and to assume the responsibilities of his station. He would be expected to take a wife, though that still did not truly tempt him. How could he settle down with a simple village girl, after having been seduced by a princess, a priestess, and a she-demon, among others? And how could any ordinary experience match that of making love to a lady spirit whose supple body could be heard and felt but not seen?

He had hoped to lead an ascetic life, or at least a simple one, while traveling, but had not succeeded for the most part. Yet perhaps that meant he was not suitable for a career of contemplation, so should give up the effort and return home to live out of his life in the normal dull manner.

Have no fear, ignorant mortal man. Life will not be your problem.

You haven't killed him yet, Ravana.

But I will, as soon as I get my move. And you will have to give me that move, when you try for your seventh seduction. And that will have to be here, because he is about to give up his quest and return home.

There are women to seduce him at his home village.

But there he'll have to marry his seductress, and complicate his life, for everything is known. Even if I don't kill him, he would soon become too dull to interest you. Home village marriage does that to a mortal man.

You are right. I must seduce him here. Now do I make my move: Leela will not rest until she has had her will of him.

The guard recognized Hari and admitted him. But when he entered the palace, it was the zamindarini who greeted him. She wore a shimmering gown whose material seemed to become translucent as it flexed with her motions. "What may I do for you, handsome traveler?" she inquired warmly.

Hari was not entirely easy with this. He remembered that Leela had an ardent nature, and a fickle one; she might have grown tired of her lover Balu, or perhaps have worn him out. "I have come to return the zamindar's medallion, as I promised, and then continue on to my home."

"Ah, but you can not do that," she said. "For my husband and Balu are out on a mission, and will not return till tomorrow. However, I shall be happy to entertain you until then."

Hari's disquiet remained. In the absence of her husband and lover, she might seek certain personal attention. "Perhaps I should depart, and return tomorrow."

"By no means, Hari!" she said, taking his hand and drawing him forward. "What would my husband think if I denied you the hospitality he surely wishes you to have? I insist on taking care of your needs this night."

That was exactly his concern. She had tried to seduce him during his prior visit here and, with no one but the palace staff in attendance, she might have something similar in mind now. She had shown that she was not a woman to be readily denied, and there would be no chance to trick her this time. Had he realized that she was here alone, without the zamindar and Balu, he would not have entered the palace.

Precisely, my love.

She moved her grip from his hand to his arm, and drew it in close to her torso so that he could not help but feel the softness of it. She gave him a rather direct stare, by this token warning him of the likely consequence of further tacit resistance. She had before threatened to accuse him of impropriety, unless he committed the impropriety, and she was evidently ready to do so again. "Then I am constrained to accept your kind hospitality," he said reluctantly. Perhaps he could sneak out when she wasn't watching him.

And now do I make my countermove: the zamindar will develop a sudden suspicion, and return secretly to verify it. When he catches them, he will of course have to kill them both, to salvage his honor. And you, marvelous creature, can abate this disaster only by touching Leela's mind and causing her to desist her seduction.

But then she would be liable to accuse him anyway, to protect her reputation.

Exactly. Leela is a dangerous tool for your purpose. Perhaps when your mortal man is dead, I will require you to enter her, and I will enter a stablehand, and we shall perform such delights as will amaze the mortal realm, not to mention the animals. Thus will I achieve variety during my century of pleasure with you.

You absolutely disgust me. I will dance for sheer glee when I am free of you for a century.

Leela brought Hari into the banquet hall. "I shall serve you the finest meal, to make you amenable."

"I would prefer to clean up and retire, as I am weary from my traveling. Any scraps will do for my sustenance."

"Ah, but my husband would not countenance such inhospitality. I shall attend to your needs with my very own hands. Let me take you into my personal lavatory and strip and clean you."

"On reconsideration, perhaps I am ready for a more formal meal now."

"How very nice!" Leela clapped her hands, and a servant appeared. Hari was both relieved and concerned to see that it was Meena, his romance of the prior visit. He would much rather have been alone with Meena, and knew she did not like seeing him with Leela, but at least she would be able to appreciate that he was helpless in the situation. Perhaps she would find a way to rescue him from it.

Did Leela know of his affair with Meena? he wondered. The two of them had been discreet, yet such news tended to circulate, and he thought it likely that she did know. So was this use of Meena to serve them a warning to him? He could not safely assume that it wasn't. Yet Leela gave no evidence of hostility toward Meena; she simply directed her to serve the meal, and to be on hand for whatever was needed.

While these thoughts percolated through Hari's troubled mind, Leela was giving Meena directions. Soon Meena left the hall, to return in a moment with a tray bearing the first course of the meal: a steaming lentil soup. "Eat, traveler," Leela said heartily. "You must have good sustenance for the ordeal ahead."

"Ordeal?"

The zamindarini sent a sidelong glance at him. "Your onward trek through the world tomorrow or a subsequent day," she explained. She moved slightly, and her gown seemed to become entirely transparent in front, showing her finely formed breasts.

"Of course," he agreed, not sure that it would be wise to feel relieved. A trek across the countryside normally was not considered to be an ordeal. He took a spoonful of the soup. It was very good.

And very highly spiced. Hari enjoyed spiced food, as did all his countrymen, but this was extraordinary. His mouth was soon on fire, and he had difficulty breathing.

"Are you uncomfortable?" Leela inquired solicitously. "Don't be bashful about eating, considering your hunger. Here, let me help you." And she took the spoon from his flaccid hand and ladled another dip of soup into his mouth. "Be sure to let me know when you have enough." She brought up a third spoonful.

Hari tried to demur, but the only sound he could make was a strained squeak. His eyes were watering and his throat was burning right down to his stomach.

"I am so glad you like this soup," Leela said warmly. "I had it made specially for my husband, but I am sure

he would want you to have it too. Have some more." She
shoved another dose at him.

This time Hari had the sense to close his mouth. The
soup, balked, splashed into his nose, which was shortly
a raging inferno. He coughed and sputtered, completely
at her mercy, embarrassing himself by his uncouth display.

"You poor thing," she said. "You are choking. I am
so sorry; it must be my fault for being so careless." And
she took hold of his head and pressed it to her resilient
bosom. This had a remarkable effect: it not only soothed
his face, it transferred the burning sensation to his groin.

By the time the agony of his head subsided, the front
of her gown was wet with his involuntary tears. He tried
to apologize, but Leela hardly seemed displeased. "Let
me just change into something more appropriate," she
said, rising gracefully. "Continue with your soup; I shall
return in a moment." She departed from the banquet
hall, and despite his distress of mouth and eyes, he could
not help observing the provocative sway of her hips.
The heat of his nether portion did not abate; rather it
continued to intensify.

As soon as Leela was gone, Meena appeared. "She did
that on purpose," she whispered fiercely. "To punish
you for preferring me to her. Here is safe soup." She set
down another bowl that looked just like the original
one, and took away the hot one. "What she gave you not
only burns the mouth, it has a more subtle effect, generating a strong desire to—" She hesitated, coloring del-
icately.

Hari realized what the nature of the other effect was.
No wonder his groin was pained! "What does she want
of me?" Hari asked, though there really was no mystery.

"She wants to seduce you, and she will beat me if I interfere."

"But you are the only one I wish to be with," Hari protested, with some slight exaggeration.

"Then stave her off somehow, and I will come to you tonight, as before, if I can escape her observation." Meena glanced momentarily down, appreciating his condition, and smiled. Then she was away with the fire-soup.

Cheered by that notion, Hari sipped his new soup rapidly, and was just finishing it when the zamindarini returned. Now she wore a gown fashioned of finely woven strips that slid aside as she moved, showing whatever aspect of her body she might choose. It was an effect that caused him to react again in spite of himself, for whatever might be lacking in her nature, it was not her physical endowments.

Meena brought in the next course, which was an exquisite salad fashioned of chick peas, onions, green leaves, radishes, and herbs. Hari sampled it somewhat hesitantly, but the seasoning was within bounds. Leela attended to him solicitously, making quite sure he had the very best of it, and every time she leaned toward him, more of her torso showed. He hoped that his eyes were not bulging from their sockets. In fact his eyes were not the only type of bulging causing mischief. He sipped freely of the wine, in an effort to conceal his re-action.

Then she served him a course of spinach and eggplant with spiced rice and curry sauce. Again he was concerned about the intensity of the spicing, but it was excellent without being extreme. Evidently she believed that one full bowl of hot soup—hot in temperature, spicing, and effect—sufficed. It was a reasonable belief; even a fraction of that bowl seemed like more than enough.

Finally she served an excellent fried pastry with honey and rose water. By the time he finished that, he was quite full, and the wine had dulled his sensitivities somewhat, so that he no longer tried to avoid the increasingly intimate glimpses of her torso her gown provided. Not even when she crossed her legs and her thigh showed all the way to the hip.

Still, he carefully fended off her suggestive remarks, pleading fatigue, and finally she consented to allow him to retire alone for the night. She did not even seem unduly disappointed. Had he been less oblivious, he would have been concerned about that oddity.

She remains as interested as ever; she is merely more subtle than he credits.

As the zamindar is more subtle than she credits. He has now returned with Balu, and they are watching from outside, having sworn the palace guards to secrecy.

He retired to his room, the same one he had had before. He was relieved, because had Leela pressed him more closely he well might have succumbed to her blandishments. He knew her nature, and certainly did not wish to betray the hospitality of the zamindar, but never before had he been subjected to such a continuous display of fine feminine flesh, while in such a state of agitation. Had it not been for the intermittent presence of Meena to remind him of his other interest, the zamindarini might in the end have seduced him right there. But perhaps it had been her purpose only to tease him, to generate a desire for her that she could then deny him, punishing him again for escaping her before. First the hot spices, then the hot temptation. He had survived both, but suppose her revenge was a triple ploy?

He lay on the bed, restless despite his fatigue of body and fullness of belly. The soup had not yet worn off. What might Leela be up to next?

He had better lock and barricade the entrance. He got up from the bed and crossed the room in the darkness. But before he found his way to the door, there was a light knock on it.

He froze. Was he too late?

"Hari," a feminine voice whispered. "It is Meena."

Meena! For the moment he had forgotten her promise to come to him if she could. She had become somewhat possessive of him during his prior visit, but he did like her, and his interest in her had freshened somewhat after absence. Also, Leela's blandishments, not to mention her soup, had stirred him to a state that would not be denied. Though he was tired, he now realized why he was restless. Meena was exactly the person he needed at this time.

He found the door in the darkness and let her in. He smelled her perfume as she entered and kissed him. "We must be quick and silent in the darkness," she whispered. "She is checking on me often, to be sure I do not receive what she does not. I can not stay long, but I could not stay away either, my love."

How well he understood! But hasty love was better than none, and his pitch of excitement was such that haste was probably inevitable. So he brought her to the bed, pausing only to lock the door, and they both flung off their garments and fell on the bed in an intimate clasp. Only the medallion swinging from the chain about his neck remained between them. Their act of passion was as swift and explosive as a summer storm, for all its silence. It was as if lightning leapt between them, igniting them, causing both their bodies to stiffen in ultimate fulfillment.

Such was their rapture of the occasion that neither one heard the slight sound at the door.

Suddenly the door burst open and three people charged into the room. One bore a bright lamp and one bore a sword.

Hari and his lover were still locked in their intimacy. Shocked, he gazed wildly around, while she hid her face.

Balu held the lamp. The zamindar held the sword. And beside them stood Meena holding the key to the door.

Meena? How could that be? Yet it did seem to be. Then who was this in his embrace?

Balu stepped forward with the lamp, grabbed the woman's hair, and yanked her head up so that her face came into view. Hari gasped as he recognized Leela. She had tricked him, pretending to be Meena, and his urgency had been such that he had never thought to question it. She had even worn Meena's perfume and made over her hair to Meena's style. In the darkness—

"So my suspicion is confirmed," the zamindar said grimly, albeit sadly. "My wife has betrayed my marriage, and my guest has betrayed my hospitality. The penalty is death."

Both Balu and Meena looked appalled, though both also looked angry, understandably. They thought that Hari had deliberately betrayed them both, but Meena did not want Hari killed and Balu did not want Leela dead. They were however helpless in this situation.

"Have you anything to say for yourselves before you lose your heads?" the zamindar asked as he lifted his terrible gleaming sword.

Ah, victory is at hand.

Leela was silent, knowing that she had no defense. Hari tried to think of a way to explain that his betrayal had been inadvertent, but he knew there was no way to prove that, and in any event he was guilty of the fact if not of the intent. And, he had to admit to himself, despite its brevity it had been a remarkably intense and satisfying event. So he gave himself up for lost.

But there was one thing he had to do before he died, as a matter of what honor remained to him. "I promised to return your medallion," he said to the zamindar. "That much I shall do while I am able."

The zamindar looked surprised. Perhaps he had anticipated tearful pleading from one or the other. "Thank you," he said gruffly.

Hari struggled to take the chain from his neck. The medallion was wedged between his chest and Leela's full breasts. He had to use one hand to squeeze a breast aside in order to get the medallion out. In any other circumstance this would be a gross impropriety, but as it was, it hardly mattered. In a moment both of them would be dead.

Finally he got the medallion up. He lifted the chain over his head and held the disk out toward the zamindar. "I thank you for the use of this talisman," he said. "It served me well."

As he spoke, his fingers rubbed along the surface of

the medallion. A notion occurred. "But allow me to make one further use of it, before I give it up," he said. Then, without waiting for the response, he spoke the name inscribed there: "*Arunakachandumunshasa!*"

"You are summoning the she-demon!" the zamindar cried, appalled. "She will destroy us all!"

"By no means," Hari protested. "I would not repay your kindness with such distress."

A low rumbling sounded and the palace trembled. Blue smoke descended from the ceiling, thickening into a column. Gradually the smoke thinned and dissipated and the plump old air demon was revealed, his turban askew as usual. He shook himself, causing his long white beard to ripple.

"That is not the she-demon," the zamindar said, amazed.

The demon's eye fell on Hari. "So you had the wit to summon me," he remarked. "What is your concern—though I have my suspicions." He chuckled.

"Merely to thank you for your past help," Hari said humbly. "I did not want to die without doing that. You were the one who informed me that the news of the za-mindar's death was false, so that I could after all return the talisman to him and maintain my honor. Now I am doing that, and thanking you. I hope you will serve the zamindar as you served me. Apparently he does not know of your availability."

The air demon looked at the zamindar. "So it seems. That explains why he never summoned me. Well, sir, allow me to introduce myself. I am the Demon of Air, bound to the nether side of your talisman as a counter to the she-demon. My power does not match hers, for I am getting old and frail, but I am knowledgeable about the present and the past."

"Why should this man summon you, instead of the she-demon, when he had the power to do so?" the zamindar asked, his lifted sword trembling.

"Sir, I will answer your questions at such time as you summon me," the air demon said. "But I am at present in the power of Hari, and will address only his concerns. However, were I to remark on your question, I might simply point out that Hari is a man of charming innocence and honor who means you no harm. He was tricked into a liaison with your wife, supposing her to be another woman in the dark. Realizing that he has wronged you, however inadvertently, he still means you no harm, and is attempting merely to acquit himself of his obligations with such honor as remains to him before he dies.

"It does seem unfortunate that his innocence should be the cause of his undoing, but this is at times the way of karma. Now I shall bid him fair parting, and await your summons when you hold the talisman again." He fixed his old eyes on Hari. "It has been a pleasure to know one as pure of intention and confused of application as yourself, young traveler. I look forward to meeting your spirit, in due course." He faded out.

The zamindar stood open-mouthed, staring at the spot the demon had vacated. "He spoke the truth?" he asked.

"He cannot do otherwise," Hari reassured him. "Now if you will take your medallion and put it away, so it will not be soiled by blood—"

But the zamindar did not reach for the talisman. "What am I to do with this situation?" he asked in bewilderment. "How can I execute a man whose betrayal was inadvertent and unintended, and who does not blame me even when I blame him?"

Then Meena spoke up. "If you will forgive my speaking, my master, I may have a suggestion. Hari seems to have done you the favor of showing you the nature of your wife. Perhaps only she should be executed, and Hari sent on his way without further action."

Did you touch her?

No. I had no need to, for she wishes no harm to come to Hari. She is prepared to give him up, in order to save him.

"Perhaps so," the zamindar agreed, evidently still confused. He turned to Balu. "What do you say, my trusted advisor?"

Leela perked up. "Trusted advisor!" she exclaimed with outrage. "Let me tell you—"

Then she broke off, for Meena had taken a step toward her with the evident intention of jamming the large key down her throat.

"Obviously it is your wife who is at fault," Balu said quickly. "She is rumored to be a passionate woman, and must have thought to achieve fulfillment from the traveler without his knowledge by visiting him anonymously in the dark. He should be let go, being innocent in intention, but death may be too good for her. For one thing, her family has connections that might prove to be awkward, if they chose not to believe her infidelity. It might be better to divorce her and enlist her silence, sparing you public embarrassment."

Did you touch him?

No. I had no need to, for the fool loves her despite her nature and wishes to save her if he can.

"How could I enlist her silence?" the zamindar asked.

"My lord, if you will marry her to me, I will guarantee it. She will never care to confess the shame of a lower-caste marriage, and will do her utmost to conceal it from her family. You will then be free to marry a woman more to your liking, and thus improve your satisfaction in life."

The zamindar looked at Leela. "Will you swear silence about what has passed this night, if I spare your life and marry you to Balu?"

Leela, realizing that this was a considerably better offer than she would otherwise receive, nodded. "I will, my lord. I will never speak word of this solitary indiscretion."

An unruly breath of air must have passed through the room at that moment, for both Meena and Balu suffered coughing fits, and even Hari felt a catch in his throat. The zamindar did not notice, however. "Then it shall be done," he decided. "Disengage and go with Balu."

Leela drew herself away from Hari, to whom she had remained embarrassingly connected, and quickly got into her gown. In a moment she and Balu were gone.

"But I do not wish to live alone," the zamindar said with a sigh. "And I do not wish to risk another marriage like the first. I need a quiet, obedient, undemanding woman who understands me."

"There is one near," Hari said as he donned his own clothing.

"Oh, there is?" the zamindar asked in surprise.

"Meena is royal born, and is as fine a person and lovely a woman as any man could ask. Have you not noticed how quiet and discreet she is?"

The zamindar turned his gaze on Meena. "Why, it is

true! You are high caste, and beautiful, and I have never had a complaint of your service. However—"

"Only at my lord's pleasure," Meena said, evidently realizing that this was an opportunity that was unlikely to be repeated. "I am not a hungry woman, in certain respects."

"Then I shall marry you, for indeed you are worthy and I trust your discretion." He turned again to Hari. "It seems I owe you not mischief, but gratitude, for you have changed my life abruptly for the better. Now I will accept the medallion back from you, and will enjoy your company for the duration of your stay here."

"You are welcome," Hari said, at last turning over the talisman.

The contest is done, horny freak. I have completed my seventh seduction, and you have failed to kill the mortal man.

Alas, you are correct. You have escaped me, luscious goddess. But there will be other centuries, and you will remain as delectable during them. You have not seen the last of my horns.

And so it was. Leela disappeared into Balu's apartment, and it seemed that he was forever disciplining her, for there were often moans to be heard at night. But she made no complaint, and spoke no word of the changed situation to others. Meena did not join the zamindar, for that would have been indiscreet before the marriage, but their betrothal was announced and she moved to a far more elegant suite where she was richly attended, as befitted her new station. Hari had many rewarding conversations with the zamindar, and showed him exactly how to pronounce the air demon's name so as to summon him, while never making the mistake of summoning the she-demon. It was an excellent time.

But all good things pass, and it came time for Hari to

move on. He had promised to return home before too long, and further delay would cause his mother and sister to fret. So he bid farewell to the zamindar and his betrothed, and set out afoot for his home village, relieved that things had turned out so well, though it was sad to leave his friends behind. He promised to visit on another occasion.

Yet now as he turned his face toward home, he experienced an abiding regret. He had sought enlightenment, and had failed to achieve it. He was still the same somewhat naive young man he had been when he started. And he still had the same desire for something more in life than just settling down in the home village with a home-grown girl and generating a family. He had associated with men of great power and dallied with royal women; how could he settle for a minor life? He knew he should, and perhaps in spirit he was willing, but his heart was loath.

✢ 14 ✢

Mohini

Heads turned and hands touched in greeting as Hari walked through the streets of his ancestral village. Maidens smiled coyly and their hearts fluttered when they saw him. Hope sprang alive in their dainty breasts, for the young Brahmin was a prize catch, one who thus far had eluded the marriage net. But perhaps now there would be an opportunity for another cast.

His mother was picking flowers in the front garden when she saw him. She dropped the blooms she had gathered, tears rushed to her eyes, and she held out her arms to him, her lips silently speaking his name. His sister, Devi, came running out of the house, her face happy and shining, and she too embraced him. He shared in their joy, glad to see them well and to be home again.

He told them of his travels, though he omitted certain details so as not to worry them. They attended his every word, Devi in wide-eyed fascination and his mother in unrevealing solemnity.

Then he remembered the rajah's gift. He located a bulge in the lining of his tunic and forced out two small objects through the threads. His mother and sister gaped in disbelief at what he held in his hand: two magnificent blood-red rubies. He gave one to each of them. If they had found his story to be too incredible, particularly his friendship with the rajah, the sight of the sparkling gems totally dispelled their doubts.

But it was the very wonder of the tale that worried his mother. She was concerned that the excitement and in-toxication of such experiences might have changed her son so that he might not be content to remain in the vil-lage, to settle down, marry, and raise a family. But she gave no notice of her concern, at least not at the moment.

Wise woman.

Later in the day a friend of Hari's, one Chandu, came by to renew acquaintances, and although Hari was glad to see his friend again, he was keenly conscious of the distance that had grown between them. Chandu's jokes about the village girls and the old schoolteacher some-how did not seem very funny anymore, and their chatty conversation seemed much like others they had had be-fore. He chose not to tell his friend very much about his travels, for he did not wish to put up with the inevitable teasing and mocking expressions of disbelief.

At twilight he sat on the back veranda with his mother watching the glow of the sun slowly fade from pink to amber. From inside the house he could hear the rhyth-mical click-clacking of Devi's spinning wheel, which seemed to say that all was right with the world. And, in-deed, the unchanging sameness of the house and village, the nearness of his mother and sister, gave him a feeling of belonging and security. He realized that the old ways were not wrong, merely dull.

But all was not unchanged. He saw the lines of worry around his mother's eyes that had not been there before, and how the streaks of gray in her hair had widened since he had gone away. She saw him looking at her and smiled.

"Share your thoughts with your mother, my son."

"Oh, I was just daydreaming. Mother, are you and Devi happy—in this house—in this village?"

"Well of course, my son. What a strange question! This was your father's house. Where else would we be happy or wish to live?"

"Forgive me, Mother. It was a silly question."

When his mother next spoke, her voice was quiet and hesitant. "Hari, there is a matter I would discuss with you, which concerns your sister, Devi."

"Yes, Mother?"

"Devi has reached the age of marriage. A suitable husband will have to be found for her. I thought of asking your uncle Arun to begin making inquiries among the Brahmin families of the village. But now that you are home, perhaps you would prefer to take on that task. Devi does not complain, but I think she may be a little anxious. It should not be difficult to locate good prospects. She is attractive and a good homemaker, and your blessed father left us with sufficient means so that a modest dowry can be provided."

Hari shifted uncomfortably in his chair.

"I would like to help Devi, Mother. But I think that Uncle Arun would probably be better. He is much respected in the village and knows many families well. I am sure that Devi would benefit from having many more candidates if the matter were placed in our uncle's hands."

"Well, perhaps so, my son. I will ask Arun, then." Hari could tell that his mother was deeply disappointed at his reply. But she assumed a positive expression and proceeded to her next concern. "Oh, did Devi tell you?" she asked in a tone of feigned cheeriness. "While you were away our next-door neighbor's youngest daughter, Valli, asked about you many times. It is no secret that she likes you. As you know, her father is a large landowner who is much respected in the village. He has arranged very successful marriages for his three oldest daughters, and I would not be surprised if one day soon he approaches me to inquire about you."

Hari inhaled deeply. "Mother, Valli is a nice girl and no doubt will make a fine wife. But I am not ready to talk of marriage. I am not at all sure I want to marry. I do not mean to disappoint you, but there are other things on my mind at the moment. I pray that you will understand."

"Perhaps your soul is troubled, my son. You left us because there were questions on your mind. I had hoped that by traveling awhile you would satisfy your curiosity about the world and find answers to your questions. But is the world really so different from our village?"

"I—I am not sure, Mother. But if I have questions, they are not the same ones I had before."

"Your father used to say that searches begin and end on one's own doorstep. Always he looked to the sacred texts to guide our lives." She took a breath that was almost a sigh. "Hari, do your mother a favor. Go to see your old teacher, the pundit Bava. He is a wise man and you were one of his best pupils. I know he would be glad to see you again, and perhaps he can advise you."

"Very well, Mother, if it pleases you."

The following morning, after making the required

courtesy calls on his uncles and aunts, and politely enduring their lectures on the joys and duties of marriage, Hari made his way to the hut of the pundit, Bava, on the outskirts of the village. As a student he had studied the Vedas as well as philosophy, logic, and mathematics under the pundit's tutelage, and he well remembered how the old Brahmin would become impatient with him because of his incessant questioning. Whenever his mind strayed into forbidden territory, the pundit would steer him back to the right path, step by step, through impeccable logic. Hari smiled to himself as he recalled that the pundit's questions, unlike his own, always seemed to have such clear satisfying answers.

Upon arriving at the pundit's house, Hari found the old teacher seated cross-legged on the floor deep in meditation. He looked exactly the same as always. His face was thin and pale and wore a look of utter calm, disturbed only by a long nose which curved gracefully downward, ending in a sharp point that nearly touched his thin straight lips. Long white hair poured down his craggy frame like a waterfall, joined by the teeming flow of his beard. He was garbed in a white dhoti, though his upper torso was bare, and his brow was stained with three ash stripes.

Hari knew that the pundit sometimes fell asleep during his meditations, but as he was considering whether to make a noise of some kind to rouse the old teacher, the pundit's eyes blinked open. The two dark pinpoints fastened on the young visitor.

"Here is a face I have not looked upon since the season of monsoons," said the pundit. His voice was thin and high, yet serene. "Come in."

Hari entered and prostrated himself before the pundit before seating himself on the floor.

"It has reached these old ears that you have been on a journey," said the teacher.

"Yes, Master." Hari suddenly realized that he had forgotten to ask the pundit's blessing before embarking on his travels and so had been unintentionally disrespectful. He felt embarrassed.

"And was your journey fruitful?"

"Well, in some ways, Master."

"Yet I see that your soul is restless. Did not your travels affirm what you have been taught?"

"I—I am not sure. No, not always."

"No? Hmm. Perhaps you were busy attending to matters of a transitory nature. I will not try to guess what they might be. But there is value in all experience—even the ephemeral can sometimes be of value in bringing about insight and realization.

"But I do not think you have come here today just to visit. That has not been your habit in the past. Something is troubling you. Tell me what it is."

Hari lowered his head. "O Master, I am not sure. I saw much pain and uncertainty in my travels. And also beauty. But to look into the eyes and soul of the world is a fearful thing. The world's soul is laden with sorrow, and now my soul too is heavy. I did not ever think the taste of worldly life would be so bitter. I would lighten the burden if I could. I thought of becoming a sannyasi, an ascetic who lives by begging, though I fear that would disappoint my family."

The pundit nodded. "Hari, the world sets many snares and shows us many false trails, which are not always easy to avoid. One does not become a sannyasi to escape, but to seek.

"In your search for knowledge your vision has been obscured by Maya, the veil of illusion. You have forgotten the lesson of the Vedas and the meaning of yoga. You no longer strive for Atman, the silent formless depth of being within us and all things. Have you forgotten that there are things that can not be learned from experience or found in books? The intellect is useful, but it too is transitory. The essence of self is not to be found in mind or body. You were taught that the senses must be cleansed if you are to achieve intuition and insight and bring peace to your soul. But you have forgotton these things. You have fallen victim to selfish desires.

"You feel disquiet, but you are disquieted by that which is changeful yet can not be changed. This earthly life is unstable. Peace and stability must be sought elsewhere. You are attracted to and repelled by the world, and yet you do not see that it is the selfsame desire and fear which troubles you. Cherish not the world of illusion. Cast out desire. The world must be rejected if it is to be surpassed, if your spirit is to be unshackled.

"I can not grasp your foot and set it upon the path to Moksha. That you must do for yourself. But perhaps I can shine a small light through a window in the house of your soul that you may see the wisdom of our sacred ways.

"Meditate upon what I have said. Then come to see me again."

The pundit closed his eyes and resumed his meditation. Hari prostrated himself before the teacher and departed. As he left he noticed that some fruit and milk had been set by the door of the hut by a villager, and he realized that he had forgotten to bring a food offering himself. Indeed he had become selfish and neglectful of the proprieties.

The afternoon was bright and lazy. Hari sat alone upon a grassy hill in the shade of a tree to ponder the pundit's words. But he found it difficult to concentrate. The breeze was fragrant with the smell of lilac, and the drifting clouds were building wondrous palaces in the sky. In the branches above his head a pair of blackbirds were busily building a nest, and their comings and goings and incessant chatter made it impossible for him to think.

As he watched the clouds in their work, his hands played idly with the grass, and he felt something rub against his fingers. Looking down, he saw sliding through the grass a small green snake trailing a half-shed skin. Its shiny new coat glistened in the sunlight in contrast to the tattered brown shell it dragged behind.

"I think we may suffer from a similar problem," he said to the snake. "But perhaps I can help you, at least this time. Next time you will be on your own."

Hari pinned the trailing end of the dead skin to the ground with his forefinger, and as the snake slid forward the old skin peeled cleanly from its body, revealing a smooth bright coat beneath. The snake stopped and raised its head. Hari could feel its unblinking eyes looking deeply into his own.

"I hope life will be a little easier for you now, my friend," he said to the snake.

The snake darted out its tiny red-forked tongue, which quivered like a striking arrow; then it lowered its head and slithered away through the grass.

That evening Hari's mother asked about his visit with the pundit.

"Did your teacher give you any useful advice, my son?"

"Yes, in a way, Mother. He is wise in matters of the spirit, though in worldly matters I am less sure. I still have questions."

"My son, there are always questions," his mother interrupted. Her tone was hard and impatient. "The world is full of questions. But one can not stop living or avoid one's obligations and destiny simply because of questions. I had hoped the pundit would reveal to you your sacred duty."

A bolt of pain shot through Hari at these words.

There was a long silence. When next she spoke, his mother's voice was soft, almost pleading.

"Hari, your sister and I love you. We want you to be happy, to take your rightful place as your father's son in the village. You are well liked and respected by everyone. The pattern of our lives is set, and the road you must follow is the same that your father walked, and his father before him. So it has been for many generations. You are our only son, and in you are the seeds of generations of our family to come.

"Why do you keep putting off marriage? And why have you not spoken with your uncle Arun about helping him manage the family properties? There is a time in life for all things. Now is the time for you to choose a wife and settle down. If you wait much longer the best choices will be taken. Will you not at least think upon this matter, my son?"

Hari sighed. "Mother, I know you and Devi are concerned about me. And there is much in what you say. I will think on it as you ask."

"Thank you, my son. As for the worldly questions you spoke of, there is a wise woman, a mataji, who came to the village not long ago. She is the niece of the old mataji, Aparna, who died but two months back. Like Aparna, the new mataji gives advice to the women of the village. She lives in Aparna's house at the southern end of the village. I have not seen this new mataji myself, but some of the other women tell me that she gives sound advice on domestic matters. Go and see her, my son. It can do no harm, and you might find the visit to be helpful."

Hari had no wish to upset his mother further. "Very well, I will go tomorrow if it pleases you."

The following morning Hari managed to find a number of unnecessary tasks to do around the house and yard, which served to delay his promised visit to the mataji. He hated having to go. The idea of consulting a domestic advisor to the village women was nothing less than humiliating. But he had promised. He prayed no one would find out.

In the early afternoon when few villagers were about the streets, Hari made his way to the mataji's house. It was small and unassuming, but well kept and quiet by itself, nestled quaintly between two grassy hillocks and covered with flowering vines. He knocked lightly on the door, hoping that no one would be at home. Unfortunately, a voice from inside answered: "Come in."

He entered into a small parlor, which was simply furnished with three chairs and a small table. A curtain was drawn across one side of the room to separate it from the rest of the house.

"Please be seated," came a woman's voice from behind

the curtain. It was soft and lilting and had a tone of quiet confidence. Hari sat in one of the chairs.

"Good day, Mataji, and thank you," he said in his most courteous voice, though it was slightly forced. He waited for the mataji to emerge from behind the curtain, but she did not.

"Please introduce yourself," she said. "I do not see many men here."

"My name is Hari, as was my father's. I live in the village with my family—my mother and sister."

"Yes, I know," said the voice. "Now I recognize you. I have heard of your family and have seen you pass by my house." There followed another long silence.

"O Mataji, will you be coming out so that we may converse? If this is an inconvenient time for me to visit, I can return another day."

"No, now is fine. In dispensing advice, I have found it better to remain behind the curtain. It is easier that way for my guests to speak freely about what is in their hearts."

Hari guessed that the real reason the mataji chose to remain hidden was because she was much younger than most of the women who sought her advice.

"Tell me, what is it that troubles you?" asked the voice. "Nothing we speak of will pass beyond these walls."

"O Mataji, I would ask about the world of the senses. The sacred texts tell us we should cleanse ourselves of our desires. Might I ask your view on this matter?"

"We are flesh, and desire springs from the flesh. We can as much separate the two as the warmth can be separated from the sun or the fragrance from the flower."

"Are our teachings, then, in error?"

"You must not be a purist. Our faith is a flexible instrument and may play many different melodies, some sweeter than others. Its virtue is that it can embrace all conditions, and by so doing has survived many centuries. Look around you. The villagers live simple lives and think not of weighty philosophical questions. They live much in the world of the senses, yet it would never occur to them that they are not good Hindus. Perhaps you ask too many questions. Accept what your senses tell you. There is virtue, and even wisdom, in the simple life of the senses—as long as excesses are avoided."

"Indeed, that has been my problem. I have sought enlightenment, yet somehow the things of the senses have overwhelmed me, and I have spent more time in the arms of young women than in converse with men of wisdom. I find myself dissatisfied with the notion of either complete asceticism or complete acceptance of the kind of life my family wishes me to have. My spirit has sought grace, but my flesh has found pleasure, and neither seems to be exactly what I wish for my life."

"Some do not readily fit in the forms of the world," she agreed. "Some are obliged to compromise, to straddle realms as it were, partaking of the virtues and liabilities of each."

"You speak well," said Hari. "Might I ask the source of your knowledge? Do you have a teacher? Which books have you consulted?"

"I have no teacher or books. There are some things that can not be learned except through experience or spiritual guidance."

"O Mataji, please forgive my next question if it is too personal, but I would ask how one who is yet young has gained enough experience to have learned so much about the world?"

A long silence followed. When finally the mataji spoke her voice was distant, almost somber.

"I was born into experience. I was nurtured on it, and I have denied it. I have seized it and exploited it. I have known its misery and its grandeur, its power and decadence. And once, in the arms of a man, I knew its sweetness and divinity. In a small village surrounded by a high wall, beneath the fallen eye of the goddess Kali."

Hari's breath caught and he leapt to his feet. Could it be? He pulled back the curtain and there before him stood Sumi. Sumi: once high priestess of Kali, she who had tried to kill him and then saved his life, she who had traded away a lifetime of power to share but a brief moment of passion with him.

He could only gape at her in utter amazement. Sumi! Here in his own village. Then he remembered her telling of an aunt in a distant village, a place where she would go to make a new life for herself. Surely the goddess Lakshmi, or Kama, the love god, must have planned this, he thought.

Close, lovely mortal man. It was an Apsara who brought her here after she had settled elsewhere. She is not really Aparna's niece, but the villagers have no way to know, and she is doing a better job than a true niece would have done.

As he stared into her eyes, his look of amazement melted into a warm, happy smile. How lovely she looked, exactly as he last saw her. She might be a goddess herself, he thought, with such soft delicate features, full breasts, and slender waist—or perhaps a temple courtesan with her full plum lips, eager flashing eyes, and dark exotic tresses.

"But now I must tell you something you may not wish to hear," she continued. "It is something I did not know myself, when I rescued you from my own anger in that far village. I spoke of spiritual guidance: what I did then was not my own devising, but was prompted by a spirit who entered me and—" She paused, her eyes dropping as if she were embarrassed. "And caused me to develop a sudden, intense, physical passion for you. Thus I acted as I did, and forfeited my power."

"You were possessed by an evil spirit?" Hari asked, amazed.

"Not evil, merely interested in saving your life. She did this by touching the mind or heart of a woman who was in a position to help you. I was that woman, on that occasion. And since, I have learned much about you from the spirit."

Hari hardly credited what she was saying, yet could not completely doubt it either. "There were other occasions?"

"Did you not wonder at how attractive women found you to be as you traveled?"

"Why no. The girls of my village find me attractive."

"But does it seem natural that a priestess or a princess or even a queen should find you so, and go to any lengths to indulge in coupling with you? These are normally quite reserved ladies."

Hari realized that she had a point. Princesses ordinarily did not throw themselves at poor travelers. "Perhaps my male vanity prevented me from questioning it. You say that a spirit caused these women to act as they did?"

"Yes, in essence."

"But why would such a spirit have any interest in me? I am not remarkable."

"She was indulging in a competition with another spirit, and it was necessary for her to cause seven different women to seduce you. Now she has accomplished that. But in the process she came to like you rather well, and wishes to associate with you further. Do you suppose you could entertain the notion?"

"Associate with a spirit? But the spirits can not be seen or heard or felt. Only the one in the cave, briefly—"

"Pudmini the Bootham, in the endless caverns. She could be heard and felt, as you discovered. But once you lessened her burden, she became completely spiritual and could no longer be detected by mortals."

"How could you know that?" Hari asked, astonished. "I told no one!"

"The spirit told me—not Pudmini, but the one who followed you."

"But how could that be, if she can not be seen or heard or felt?"

"She can enter the minds of mortals and stir in them thoughts or emotions. Because I was a priestess of Kali, she was able to enter my mind more deeply, and reveal the thoughts she wished to communicate to you. Now she wishes to know whether you are willing to come to know her better, knowing her for what she is."

"But if *I* can not sense her, how can I know her?"

"By the women she possesses for you. Her powers of influence over mortals are limited. She can enter only females, and can instill only certain feelings, which are usually temporary unless the woman has a basic affinity for the type of feeling generated. But should she find an amenable host she could do considerably more, becoming for that time almost mortal. That is the case with me: I am allowing her into my mind and speaking for her, because of the reward she offers me in return. But she could do it with any other woman, if you truly accepted her, and—"

Hari remained confused and troubled by these revelations, but part of him saw the rationale of it, and saw how well it fitted in with his experience. He was beginning to believe. "And—?"

"And loved her."

"Love a formless spirit?"

"Her form would be that of the woman she possessed at the time. Her words would be her own."

Hari shook his head. "It would not be love for the woman I saw, but for the spirit who possessed her—who might at any time fly away to possess some other woman."

"Which other woman would then have the same love for you the spirit does, being then the same person."

"But that would mean that my love was any woman, or no woman. How would I know her?"

"By her words and actions. You would not mistake her, whatever her form of the moment."

"But I could not settle down with a different woman each day! The village would never allow it."

"True. You would have to select a local woman to be your apparent wife. She would have to agree to let the spirit possess her and speak and act through her, as is the case with me at present. And to allow you to be with whatever other woman the spirit possessed for you."

"For me?"

"She would seek only to please you, by the intensity of her desire for you and the variety of forms she could assume for your pleasure."

The belief was solidifying, and so was his interest. "As was the case when I traveled?"

"As was the case, from Meena on through Leela. Did you not find them to be varied and accommodating?"

"I tried to avoid Leela! She tricked me in the darkness, just as I tricked her before."

"But in that darkness, before you knew—did you have any complaint of the occasion?"

Hari remembered the overwhelming intensity of the event. "It could be like that, again?"

"With any mortal woman you wish. If you give the spirit the power."

That made him wary again. "The she-demon wanted me to speak her name a second time, to give her power, but I would have regretted it had I done so. How can I trust this other spirit?"

"Trust can come only with time. But she can have mortal power only with your acceptance and love. If she betrays you, your love will wither. Then she will fade."

"I must think about this," he said uncertainly.

"Of course. It is your decision. She will accede to your desire of whatever nature, for the duration of your life, for it is but an instant to her. Simply tell her what you want, for once she possesses a mortal woman she cannot divine your thoughts directly."

"She can read my thoughts when she is in the spirit state?"

"Yes. She is unable to enter and control a man, but she can fathom his thoughts."

"Then she will know what I decide."

"Yes. I have presented her case; now you must do as

you see fit. She bids you parting, for now, but she will return the instant you wish it."

Then something changed in Sumi. It was subtle, but Hari could tell that a quality had departed from her.

"But I had another question," he protested. "Perhaps two."

Sumi raised her eyes. "Perhaps I can answer them."

"What is her name?"

"Mohini the Apsara."

"Mohini," he repeated, liking it. "And what of the women she possesses? What of their own spirits?"

"They are present, but in reduced circumstances. That is why they must agree to her possession, for they can rise and hurl her forth from their bodies if they wish. It is only when she puts a notion into their minds that they think is their own that it has full effect. When they know her, they have power to expel her."

"How can you be sure of this?"

"Because I have been knowingly possessed by her, after being unknowingly prompted to passion for you. I have experienced both forms of her involvement. I know their natures."

"And now you are yourself again?"

"Yes. My task is done."

Hari remembered how the guru Sundar had transferred his spirit to Hari's own body, so that he might indulge himself in one act of love with his dutiful young wife, Sharmila. That participation had not been burdensome to Hari, and indeed it had had its own reward. He appreciated how Mohini the spirit could similarly enter the body of a woman and partake of her activities without harming her in mind or body. The guru had been old and frail; Mohini lacked substance. Their needs were in their fashions similar. There seemed to be no reason to distrust the process, though it was not a thing it would be easy to explain to others.

True.

Hari thought of another question. "What reward did she promise you?"

"I think you know it."

He read a question in her eyes, a question rimmed with tears, to which his heart well knew the answer. No doubts assailed him now as they came together and embraced. Gently he pressed her to him and set his lips to hers. All was feeling: the soft warmth of her body as it bent willingly against his, her pounding heart and swelling breasts, the passion in her kiss. And like a candle flame-kissed, the weight upon his soul melted away, even as his spirit took flight, soaring into the timeless oblivion of pure delight, to that blissful dimension the gods had set aside for mortals that they might glimpse the infinite and touch the edge of eternity.

Sumi gave wholly of herself, and long did Hari linger in her arms. And in those moments of sweet calm between the sea-waves of passion, Hari became aware of Sumi's true feelings toward him. Her gentle caresses, her tenderness, the adoration in her eyes, her soft whisperings, all spoke of love. It was a message his heart could not help but heed, and which his mind was powerless to deny.

"Yet, this is temporary?" he asked when the edge of passion had been blunted.

"Perhaps. I was, it seems, more than ready to accede to her nudge."

"Then maybe it should be you whom—whom I marry.

She considered. "I think not."

"Not?" he asked, surprised. "Why?"

"Because I am a jealous, hot-tempered woman. I would be enraged if I caught you in the embrace of another woman after you had pledged yourself to me. That would interfere with much of what Mohini offers you."

"You love me, yet you tell me this?"

"I tell you this *because* I love you. Because I also know that my love may fade, being perhaps artificial, and that you deserve what Mohini offers. It is in your nature to crave more variety than any one mortal woman can provide."

"But if I marry some other woman, then you will not have even this much with me."

"I will—if you choose me as an alternate woman."

"You would prefer to be an alternate, to being the primary? Will you not be as jealous whatever your state?"

"No, for my expectations will differ. I will know that when you come to me, it is only because you truly desire me, not because you are committed to me. I crave your love, not your commitment. Meanwhile, I shall have a good position here, that is fulfilling in other ways, and is perhaps more appropriate for one who is unmarried. So I think you should go and find some simple village girl who will gladly settle for what you offer and not be jealous."

Hari considered that. "Perhaps you are right, Sumi. I thank you for your assessment of the situation."

"Understand, Hari, if I thought for a moment I could be what I needed to be, I would instantly marry you. But

I have learned much realism recently, and believe I know what is best for us both. I am not denying you passion, only marriage."

"I thank you again. Surely there will be another occasion, soon."

"I thank you for that belief," she said, smiling a bit wanly. It had clearly been a difficult decision for her.

That evening on the veranda Hari's mother cast anxious glances at him, but said nothing. He observed his mother's uneasiness and knew its cause.

"Did you visit the mataji today, my son?" she asked finally.

"Yes, Mother."

"And was she as wise as the village women say?"

"Well, yes, in her way. But she is yet young, not much older than Devi, and so still has much to learn." He knew it would be unwise to tell her of the true nature of his dialogue with Sumi.

"Was she of no help to you, then?"

"She was extremely helpful, Mother. It is sometimes useful to have the detached view of one who knows of life's day-to-day problems."

"Yes, my son, that is quite true. There is a practical side to life which can not be ignored. If the mataji made you see that, then she is clever indeed. Yes, our traditions also come from the earth, not only from the hands of the gods in Swarga."

A period of silence followed, broken only by the chirps of the crickets beneath the veranda and the click-clack of Devi's spinning wheel.

"And have you thought further on the matter we discussed last evening, my son?"

"Yes, Mother. I have a better understanding now of some of the questions that have been on my mind. And I have made some decisions. I will marry, perhaps soon. But it will be a woman of my own choosing."

His mother's hands and body shook with her pleasure. "Oh my son, you have brought great joy to your mother's heart. Devi too will be pleased, as will your aunts and uncles."

"You mentioned that Valli may be interested in me. I have not heeded her at all recently. As I recall, she is a rather pretty and agreeable girl."

His mother smiled, immediately aware of the change in his interest. "You have indeed not been observing her, my son. She has in recent months become uncommonly beautiful, yet remains quite pliable. She would not give you any argument about anything, ever. Unless by some ill chance you wished not to beget children."

Hari smiled. "There will be no such ill chance. Perhaps we should invite her to dinner tomorrow. I think I may have something of import to discuss with her. Is that all right?"

"Yes, of course. Her family is well respected in the village and we will be honored."

O my darling mortal man! You have decided. You will never regret this.

For Hari was thinking about the prospect of having a stable, socially acceptable marriage, while also having the apparent love of any woman he might choose, wherever he might travel, including one or two or even three lovely princesses. He rather thought he could learn to love the spirit behind the form, as well as the woman who enabled him to participate. Mohini—already the name was assuming significance. Valli, who would be there when the spirit was not, to bear his children and care for them. He could be a responsible citizen without giving up his wayward dreams.

He was definitely not cut out to be an ascetic, he concluded.

Definitely not, my precious one.

Authors' Notes

Piers Anthony

This may be hard to believe, but I have been trying to avoid collaborations. So how is it that at this writing in June 1993 the last three novels I have done have been collaborative? Well, I consider each case separately on its merits. I do turn down most offers of collaboration, and sometimes there are hurt feelings about that, but I accept those that seem to have merit, and that I think I can contribute to meaningfully. Sometimes in Authors' Notes I spell out exactly what each collaborator did, and sometimes I don't. I will say that in this case I wrote some of each chapter and all of one chapter, while Alfred Tella wrote all the rest. His was the original manuscript; I did the revising. This is the general pattern of most of my collaborations. I'm quite reasonable about it: all I want is to have everything my way. And no, I did not originate the vegetarian theme, though I am a vegetarian.

Because my collaborator did most of the work, this project did not take me long. Not much happened to me in this limited period, except that I broke my glasses on the way home from attending my wife and daughter's joint birthday celebration; the case got caught by a closing car door. Naturally the same-day-service type of optician did not have in stock the standard frames I had gotten four years before and had to special-order them, leaving me to struggle through using my heavy computer glasses full-time for how much over a week is not known at the moment. A sore nose can be marvelously irritating and unconducive to thoughts of spirituality.

But I also read a novel. I mean someone else's novel. I was curious about *The Bridges of Madison County* by Robert James Waller, then over forty weeks on the national bestseller lists and still #1. What's the secret to such success? It's a small novel, simply told, about a four-day affair between a wandering photographer and an Iowa farmer's wife. Not much there, obviously. But by the time I finished it, the story had gotten to me, and I was in a daze. Evidently my reaction is not unique; there's just something about that story. So for those who are curious whether a rattlesnake will be poisoned if bitten by another, or whether a commercial writer can be moved by someone else's commercial writing, the answer is yes. Am I jealous? Of course.

Alfred Tella

I was dubious about collaborations in fiction until I read the magnificent trilogy of novels by George S. Viereck and Paul Eldridge entitled *My First Two Thousand Years*, *Salome*, and *The Invincible Adam*. Since then I've read other coauthored novels that worked and have become curious to make the experiment. Different authors have different strengths, and the right combination can bring synergy to a common product.

Why Piers as a partner? Because he is a gifted writer whose novels I enjoy, and because we share certain values, among them an appreciation of history and an affection for nature, critters, and our planet. If we're not quite kindred souls, the spiritual overlap is considerable. We've been corresponding ever since Piers blurbed my 1990 novel, *Sundered Soul*.

Asian cultures, mythologies, and tales have always held a special fascination for me, and the Indian setting of *The Willing Spirit* was inspired by such classics as the *Panchatantra*, the *Ramayana*, and the *Vickram* stories, and also by my friendships with Indo-Americans. The stories and fables from the ancient Sanskrit are timeless, and in many ways are the progenitors of modern fantasy.

If you're wondering about all those pigeons in Chapter 7, it's because I have a pigeon loft at home—actually, a converted garage with a built-on aviary. (The car stays outside.) The birds are the fancy varieties, in many colors and sporting lovely body ornaments—crests, hoods, and feathered feet. If you're curious, take a look at the striking color photographs in Wendell Levi's book, *Encyclopedia of Pigeon Breeds*. Even better, visit a local pigeon show!

My wife and I live in northern Virginia surrounded by trees and wildlife, friends all. Some of our more unusual visitors have been a stripeless skunk, a white deer, a maskless mother raccoon (with masked babies), a house-eating woodpecker, and a television-addicted flying squirrel who watches from a tree outside our living room window.

An acknowledgment: Some of the ingredients used in the divine creation of women (Chapter 7) owe to F. W. Bain's translation from the ancient Sanskrit, as given in a recipe in his 1898 book, *A Digit of the Moon*.